SECOND
SONS

SECOND SONS

David Ylhainen

ISBN: 978-1-64570-194-1   (Paperback Edition)
ISBN: 978-1-64570-195-8   (Hardcover Edition)
ISBN: 978-1-64570-193-4   (E-book Edition)

Book Ordering Information

Phone Number: 347-901-4929 or 347-901-4920
Email: info@globalsummithouse.com
Global Summit House
www.globalsummithouse.com

Printed in the United States of America

ACKNOWLEDGEMENTS

First, I would like to thank God, through which all things are possible. He has driven me to be all that I am and I pray that I can continue to do what it is that He has set before me. Many thanks to my family, friends and my first fan, Jan. Most of all I would like to thank my mother for constant encouragement and willingness to help out when I needed it.

CHAPTER *1*

Wind and rain pelted the house as the storm raged on till just past midnight. As if on cue, Mason jumped up from his fitful sleep as a thunderclap roared. Covered in sweat and panting heavily, Mason took in his surroundings and sat on the edge of the bed. Then, cradling his head in his cupped hands, he let out a large, heavy sigh. Just then, a hand gently touched his shoulder from behind.

"Nightmare again, hon?" a concerned female voice said.

He turned slightly and nodded as he spoke. "I'm fine, sweetie. Go back to sleep," he replied in a half sigh.

Patting her hand softly, he stood up and walked into the nearby bathroom, flipping the light switch as he entered. He turned on the faucet and repeatedly rinsed his face with cold water and then paused to look at his reflection in the mirror. Staring at himself in a half daze, Mason replayed the memory that had become such a horrible, recurring nightmare.

The night it happened wasn't all that different from tonight, he thought to himself. A heavy storm had rolled in, making the tree branches sway in the front yard and pelting the glass heavily with large drops of rain. Of course, the day hadn't started out that way. Earlier that morning, Mason's father had taken him and his older brother, Jason, to the park to fly kites. The wind had been good, and they had had no problems getting their kites to fly. Mason remembered it had taken all his strength to keep the kite from dragging him across the field; after all, he was only five.

It had been a good day—and the last one he would spend with his family. He often thought of what he would have done differently had he known what was going to happen. Later that evening, just after midnight, Mason woke up with a strong urge to use the bathroom.

He got up from his bed, half glancing at his older brother across the room, who was in a deep sleep. As he walked down the hall toward the bathroom, he paused, thinking he heard a muffled noise coming from his parents' room, but he continued on, assuming the noise was from the storm.

Just before he entered the bathroom, he noticed that the floor was wet and the window was open at the other end of the hallway. Not only that, but it appeared that part of the glass had been broken too. As he approached the window, he moved the blowing curtains out of the way to look outside. A cat that was soaked to the bone looked up and mewed at him. Their cat was strictly an indoor cat but never missed an opportunity to sneak outside if given the chance. Unfortunately, the cat's curiosity got the better of him this time. Leaning out the window to climb outside, Mason scolded the cat.

"Jasper, you know you're not supposed to go outside!" he yelled, nearly closing his eyes to protect them from the downpour.

Using the drainpipe that was right next to the window, Mason shimmied down the three or so feet it took to get to the ground. As he cradled the cat in his arms and looked back through the window, he saw something that would haunt him for the rest of his life. The door to his parents' room swung open, as if kicked, and his mother flew out, hitting the wall with such force that blood began to run from her nose. Mason was about to scream but was silenced by fear as he saw what followed behind her. Three figures dressed in black came out of the room after her as she scrambled to a crawl on the slippery, wet floor. As they approached her, she wiped her hand across her face in an effort to clear it of the blood now gushing from her nose.

"Please! Don't hurt my children," she pleaded, glancing up at her closest attacker.

One of the figures reached down, and to Mason's horror, it took a knife and, with one swift motion, slit her throat. A look of shock filled her face as she grabbed the wound and slowly slid to the floor. As if signaled by the act, the other two figures went into Mason's room and came out with his older brother moments later. His hands and feet were bound, and his mouth was duct taped. The two figures carried him down the hallway toward the window where Mason was watching, and then they turned to go out the front door.

Mason hadn't even realized until then that it was still raining. As he squinted his eyes and looked down the side of the house, he could see the two figures loading his brother into a van. Mason was shaking; he was wet, cold, and scared, and he had no idea what to do. The cat squealed and squirmed in his arms, begging to be let free of his grasp. He had been gripping the cat so tightly that claw marks were left on his arms where the cat had desperately tried to flee from Mason's tight grip.

After letting Jasper go, Mason looked up to see the two men returning to the house. He glanced up through the window carefully to see what would happen next. The one who had killed his mother was barking orders at the other two, after which they started to knock things over, break things, and make a mess of the whole house. One of the men went back into Mason's parents' room and came out with his mother's jewelry box and a VCR. Another grabbed a CD player off of an entertainment unit and then kicked it over, sending everything on it crashing to the ground.

Then one of the men approached the window, and Mason thought for a terrifying second that he had been spotted. However, the figure stopped short of the window to pick up a wallet that was on an end table nearby. He was wearing a long-sleeved shirt and gloves, but when he stretched down to pick up the wallet, the top of his wrist became visible. There Mason saw a small tattoo, perhaps one inch by one inch. It consisted of a red pyramid with a black snake coiled around it. After motioning to the other two, the man grabbed the wallet, and all of them headed back out to the van.

Lips shivering from the rain and pale with fear, Mason slowly got up from his spot in front of the window to check if the assailants had gone. As he crept to the front of the house, he could see no trace of the van his brother had been loaded into. Mason then turned and ran as fast as he could through the front door, which had been left wide open by the intruders. There on the floor in front of him was the limp figure of his mother.

"Mom?" Mason asked despairingly. "Mom?" he shouted louder, with tears in his eyes. Then, as he got to her body and the pool of blood that surrounded her, he realized she was dead.

"Mommy!" he shouted in uncontrollable grief.

As Mason sat next to his mother's body, tears rolling uncontrollably down his face, he realized that throughout the whole incident, he hadn't seen or heard his father. He got up from his mother's body, leaving a trail of bloody footprints as he went, and cautiously entered his parents' bedroom.

"Dad? Are you in here?" Mason asked cautiously.

It was dark, and as he approached the bed, he saw a figure, but he wasn't close enough yet to see who it was.

"Dad, is that you?" Still there was no reply.

Suddenly, a gasp came from the figure under the sheets.

"Mason . . ." his father wheezed.

"Daddy!" Mason squealed, running forward to embrace his father.

But as Mason got closer, he realized that his father had been brutally beaten. His face was hardly recognizable and covered in blood, with one eye half open and one swollen shut. Mason stopped just short of his father, staring in shock and horror.

"Listen to me, son," his father said, motioning him to come closer.

"I want you to dial 911, like Mommy and I showed you, okay?" He swallowed hard before continuing. "When the policemen come, they will ask you a lot of questions, so tell them everything you know. Never forget how much your mother and I love you, son. Also," he said in hardly a whisper, "remember your brother—remember they came for him. God . . . be . . . with . . . y—" The last gasp of air was not enough to finish the word, but Mason heard it nonetheless.

As soon as the police arrived, there must have been three or four detectives who asked Mason the same questions over and over. After telling his story, Mason was taken to his uncle's house, who happened to be a police officer himself. Uncle Joe was Mason's godfather and the only family Mason had left. Later the case was classified as a robbery/homicide/kidnapping. The police figured Mason's brother had been taken for leverage in case they were caught, but Mason never believed that; he knew there was more to the story but as of yet had not been able to put it together. The police, working with the press, left names out of their public report and stated that the youngest child was not present in the home during the attack, which was technically true; he was outside the house when the crime occurred. However, this and his eyewitness account were kept from the media to circumvent any attempt of the murderers to track him down and finish him off. Although the police believed this was unlikely, Mason's uncle insisted on it.

Of course, the police did everything they could to find the suspects, but with so little to go on and only the testimony of a five-year-old, the case quickly became cold. Mason's brother was never found and was presumed dead. Even though it had happened over twenty-five years ago, it still haunted him to this day. The incident had led to Mason's career choice. He had become a private investigator, specializing in locating missing children. It wasn't a lucrative career by any means, but it allowed him to help calm the demons of guilt inside him, and when he had spare time, he would continue to work on his own case. In recent months, a peculiar second part to his dream had emerged, one he knew he had not been witness to, but he was positive it was connected, though he couldn't explain why.

In his dream, Mason, as if hovering above the scene, saw a stone altar in the middle of a circular room. With the exceptions of torches lit periodically on the wall, it was very dark. In fact, there were no windows or other light sources inside the room. The altar was made of a large slab of stone and was flat on all sides but one. Toward the front, it had what seemed to be a drain, as if meant to catch blood or other liquid from some sacrifice. Also, on each corner were shackles or restraints of some kind. Toward the middle on one side was a large carving of a huge serpent with its mouth open wide. In its mouth, it held what looked like a large, golden bowl.

Then, as if appearing from darkness, a procession of shadowy figures appeared. They were marching in a single-file line, forming a circle around the altar. They were chanting in a language he didn't recognize and wearing black hooded cloaks, so only their mouths could be seen clearly. At the end of the procession, two of the cloaked figures were carrying Mason's brother. He was gagged but free from his restraints. They placed him on the stone altar, shackling his arms and legs.

Then one of the figures, who seemed to be the leader, moved to the head of the table, leaning over Mason's brother's head. When the leader raised his hands, the chanting ceased. Then, with a dagger of strange shape held high, he yelled out, again in a language Mason didn't understand, but he caught the last word, which sounded like a name: "Apep." Reaching down, the cloaked figure slit Mason's brother's throat. Blood ran down the back of his neck and into the caldron below, all the way down until it came out the serpent's head and filled the golden bowl. The leader walked over, grabbed the golden basin, and lifted it to his mouth to drink.

The chanting began again, but this time it grew louder and louder. The cloaked figure continued to drink until the blood trickled down the side of his mouth. When he lowered the basin, blood stained his lips; he smiled, as if knowing Mason was watching him. Then Mason looked at his brother and saw him turn his head, as if looking at Mason for assistance, and then he gurgled on what was the last bit of blood in his body. It was always at this point that Mason quickly awoke. The death he saw his brother experience only made the guilt he felt for doing nothing more real.

After rinsing his face, Mason decided a return to dreamland was out of his grasp, and he decided, as he always did, to go to his office. The stairs creaked as he walked down and headed to his study. He knew he wouldn't wake up Tyler, his wife. She had been through this too many times to worry about him. She knew the best thing she could do was listen if he wanted to talk and leave him alone if he didn't. With that comfort in her mind, it was easy for her to fall back into a deep, restful sleep.

Mason turned the lights on as he casually entered the study. He had converted this room into an office and actually used his own home as his business address. Though meager in surroundings, once his clients were inside the room with the door closed, it looked like a typical office building. Lying on his desk was his briefcase, along with a lamp, a phone, and other assorted office décor. After sitting down at the desk, he reached for his briefcase and unfastened the latches that held it closed. From within, Mason pulled out a manila folder that was packed full of paperwork and photographs.

The case he was working on recently struck a chord with him. It had an eerie similarity to his own experience, but unlike the other cases he kept in his personal file that seemed to be like his own, this was the first time the tattoo he recalled seeing as a child had also been seen.

He flipped on his desk lamp and opened the manila folder to review the case. The name of the boy who had been taken was David Grafton. David's mother and father, Teresa and Ian, had approached Mason a week ago, hiring him for his services to investigate and hopefully recover their only son. After reviewing the story, based on his interview with the Graftons, Mason was sure this connection was why his nightmares were starting up again, more frequent than ever.

It had all begun two weeks ago on a cool summer night. Ian and Teresa had returned home from a night at the movies and a nice dinner. It was their eighth wedding anniversary, and they had hired the next-door neighbor's daughter, Debbie, to babysit their son. From the moment they pulled into the driveway of their home, they knew something wasn't right. They could see from the street that the porch light was out. Ian was positive he had switched that light on when they had left earlier that evening. Once they got to the front door, they could see it was slightly ajar, and the lock had been broken.

As they rushed inside and broke the deafening silence, they yelled out for their son and the babysitter. Searching the house frantically, Teresa came into the hallway that led to the bedrooms. She searched the wall with her hand, feeling frantically for the light switch to illuminate the pitch-black house. After finding it, she turned it on and scanned the hallway. She saw a pool of blood at the end of the hallway and screamed to her husband, Ian.

Ian made his wife stay where she was at, wanting to protect her from anything left in the house. He walked to the end of the hall and could see that the pool of blood on one side left a trail that led into the master bedroom, as if something had been dragged through it. After following the trail into the bedroom, he saw the lifeless body of Debbie. The babysitter was stretched out, lying motionless on her stomach. He ran to her side, shaking her and repeating her name over and over, eager for a response. He felt for a pulse, but her body was cold, and he knew it was too late to save her.

Her throat had been cut, but it seems she dragged herself into the bedroom before dying. Next to her, on a piece of junk mail, was a note she had written. It was obvious she had written it because the pencil was still stuck in her hand. After pulling the paper from underneath her cold grasp, Ian looked to see what she had written. It simply said, "They took him," and underneath her written statement, she had drawn a pyramid with a snake curled around it. She had used what was left of her life to write down all she knew about her attackers and what they had done with the Graftons' son. Mason remembered the first time he had seen the photocopy of what the girl had written. He tried to hide his amazement, but although the sketch was rough, there was no mistaking that it was identical to the tattoo he had seen on the night his brother was taken and his parents murdered.

Mason didn't share his past or the vision of his brother's sacrifice with the Graftons. He gave the typical, "I will do the best I can," speech, but in his heart, he knew the boy was probably already dead. He also didn't want the people who hired him to think he should be put in a padded cell. Throughout his investigations, especially when working with the police, he had been given looks of ridicule and smirks that taunted him for his bizarre notions of tattoos and cloaked figures. He didn't want his clientele to be affected by his bizarre theories or visions.

Mason closed the manila folder, reached down, and opened up the desk drawer on his right. There, amid paperclips, pens, and other miscellaneous office supplies, was a Bible. As he pulled the book from its resting place, it was clear that it was well used. The cover was worn and the inside of the spine was starting to flake, giving in to the many times it had been opened and closed. The Bible had belonged to Mason's father and contained many side notes and underlined passages. Mason read it daily but always found himself going to one particular passage his father had underlined, Proverbs 12:6-7: "The words of the wicked are to lie in wait for blood: but the mouth of the upright shall deliver them. The wicked are overthrown, and are not: but the house of the righteous shall stand."

Mason's father had outlined many passages, but this one in particular seemed to fit the most recent editions of his nightmare. Even though he had worked on many cases, in the end they all came back to his. Every child he was hired to find or investigate was, in his mind, another chance to save his brother.

After finishing his study, he prayed, turned off the lights, and headed back upstairs. Mason was confident that the connection in this latest case was not just a coincidence. There was something going on—something very large and very evil. As he took the last of the stairs, he remembered his father's last words: "Remember your brother; remember they came for him . . ."

Mason was sure there was something more here; he only needed to dig. Tomorrow he would begin that process by visiting local tattoo parlors to see if they were familiar with the symbol. Mason knew it would be an arduous task at best, but he had to start somewhere.

CHAPTER 2

After awaking early the following morning, Mason was eager to begin his investigations on the symbol that was a dying babysitter's last message. It had been twenty-five years since he had seen the tattoo on the wrist of his parents' killer. He had just about reached the point where he thought he had imagined seeing the tattoo that night. After all, he was only five at the time his parents were murdered—maybe he had imagined it—but the drawing proved that he wasn't imagining things. It also proved that after many dead ends, this was the best lead he'd ever had. It was his best hope for putting a rest the mystery of who was responsible for the attack on his family.

After finishing his morning routine, he headed downstairs to grab something to eat before he left. He could hear Tyler downstairs cooking breakfast and could smell the freshly fried bacon from the hallway.

His wife worked as a Registered Nurse at a local hospital. Recalling the first time they met, a smirk came to his face as he remembered coming into the ER with a broken wrist. He had been talking on the phone while leaning backward in a chair faced in the opposite direction from the phone and fell backward. He had placed his left hand back to break his fall, but his wrist was unable to hold the weight of his body, and he heard a snap like the branch of tree breaking under heavy weight. He had driven to the hospital with one hand—lucky for him he had an automatic—and checked himself into the emergency room.

After waiting for what seemed an eternity, a beautiful young lady came to the ER entrance and called his name. After viewing his injury, the RN asked for an explanation of how it had happened.

Mason turned beet red and then relayed the story of his exciting phone call adventure. He could tell the RN, Tyler, wanted to burst out in laughter, but she composed herself nonetheless. As he was being wrapped up in a cast, she came back in to finish up his paperwork. They chatted for a little while, and he asked for her phone number. Things only progressed from there, and within two years they were married. *Funny how God works,* Mason thought. That was over six years ago, and he still got embarrassed every time either one of them brought it up.

As he came into the kitchen, he could see Tyler had already set a place for him at the table with a hot, fresh cup of coffee waiting for him. This was not what he expected, but he knew that this was her way of letting him know that she understood his nightmares and was there to offer her support.

"Smells great, Ty," Mason said with a large smile on his face.

"I thought you could use an extra boost this morning. I know you didn't sleep very well last night," Tyler replied.

Walking over to his wife, Mason gave her a peck on the cheek and then proceeded to sit down at the table.

"God definitely broke the mold when he made you. Sometimes I don't know how I got so lucky," Mason chirped.

"I believe it had something to do with your balance?" Tyler replied with an instigating smirk on her face.

Mason could only return the smile since he literally had no ground to stand on.

After filling a plate with bacon and eggs, Tyler went to the table and presented the "extra boost" breakfast before her husband.

"I'm sorry I can't stay and eat with you. I have to get to the hospital early today to cover for Martha." After pausing for a moment, Tyler continued. "So . . . what time do you think you'll be home tonight?" she asked cautiously.

"I'm not sure, but I will be back in time for dinner," Mason said.

Since Tyler had to leave, they prayed, as they did every morning, and she left for work. Mason looked down and began to gobble down the wonderful breakfast his better half had made for him. While finishing up the remainder of his coffee and breakfast, Mason turned his attention to the newspaper. The Happy Rock times, named after the small suburb of Kansas City, Missouri for which it reported on, was a town that was fairly small, yet half rural and have urban. It lacked the big city appeal and had many farm houses and large estates with livestock and horses, but also contained quaint sub-divisions and large shopping malls not far away. Mason had grown up here and loved the four seasons. It was great to see the scenery change so dramatically every quarter and he never gave any thought to living anywhere else, especially with ties to the community and his own past, he definitely wouldn't be going anywhere until he found peace in the form of answers. Continuing to read through the headlines of the local paper, his eyes widened as he came across an article that had an all-too-familiar ring to it. The headline read, "Child Missing, Parents Found Slain." Mason zoomed through the article, looking for specific details. It could be nothing, but he saw some of the minor details were too similar to overlook. Both parents had been stabbed to death, and besides the kidnapping of their only child, the place had been burglarized. Unfortunately, no names or details were provided because it was considered "still under investigation," but since Mason's uncle used to be a sergeant in the police department, he was able to get inside information on some of his cases. He grabbed the phone, deciding to put in a call to his uncle to see if he could get any further information. His uncle had taken him in after his parents were murdered, and although he was his father's brother, Mason considered him more of a father figure.

"Uncle Joe? . . . Yeah, Mason here . . . Listen, did you see the paper this morning? . . . Guess you knew I would be calling you then . . . Can you do me a favor and check in with your buddies at the precinct? I have a feeling this one's connected. Let me know what you find out . . . Okay, bye," Mason hung up the phone, still thinking about the article.

Suddenly he realized something: if this and other cases were connected to his own, all of them hid behind the guise of burglary.

"All of that stolen property has to end up somewhere," Mason said out loud.

Mason held that thought for a while but also realized the kidnappings never left a trail to be followed. After all these years, the tattoo was still the only lead he had. After taking one last swig of coffee, he grabbed his coat and headed out the door. As planned the night before, he decided to start checking out the local tattoo parlors to see if anyone recognized the symbol. Using a photocopy of the note the babysitter had left and his own memory, Mason redrew the symbol on a single sheet of paper. He didn't want to alarm those he asked about the symbol, and he thought it best to keep his questions about it from a standpoint of interest, not investigation. He believed the latter would make people suspicious, and that's the last thing he wanted.

It was midday, and Mason had visited more than a dozen tattoo parlors in the city. He thought it very amusing that tattoo parlors were thought to be rare, stereotypically speaking. But in actuality, they were found as easily as your local drugstore. He would have a lot of driving to do to cover them all. So far, no one had recognized the symbol of the snake curled around the pyramid. He got a few suspicious looks, but because of his experience, he could tell none of them were lying when they told him they had never seen it before.

Mason decided a change of venue was in order for the rest of the afternoon. Instead of finishing up the tattoo shops, most of which were downtown and too numerous to visit in one day anyway, he would go to the local library. Perhaps he would get lucky and stumble onto the meaning of that last phrase he heard in his latest nightmare, "Apep." Although it could be nothing, he couldn't get the thought out of his head that his dream was connected to this somehow. Besides, he was getting a bit tired of driving around all day.

He had been to the library many times before, hoping to stumble upon the symbol in encyclopedias or some book on ancient Egypt, but he never found anything. He had never taken the time, though, to research this latest part in his dream and felt it was worth looking into. It was a long shot, but at this point he was willing to give anything a try.

He arrived at the large, brick library a little after one o'clock and began his trek for historical references. The library was one of the oldest buildings in town. It had been built sometime in the 1920s, and although it had been remodeled, it still had that old architectural nostalgia attached to it. Mason recalled when he was a child there were rumors of it being haunted. There was even an article in the paper once because someone had been found dead inside. Of course, it turned out to be nothing but a heart attack. There's nothing like War *and Peace* to send your heart racing. Somehow, though, Mason always felt strange when he came to the library. He would suddenly get the jitters, as if he were standing on a grave site. Quickly giving his conscious the cold shoulder, he continued down the entryway.

He saw the librarian look up as he came through the entrance. She did a double take, as if recognizing him, and then smiled and waved. Mason remembered her from the last couple times he had dropped by.

She must work here full time, Mason thought.

After arriving at the history section, Mason began to scan and pick off a few books to bring to one of the many round tables that were placed throughout the library. As he sat down, he noticed there was hardly anyone around, but it was a weekday, and since school was in session, there were no children there either. After picking up the first book, he started scanning for any references to Apep. He was about to open the second of the books he had brought with him when he felt a tap on his shoulder. It startled him a bit, but after turning, he saw it was the librarian. Though wearing glasses, she was not what you would a call a stereotypical librarian. She had long, black hair, brown eyes, and an attractive face. She was also wearing a shorter-than-average skirt and blouse that tightened around her thin waist and chest a little more than it needed to. Mason gave her a smile as she spoke.

"Sorry to bother you," she said softly, "but it looks as if you're looking for something specific." She gestured toward the stack of books Mason had piled on his table as she spoke.

"Is there something I can help you find Mr . . . . ?" she inquired.

Mason was not sure how to respond. He had never seen such personal attention in a library before. Perhaps she was hitting on him? He dismissed the thought immediately. His large wedding band was more than noticeable, not that this would stop all women, but he thought it to crude for a librarian.

"Krane . . . Mason Krane, but please, just call me Mason," he replied and she gave him a smile.

"Okay. Is there anything I can help you with . . . Mason?" she inquired delightfully.

"Nope, just poking around . . . I wouldn't want to waste your time," he replied.

"Are you sure? It wouldn't be any trouble?" she pushed.

"Well . . . okay," Mason said giving in. "Have you ever heard of Apep or seen a picture or tattoo of this nature?" he asked, showing her the picture he had drawn of the tattoo.

As soon as she saw the picture, she stood up and used her left hand to rub the back of her neck underneath her hair. She also, for an instant, seemed alarmed, but he figured it a normal reaction to such a strange drawing. After recomposing herself, she glanced at the image intently before giving a reply.

"I've never seen anything like that before, nor have I heard of the word Apep, but it looks like you have picked up the right books to look for answers." she stated, as if trying to get out of the conversation. "Well, I will let you get back to it. I will be up front if you need anything, Mr. Krane . . . ur, uh, Mason, I mean," she said with a hesitant smile.

"Thank you, Mrs . . . . ?" Mason replied.

"Oh, my apologies—just call me Amy," she said as she left.

Mason thought the encounter very odd. He was sure she recognized the symbol, but then again, maybe that was just his mind wanting so much for someone else to verify what only he and a dead babysitter had seen.

Mason continued scanning through the book, looking for anything that might be related. He was in a chapter of a book on Egyptian mythology and gods when he came across what he was looking for. At first he couldn't believe it. He thought perhaps he had misread it, but there it was. Among the other gods of Egypt, there was one called Apophis or Apep for short. This god embodied all the destructive forces of chaos. At this point, Mason thought this was pure coincidence. He was looking for one word, and he found it. For all he knew, Apep could be in the English dictionary, but what he read next changed his mind. Apep was always represented symbolically by a serpent or dragon.

"Could it be?" Mason caught himself asking out loud.

Continuing to read, Mason soaked up everything he could on the Egyptian god Apep. One of the ancient Egyptian texts, *The Book of the Heavenly Cow*, described Apep as a serpent or arch-demon who was the most dangerous inhabitant of the Egyptian underworld. Apep, according to the ancient text, was said to be thirty cubits or forty-five feet in length. His voice was so terrifying that it even scared the sun god, Ra. The text went on to describe a god of chaos who could reduce the temple buildings that symbolized order to ruin within seconds.

At this point Mason was half filled with excitement and half filled with confusion. What did any of this have to do with the kidnapping of his brother and the death of his parents? There was something deeper and darker here, and Mason felt as if he had only brushed the surface.

After pausing to think a moment, he nearly jumped out of his chair when his cell phone started to ring. He hadn't realized how quiet it had been until that moment, and again he felt ill at ease in this place.

"Krane here . . ." Mason stated flatly as he answered his phone. "Uncle Joe . . . Sure, I can come around . . . I'll be right over . . . 'Kay . . . Bye," Mason finished up the call quickly.

Uncle Joe had received a few more details around the article Mason had read in the paper earlier and urged him to come over to discuss them. Mason got up and exited the library, but he had so much on his mind, he had forgotten to put the books he had pulled back on the shelf. This was an all-too-familiar sight for the librarian, and as she walked up to the table Mason had been seated at, she reviewed the last page, which was open. Her eyes widened, and a look of discontent slid across her face as she read it. Slamming the book closed, she gathered up the books and began to put them back in their proper place on the shelves.

Mason arrived at his uncle's house on the other side of town. As he pulled into the driveway of the ranch-style house, he remembered the night the police brought him here to stay. It was the night he saw his mother murdered before his very eyes.

The police had brought him to his uncle's house after hours of questioning, but it was still dark outside. Mason remembered his uncle's house being lit up like a Christmas tree by the police lights. There was a large oak in the front yard with a swing on it. Mason and his brother, when visiting, would compete to see who would dare swing the highest.

Mason looked to his left at the big oak to see the swing had long since been taken down. Mason remembered asking his uncle to take down the swing shortly after coming to stay with him. Without his brother, it was just a reminder of what had been lost, and brought only pain to even look upon, let alone use. His uncle had made some cosmetic changes since then, but Mason saw the same house he was brought to on that horrible night his family was destroyed. It was the house he had eventually learned to call home.

Mason hadn't visited his uncle in a quite a while. In fact, he felt a little guilty since recently the only time he had contact with him was when he needed to leverage his uncle's experience and contacts as a former cop. His uncle had always been available to him and never let him down when it came to schmoozing his old police buddies for information. However, recently Mason got the feeling that his uncle was getting a little concerned with the many requests Mason had been making.

As he got out of his car and headed to the front door, Mason realized how much of an influence his uncle had had in his life. Uncle Joe had raised Mason as his own son and did the best he could with the resources he had. Uncle Joe was a beat cop, working the streets for basic calls, domestic violence, speeding tickets, etc. He had even had a short appearance on a reality TV show, but he never pursued anything of a higher level within the department. He loved being on the street, working with the people and helping to make his community safe. He had retired ten years ago from the force with full pension. But even though he was retired, he still participated heavily in neighborhood watch programs and other community events.

Though Mason was sure raising a five-year-old alone had worn his uncle out, you wouldn't be able to tell by looking at him. He was about six foot one, with brownish gray hair and a little bit of belly hanging over his belt. He would tell Mason, when Mason was young, that for each bad guy he caught he got a piece of candy, and that's how he got so big. He always had a warm smile and never shunned an opportunity to help a fellow neighbor or stranger, for that matter.

As he walked to the front door, Mason was eager to meet with Uncle Joe and find out if the murder/kidnapping he read about in the paper might be another possible connection to his own cases. He reached the front door, but before he could knock, the door opened and Uncle Joe smiled at him as he welcomed him in.

"Come in, Come in," his uncle pressed.

After entering the house he had come to know so well, Mason and Uncle Joe sat opposite from each other at the small kitchen table. His uncle was not a rich man by any stretch of the imagination, but he had made a decent living and was very content with the blessings life had brought him.

"You hardly come to visit me anymore," he scolded, half in jest. "I haven't seen Tyler for a long time," he said with a smile.

"I know, we need to plan a BBQ or something soon," Mason replied, avoiding his uncle's gaze as again a feeling of guilt washed over him.

Rapidly changing the subject, Mason launched a question, eager to find out what his uncle had learned. "So what did you find out about that article?" Mason asked anxiously.

"Not much, I'm afraid. It looks as if a thief or thieves entered the house from a basement window in an effort to burglarize the place. Based on where the bodies were found, they believe there was more than one intruder. The father was found in the bedroom with his throat slit, the mother in the hallway." After pausing a moment, his uncle continued.

"Something that's odd about this whole thing, though. There was no sign of a struggle. It's almost as if the victims were volunteering to be murdered. There were no scratches, bruises, or any other signs that they fought their attackers. The theory is that these would-be thieves used the victims' child to keep them from instigating any kind of a struggle," Uncle Joe concluded with an unsatisfied look on his face.

"Is there any trace of the missing boy?" Mason asked.

"None," his uncle replied shortly. "It's as if they, the child, and the stolen items disappeared without one speck of physical evidence."

Mason looked down as he contemplated the information. He knew in his gut that this was another case that fit the crime scene of his parents' death and the Grafton kidnapping. Looking down, he suddenly spoke to himself out loud, forgetting that he was in the company of his uncle.

"There has to be a connection!" Mason stated passionately.

Looking up into the face of his uncle, Mason knew what was coming next. His uncle had a look of concern on his face. Mason had seen it before, but whatever thoughts or feelings had brought it up in the past, Uncle Joe stayed silent, but this time he knew the silence was about to be broken.

"Mason, it's been twenty-five years since that night," he said, folding his arms in front of him as he spoke. "As far as I am concerned, the one good thing that came out of that night was the fact that God guided you to a career where you could help people locate their missing children. Look at all the cases you have solved, the families you have brought back together. You have done some wonderful things that probably never would have happened had your family not been taken that night, but you need to let it go. You're a grown man, smart enough to make your own decisions, but I can see what this has been doing to you lately. You're going to drive yourself crazy looking for answers you're never going to find." He paused a moment, lowering his gaze.

"You forget that I lost family that night too . . . that was my brother who was murdered. I did all I could to find those who were responsible, but after all this time, I have learned something very simple. Although difficult for us to understand, God is going to take care of it, and in the long run there will be a judgment for those responsible, but it's not me, and it's not you who will be the ones to seek out justice for God. You will own do yourself damage by trying to take on that role." Uncle Joe stopped, looking into Masons eyes, with tears almost welling up in his own.

"Uncle Joe . . ." Mason started. "I'm sorry, I know it seems that way, but I remember my father's last words as if they were spoken to me yesterday. I remember everything, and it was more than a murder. It was a set up, and I believe there is a reason I have seen the things I have. I know something is going on here, and if someone doesn't get to the bottom of it, more people will die. You're right when you say God put me in this place for a reason, and I am more confident of that now than I've ever been." Mason got up from the sofa, turned, and put his hands in his pockets, staring at the wall that happened to be covered with family photos. He was looking at one particular photo of his parents, his brother, and himself as he continued.

"I don't mean to upset you, Uncle Joe, but there is an answer out there, and I am convinced I am the one that has to find it—not just because I want answers about what happened that night but because if I don't, this is going to continue to happen." With that said, Mason returned to the seat opposite of his uncle.

There was an uncomfortable silence between them for a moment, and then Mason's uncle smoothed it over.

"Well . . . I've said my piece. You are the one who needs to do what you think is best, and if God has put you on this path, then I will do whatever I can to help you. You are like a son to me, Mason . . . I know you know that, but sometimes it's good to say it out loud every once in a while. I am very proud of you, and your mother and father would be too," he said with a warm smile.

From there the conversation turned casual between Mason and his uncle. They talked about the weather and how their favorite football team was doing, throwing out a joke here and there. The encounter ended on a good note, and Mason felt good that they had had a chance to talk. It was getting near five o'clock, and Mason left his uncle's to try to beat his wife home from work. He usually did his workout before dinner. It was a good tension reliever, and he had a lot to unload today.

As he pulled into the driveway, Mason saw that in fact he had beaten his wife home from work. After entering the house, he quickly went upstairs and changed into a T-shirt, shorts, and some tennis shoes. After stopping at the kitchen to fill up a container with water, he went downstairs to the basement. Mason had converted the basement into a miniature gym. It was about twenty feet by twenty feet with a ten-foot by ten-foot mat in the center. In one corner was a speed bag hanging off the wall and in another corner was a wooden dummy. If you didn't know any better, you would think it was a place to hang your coat and hat, but it was in fact a device used to train in the art of Kung Fu. In the center of the room, hanging from the ceiling of the basement, was a full-size punching bag.

Mason walked out onto the mat, got on his knees, and began to pray.

"Dear Lord," he started. "Thank you for the blessing of your love, guidance, and protection. Please guide me in all my ways, in all my thoughts, and in all my actions. If I am ever forced to use my skills, Lord, please guide my movements, that they may strike true and never falter. Give me discernment, Father, that my actions may always bring you glory. In the name of Christ your Son I ask it. Amen."

You wouldn't know it to look at him, but Mason was very capable of handling himself in a fight. He was Caucasian, five feet, nine inches tall, and weighed roughly 165 pounds. With his brown hair, blue eyes, and elegant look, most people took him for a corporate yuppie, but as they say, "Don't judge a book by its cover." Mason's uncle had started him on martial arts as soon as he came to live with him, and at the time, it was a welcome distraction from his parents' death. Mason had been in Tae Kwon Do since he was five and had also taken Kung

Fu and Brazilian Jujitsu, which was basically wrestling, but instead of pinning your opponent, the object was to make him submit.

Mason always prayed before he practiced his arts and always asked God to provide him with the same guidance. He knew that, while he had the ability to protect himself, he could also do a lot of damage to another person. He took this very seriously, especially after one incident where a drunk mistakenly mistook Mason for his wife's lover. Mason had no choice but to defend himself when the man attacked, but while Mason's skills left him unscathed, the drunk suffered a broken nose and a slight concussion. Mason didn't enjoy hurting people, but in this line of work it paid to be prepared.

To keep himself from getting cramps, Mason started by doing some basic stretches. When he was done, he moved toward what his wife called the "Stick Man." The wooden dummy, known as a Choy Li Fut in Chinese, was basically that—a man-like figure made of wood. It had two arms stretching out from the sides and a padded post in the center. Basically you used the wooden arms to simulate blocks and used the pad in the center to simulate counterpunches to the gut, chest, and face. Mason started slowly, using very fluid movements and simulating blocks and counterpunches, but it wasn't long before he was striking swiftly at the arms and the head portion of the padded post. Though moving quickly, it was clear his movements were not random but honed for accuracy, almost as if he were playing patty cake with the dummy. Finally, he stopped and spent the next half an hour utilizing the speed bag and the punching bag to practice his various techniques. After hitting the bag one last time, he could hear the front door creak open and knew Tyler was home from work. With that he headed upstairs, eager to see her after such a long day.

Mason watched her put her purse and keys on a table just inside the door. She looked as if she were in a trance and was oblivious to his presence.

"Hey, you," Mason said lovingly as he entered the living room.

She snapped out of her glazed look, and a smile came across her face as she walked up to greet him.

"Hi," she said, giving him a kiss first.

"Everything okay?" Mason asked curiously.

"Yeah . . . Yeah, I just had a long day, that's all," she stated, brushing his concerns aside.

They continued their discussion on how their days went for a while, had dinner, and went to bed. Mason was certain something was bothering her, but for all his smooth talking, he couldn't get it out of her. He knew her work sometimes got a little stressful, but something told him there was more behind her feelings than work. But then again, maybe she just didn't want to unload her thoughts on him. She did that from time to time, not wanting to burden him, but he understood her need to vent and tried his best to encourage her to speak her mind.

As Mason was lying in bed, he planned to continue where he left off on visiting the tattoo parlors. After what he had found in the library, he was confident there was a connection between the symbol and the Egyptian god Apep, but where that connection would lead him, he couldn't begin to fathom.

CHAPTER *3*

After having a very fitful night's sleep, Mason awoke early to continue visiting the local tattoo parlors. He had been to several so far, with no luck in finding anyone who recognized the symbol, though he did get many offers from the artists saying they could duplicate the design very easily if he wanted it done. Mason always declined politely to their offers, which always brought a look of confusion to their faces. After all, he had just told them that he was interested in the design and was curious if any of them had done it before. His refusal made them suspicious immediately, and the last couple places he went to were not in the best part of town. In fact, Mason scolded himself for the way he had dressed; he definitely stood out in his ironed slacks, long-sleeved, button-up shirt, and sport jacket. It was clear to anyone in this part of town that he wasn't local.

By noon, Mason's stomach started to rumble, so he decided after this next tattoo parlor, he would stop for a bite to eat. After parking in the street in front of the shop, Mason got out of his mid-'90s sedan and looked up at the sign above the store. The sign read, "Dragon Tattoo" in black, red, and blue, swerving text. Mason entered the parlor, seeing exactly what he expected based on the many other parlors he had visited. On the walls were several designs, as well as different styles of fonts, animals, and human artistry, the human portion being a bit more than Mason wanted to see of the female anatomy. He scanned the wall for the symbol while at the same time making his way to the counter. He saw a short, stocky, bald man with a goatee smoking a cigarette and staring at Mason with a suspicious look on his face. He had a brown complexion and had on dark sunglasses that covered his eyes. Although he was wearing a shirt—a tank top—it was obvious that the whole upper part of his body was covered in artwork. Suddenly, the man got up from his seat and started walking toward the front desk to confront his would-be customer. He did not look pleased and Mason immediately got the impression he wasn't welcome here.

"I told your boy yesterday, homes!" the man shouted with a Latino accent. "I will have the rent to him by Friday, and it don't make no difference who he sends in here. He ain't going to get it no sooner," he stated, pointing his cigarette-holding hand at Mason.

"I'm sorry, but you must have me confused with somebody else," Mason said with a confused look on his face. "I'm just looking at tattoos . . . In fact, I wondered if you could help me with a certain design," Mason said as he pulled out the drawing he had made. "Have you ever done a tattoo like this before?" Mason asked, watching the man's reaction for any sign of recognition.

The man relaxed a bit and then took the paper from Mason, pushing his dark shades up to his brow to get a better look at the design. Then he turned back to Mason to speak.

"What are you a cop or something, essé?" the goateed man said jokingly, and then he continued without giving Mason a chance to reply. "I ain't seen nothing like this before, but it looks pretty easy to do if you want to get in the chair, homes. I'll set you up." The man gestured to the chair in jest, knowing full well that Mason was not there to get a tattoo.

"That's okay, but thanks for the offer," Mason replied politely, taking the paper back and turning to walk out of the store.

"You better hide your Rolex before you leave this neighborhood, essé!" the man shouted jokingly at Mason as he was leaving.

Again, Mason kicked himself for his inability to blend in, but he could tell that the tattoo artist had never seen the design before. He may have been bad mannered and rude, but Mason could tell by his reaction that he had no information on the drawing of the red pyramid with a black snake coiled around it.

Mason had just exited the shop and was about to get into his car when he heard a commotion coming from the side alleyway of the tattoo shop. After walking to the edge of the alley and looking down, he could see that toward the back of the shop three figures seemed to be kicking and punching a fourth, who was on the ground. He wasn't sure what was going on, but he could tell as he walked forward that the young man that was being beaten was in real bad shape. Mason stopped ten feet short of the scene before he spoke.

"What's going on here?" Mason asked loudly.

The three figures turned toward Mason, obviously annoyed by the interruption.

One of the figures, a tall black man, stepped forward. Mason could tell by his body language and the shifting of the other two figures next to him that he was the leader. He was about six feet tall, with a blue handkerchief wrapped around his head and a cold, hard stare on his scarred face

"This is none of your business, Uncle Tom. Just mind your own biz before we have to hurt you *bad*," he said, with great emphasis on the last word.

Mason eyed the other two carefully, sizing them up. The man to the left of the leader was white, about five feet five inches tall, with a baseball cap on backward. He was holding a small wooden club in his right hand and was slapping it repeatedly into the palm of his left hand. The other was black and very wide and had a baseball cap on sideways. Mason paused before responding, trying to get a better look at the other figure on the ground, which could now be heard whimpering.

"I don't want any trouble . . ." Mason stated. "It just looks like your friend there is hurt pretty bad and uh . . . I would like to get him some medical attention," Mason stated, but he could tell none of the men were buying his story. Seeing that they were not wavering at all, Mason tried a different approach. "Also, that's not really fair, three on one, don't you think?" Mason said cautiously.

The leader glanced at the others with a smirk on his face and then turned toward Mason to speak.

"I guess they don't teach you up town folks how to count too good. Looks like five to one to me," the leader said, laughing.

Then Mason knew why they were laughing. He could hear the footsteps behind him and turned to see two more gang-like dressed hoodlums. One had a switchblade in his right hand, and the other was carrying a baseball bat.

The leader and the men on each side of him took a step forward, surrounding Mason. It was then that Mason could see a young man curled up in a ball on the asphalt behind them. He was a young black male, sixteen at the oldest. He was skinny, and one of his eyes was swollen shut. He also had blood dripping out of his nose and onto his blue T-shirt. He quickly slid backward on the ground when he saw his attackers turn their attention toward Mason.

Mason thought about what to do. He couldn't call the police; it was far too late for that. Though he was able to handle himself, five to one was a lot to ask of anybody. Mason decided the practical approach was to offer them money. Mason pulled out his wallet as the men came closer to form a five-point circle around him.

"Listen, guys . . . take anything. My money, my car, whatever you want," Mason stated quickly, holding out his wallet and spreading the bills inside so they could be seen. As the leader approached, Mason braced himself for anything. He didn't want to fight, but if they left him no choice, he would protect himself.

"Oh we are going to take what we want, all right, but we're going to have some fun first," stated the leader, laughing while leaning an elbow on the man to his right.

Trying to catch Mason off guard, the leader suddenly threw a punch with his right hand. Mason ducked low to the ground and did a sweeping kick to the man's shins. Having his legs kicked out from under him, the man fell to the ground so hard that his body made a thud as it hit the dirt. When Mason stood up, he felt a large blow to his back, he guessed by the thug with the bat, which sent him crashing toward the ground. Knowing there would be more if he didn't move, Mason quickly rolled backward and got to his knees quickly. The man with the switchblade lunged directly toward Mason's head, but he saw it coming and rolled backward, kicking the blade from the man's hand as he did. His attackers paused a moment, obviously stunned by Mason's abilities. This gave Mason enough time to get back to his feet and prepare for another exchange.

The leader was on his feet again, leading the other four, but now all of his attackers were in front of him. The leader cursed and threatened Mason with a growl.

"Your own mama ain't goin' to recognize you when we get done with you!" the leader shouted angrily.

At this point, Mason changed his tactics. He was clearly in danger, and the odds being what they were, he took an offensive approach instead of a defensive one. As they approached, the leader hung back while the man with the bat attacked first. The man wielded the bat and tried to hit Mason in the head, but Mason caught the man's bat-wielding arm underneath his own left arm and then came up hard underneath it with the palm of his right hand. The blow was so intense that it not only made his attacker drop the bat, but he also stumbled back screaming, seeing that his arm was bent in the opposite direction and had made a snapping noise as well.

The others appeared a little weary at this point, but Mason wasn't going to wait for one of them to come at him again. After running up to the heavy one, Mason did a roundhouse kick to his face so fast, it sent the man reeling to the ground.

Two down, Mason thought as the others approached.

Next the man who had earlier tried to stab him with a switchblade approached. He came up to Mason and threw a punch with his left hand, but again Mason dodged low and in the same fluid motion hit the man with a hard uppercut to the groin area. The man grunted and fell heavily to the ground, moaning in pain.

The leader and the white one were about to attack Mason at the same time when from out of nowhere the young man who had been beaten jumped on the leader's back, holding a switchblade to his throat.

"Now who da man! Huh, sucker?" The youngster asked tauntingly as he continued to badger his attackers while holding the knife at the gang leader's throat.

He must have picked up the knife during the skirmish, Mason thought.

"I think it's time you all went home now, before I start to get the shakes," he stated, sliding off the man's back but still in a very good position to stab the leader in a vital area.

The leader backed up slowly, staring at his adversaries as he walked.

"You better watch your back, Jordan, and you too, whitey," the leader said, pointing his finger at Mason.

Mason watched as one by one each of the men followed after the leader. One was still howling in pain from his broken arm as he fell in line.

"Punks!" The teenager suddenly blurted out while at the same time sizing up Mason.

"You did pretty good, man. Where'd you learn that stuff, at Princeton?" the young man said jokingly while he wiped the blood from his face with his shirt.

Mason took a good look at the young man, who apparently was not as bad off as he first appeared. Now Mason understood the young man's strategy. The more damage his attackers felt they inflicted; the quicker they would leave him alone. Mason also noticed needle marks inside the youngster's left arm and suddenly realized he may have inadvertently got involved in a drug deal gone wrong. It was then Mason realized that his back was throbbing with pain from the blow he had taken from the bat. Stretching back and putting his right hand on his spine, he inquired if the young man was okay.

"You need an ambulance or anything?"

The young man, who went on to introduce himself as Jordan, looked at Mason with a taken back expression on his face.

"Man, I don't need nothin that a quick fix won't patch up," Jordan replied.

Mason looked at Jordan disapprovingly as he spoke.

"That stuff will make you suffer more than those guys did. You should stay away from that junk."

Immediately, Jordan got defensive.

"Who are you? My mother? I didn't ask you to step in . . . In fact, you would be dog meat if it hadn't been for me."

Jordan paused before continuing. "In fact, I think you owe me Jack. I think twenty bucks should cover it," he said, holding his hand out with a smile.

"There's no way I'm giving some kid with a drug habit money to support it. There are plenty of ways you could make an honest living instead of hanging out with guys like that, doing drugs, and messing yourself up," Mason stated flatly as he continued to nurse his sore back.

Jordan turned sincere and spoke softly as he replied.

"Yeah, and I suppose I had all the same opportunities you had, right? I bet you lived on the streets since you were ten. I bet your mother was a junkie, selling herself on the street corner so she could buy groceries and pay rent on a roach-infested hotel, right?" Jordan's voice started to escalate.

"Oh yeah, and I bet your father left when you were five and you didn't have nobody to go to, right? No school, no parents, no job . . . heck, I bet you went through life with all those things, huh?" Jordan waved his hand as if in disgust as he turned to walk away.

Mason felt horrible; he was not good at seeing things from other people's perspective. In his mind, everyone had the same opportunities and the same chance to live a successful life as he had. Therefore, his pity meter always ran low, but every now and then, as in this case,

God would pull the rug out from under him, letting him know that he didn't rate any better than this young man.

"Wait," Mason called out after him.

Jordan turned with a sarcastic look on his face as Mason spoke.

"Listen . . . I'm kind of hungry. Getting the stuffing beat out of you works up quite an appetite. You wanna grab a bite . . . my treat?" Mason asked with a smile on his face.

Jordan didn't look enthused, but his face soon smoothed over.

"All right, I know a joint around the corner," Jordan replied.

Mason and Jordan headed down the street to a diner that was just up the block from where their altercation had occurred. It looked like a Denny's only it was called Denise's Diner. As they entered the establishment, a waitress came up, quickly staring at Jordan with a look of dissatisfaction on her face.

"Jordan, you know I ain't letting you in here," she barked.

"No, no, no . . . you got it all wrong, my friend here is buying." Jordan motioned to Mason as he replied.

The waitress eyed him up and down and then stared, as if awaiting confirmation he had money to pay for the meal.

"Yep, it's on me," Mason said with a fake smile on his face.

"I don't know how he hustled you, but money is money. Have a seat over there and

I'll be right with you. And, Jordan, go to washroom and clean that face of yours, boy. That's all I need is to have you bleeding up in here," the waitress said sarcastically.

Mason sat in the booth the waitress had pointed out while Jordan went to bathroom to clean up. Mason stared at the menu as Jordan returned, and he inquired about Jordan's familiarity with the restaurant.

"Been here before, I see . . . you carry a real good reputation around with you, don't you?" Mason jabbed.

"Oh that's just Eisha. She loves me; she just don't know it yet," Jordan returned with a small giggle and grin.

Mason nodded, and then, folding his hands on the table, he bowed his head and began to pray to himself. When he had finished, he noticed Jordan was staring at him as if he was crazy.

"No wonder you're so high and mighty; you got that high-class religion, eh?" Jordan poked.

Again, Mason felt ashamed at his behavior earlier. Being an advocate against the stereotypical, white, Christian male, he suddenly found that he was nothing but a hypocrite.

"I'm sorry about that. I have no right to judge your life," Mason replied, swallowing hard afterward.

"Ain't no thing, man, I heard that jive a million times," Jordan stated flatly, but Mason could tell that his words had hurt him, even if he had been scolded about his drug use frequently.

"What was all that about back there anyway?" Mason asked.

"Well, that tall one, Tyrone, tried to stiff me on some dough he owed me, so I just kept his junk instead of selling it," Jordan replied indignantly.

"You better be careful, he didn't look to happy when we left. Are you sure he won't come after you again?" Mason inquired further.

"Shoot . . . somebody's always after me for one thing or another," Jordan retorted.

Just then the waitress came and took their orders, and silence reigned for the rest of the meal. Mason noticed that Jordan wolfed down his food in an instant. He couldn't understand how such a skinny body could hold all that food. Jordan had ordered two meals and finished them both off by the time Mason had finished his. Well on his way to finishing off a slice of apple pie he was eating, Jordan looked up and stared at Mason for a second.

"So what brings you down here anyway, man?" Jordan asked, his mouth half full of apple pie. "I can tell you aren't a regular in this neighborhood," Jordan continued.

"I was looking for something," Mason replied, not wanting to go into detail.

"What?" Jordan asked as he shoveled another fork load of pie into his mouth.

Mason, frustrated with no leads, not to mention the day's highlights, gave in to Jordan's pestering.

"A tattoo," Mason returned flatly.

"A tattoo?" Jordan's eyes widened has he started to cough and laugh at the same time.

"Why you coming all the way down here to get a tattoo? They don't have tattoo shops uptown?" he questioned, spitting pie crumbs out as he spoke.

"No, it's not that. I am looking for a specific tattoo. I am trying to find the guy who did it originally," Mason replied, eager to end this conversation and return to more familiar surroundings.

"What's it look like?" Jordan continued to press.

Mason, certain this would bring an end to the persistent questioning, pulled out the drawing of a symbol he had made and handed it to Jordan.

Jordan took the piece of paper, and as he looked at it, he started to chew very slowly. Mason didn't notice at first, but then he could tell that Jordan seemed to show some kind of recognition.

"Yo, yo . . . I've seen this before, man," Jordan said excitedly.

Mason wasn't sure of him at first. He thought this might be another ploy to extort something from him, but he decided to give Jordan the benefit of the doubt.

"Where did you see this?" Mason inquired.

Jordan looked down, as if ashamed, for a moment before he went on.

"Well, uh, I was in this alley way taking some garbage out and a . . ." Jordan stopped, seeing the sideways glance that Mason was giving him, obviously not buying his story. "Okay, okay," Jordan gave in. "I had just had a fix and was kickin' back in this back alley I sometimes sleep in," Jordan said.

Mason's heart once again leaped into his throat out of sympathy with the life this young man led. He suddenly felt guilty for the many things he had always taken for granted, most of which would have been luxuries to Jordan. Mason had run into some trouble with drugs when he was younger, but Uncle Joe straightened him out quickly. Jordan didn't have an uncle or anyone else, for that matter, to help him. Right then, Mason made a decision to help Jordan, even if the information he was providing was bogus.

Jordan continued on with his story as Mason took out a tablet and started to jot down notes. It was late in the evening a couple months ago. Jordan had fallen asleep behind some large containers that were next to a Dumpster. The alleyway was quiet, and hardly anyone ever came back there because of the stench. As he slept in the alleyway, he awoke to a vehicle driving closer toward the dead end alley. Thinking at first that it was the police, Jordan quickly got up and ensured his body was well hid. Then, as he looked in between a crack in the stack of containers, he saw a light blue Chevy Impala pull up to the Dumpster. The headlights from the car lit up the alleyway, but suddenly the headlights shut off and the only light was coming from the parking lights of the vehicle.

A man stepped out of the car. He was of average height, weight, and build and was wearing a suit and gloves. After stepping out of his vehicle and heading toward the back of the car, he popped open the trunk. At this point, Jordan thought the man was just dropping off some garbage. A lot of people did that who didn't have room in their regular trash cans for bigger items. As Jordan continued to watch, the man appeared on the other side of the vehicle carrying what looked like a stereo receiver and other audio/video equipment. Also, he didn't have his jacket or tie on anymore. Instead the man's sleeves were rolled up and his shirt slightly unbuttoned. As the man approached, he leaned over the rail of the Dumpster to place the items on the top of the stack of garbage.

As the man rose back up, Jordan noticed a tattoo on the man's chest centered directly over his heart. It was a tattoo of a red pyramid with a black snake coiled around it. The man made two more trips to his trunk before leaving the alleyway. The only reason Jordan remembered any of this at all was the fact that all the items the man had thrown out appeared to be in perfect condition. The next day Jordan had sold or traded all of the equipment for drugs, food, and Lord knows what else.

"Did you see what this guy looked like?" Mason inquired with excitement.

"Not really . . . he had short brown or black hair and glasses. That's all I can remember." Jordan replied.

"Wait a minute!" Jordan stated quickly. "I do remember one other thing. The dude's ear! . . . Yeah, the dude's left ear looked like the top of it had been chopped off clean."

Mason kept scribbling as he asked Jordan another question. "The equipment that you sold—what were the items, and who did you sell them to?"

"I took most of it to Ray's Pawn Shop over on Fifth Street," Jordan replied flatly. He continued on to describe the DVD player and a stereo receiver he had taken there. There were additional items, but he didn't remember enough about those to give Mason any decent leads.

Mason kept going over his notes to ensure he had everything, double checking all the facts with Jordan before moving on to the other notes he had taken. Mason's heart was pumping a mile a minute. This was the first real lead he had had in his parents' murder and the kidnapping of his brother and the Grafton boy. His next step would be to visit Ray's Pawn Shop to see if he could recover any of what he believed were stolen goods from the murder/kidnappings. Mason suddenly realized that in all his excitement he forgot about Jordan. Looking across the table, he saw a young man who needed help desperately, but it had to be a two-way street. Mason knew that he could only help Jordan if he wanted to be helped.

The waitress made a checkup visit on them and to make sure the bill was going to be paid. Mason ordered an additional lunch to go for Jordan and saw a smile cross his face when he did so. The waitress left, and they continued to sit, waiting for the order to be completed.

"Thanks, dude, you're all right for an uptown Jo," Jordan chuckled.

Mason smiled briefly as he reached into his jacket pocket and said, "Jordan, this is my card. I want you to call me if you remember anything else or see anything else related to what we talked about today." Mason handed him the card and swallowed hard before he continued. He did not want to mess the next part up.

"Also, if you ever decide that you want a change, that you want to live a different life, let me know. I don't know how hard your life has been, but I can tell that it hasn't been easy for you. I would like to help you if I can, but you have to want it first. At the very least, I would like your permission to keep you in my prayers."

Mason was sincere about the offer; he felt in his heart that God had put this young man before him to reveal more than the mystery he was trying to solve, but he also knew Jordan needed help. He needed someone to lift him up and give him a chance.

Jordan accepted the business card from Mason's hand cautiously.

"Sure. I'll let you know if I sees or hears something, man," Jordan replied, shrugging off the sincerity of Mason's offer. "As far as the rest, you can pray for me all you want. I like my life, and any trouble I have gotten into God hasn't seen fit to help me yet, so I don't pay him no mind either."

"Just the same, if you need anything—a warm bed, a meal—you call me," Mason restated.

Looking down, reviewing the business card Mason had just given him, Jordan's eyebrows lifted in surprise.

"You're a private eye?" Jordan said, smiling. "Like Magnum, PI, right?"

"Something like that," Mason returned.

"Well, I knew you weren't no cop—at least no cop I've ever seen could fight like that," Jordan said.

It was then that the waitress returned with the to-go lunch and Mason's change. Mason pushed the bag full of food toward Jordan as he got up to leave. Letting him go in front of him, Mason left a tip on the table. As they walked outside, Mason felt that Jordan was headed in the opposite direction he was going. Sure enough, Jordan turned around and held up his right hand.

"Hey, man, we really gave it to 'em, didn't we? Give me five," he said, gesturing Mason to high-five him. Mason smiled as he slapped the young man's hand.

"I am outta here, man. I'll holler if I remember anything else," Jordan said.

"You take care of yourself now," Mason replied.

Jordan dropped his act for a moment, and Mason could see Jordan's face dive back to sincerity as he turned and walked down the street. Mason was sad to see him go; he never thought he would come across somebody like Jordan and have such an instant connection. He could only hope and pray that he would see him again.

As he recalled the day's events, Mason shook his head in disbelief as he looked up at the sky. "Lord, you sure do work in mysterious ways," he said with a smirk.

Mason was about to leave when the waitress came out the door. "That was a waste of money, if you ask me," she stated sarcastically. "You know how many times that little punk has stiffed me?" she stated in disgust.

Mason reached into his wallet and pulled out a hundred-dollar bill, shoving the money into the waitress's hand as he spoke.

"Probably as many times as me, you, and others treated him like a criminal instead of a lost soul. That should cover any outstanding orders, perhaps even a few extra if he wanders in again," Mason returned, giving the waitress his own look of disgust—not just for her but for himself and the way he had behaved earlier.

The waitress looked at the money Mason had shoved into her hand, speechless at the act of mercy he had shown.

With that, he turned and headed down the block back toward his car. It was then that the pain from the blow he had taken from behind returned. Somehow it had been there the entire time, but he had paid it no mind until all his distractions were gone. When he reached his vehicle, he unlocked the door, and his face contorted in pain as he sat in the driver's seat.

Pausing for a moment, he thought about what his next steps should be. After pulling out his notepad, he reviewed the information he had jotted down from his conversation with Jordan. Jordan had said he had taken some of the items to a pawn shop; perhaps some of them might still be there. If he could get one or both of them, he might be able to link them back to the crime scene, and fingerprints taken from the stolen audio and video equipment might lead to a suspect.

Closing the notepad, he realized there was something else he had to take care of. It had been a couple weeks since he had last spoken with the Graftons about their case on their missing son, David. He didn't know what to tell them at this point. All he had were theories and this lead on the possible stolen goods. It was a long shot at best, but Mason believed in giving his clients regular updates, even if he didn't have anything new to tell. One thing was for sure: if he could get one of the items from the pawn store and positively identify it as something stolen from the Grafton house, it would prove that there was another motive behind the crime. Why would someone go to all that trouble to steal something and kill a babysitter in the process just to throw it away? This was getting more complicated by the minute. The more information he uncovered, the more unanswerable questions he was left with.

Starting the car, Mason vowed to visit the pawn shop the following Monday. Tomorrow was Sunday, after all, and he really needed the energy he knew being in God's house would give him. Also, he needed to spend some time with Tyler. He had missed her lately with all his trips, and he had a lot to share with her on some of the things he had learned—not just about the case but about the remarkable young man he prayed he would see again.

CHAPTER 4

Mason had soaked in a hot bath the night before, but the throbbing pain nailed him hard when his alarm clock went off, again, Sunday morning. He had already taken a rather long verbal berating from his wife for getting involved in a fight and nearly getting himself killed. She had also complained that she was going to have to sleep with a Ben Gay factory all night. He knew she was right, but all things being equal, he looked at the pain and foot-long bruise across his back as a bonus.

Grunting heavily, he got up slowly to sit on the edge of the bed. After rubbing his eyes and yawning, he realized he hadn't had any nightmares last night, but the pain from his injury had been more than enough to make him lose a few hours of sleep.

"All right, mister. That's the third time that snooze alarm has gone off, so you're getting up now whether you like it or not," Tyler commanded as she entered the bedroom.

She was a light sleeper, and Mason had no doubt that her slumber had ended the first time his alarm had gone off. She didn't mind so much if he actually got up, but if he hit that snooze button and went back to sleep, he knew he would hear about it later.

Mason was still plagued with thoughts about yesterday's events, especially Jordan. Tyler had listened intently the night before, and although she wasn't happy about the fight, she was very supportive of his actions, especially when it came to Jordon. Mason had pitched the idea about taking Jordan in, giving him the help and guidance to be whatever it was God truly wanted for his life. He was sure it was what God wanted him to do, but Tyler was a bit hesitant about taking in a complete stranger, especially one with such a scarred past. Mason understood her position and resolved to continue praying that

God would open the doors necessary for whatever course of action needed to be taken.

Mason and Tyler continued with the morning festivities and headed off to church. Mason was looking forward to it and was also eager to see Uncle Joe. Yesterday's events gave him a new perspective on all his uncle had done for him, and he was sure he hadn't thanked him enough for all he had done in his life. He didn't even want to think about the person he might have become had his uncle not been there for him. This only served to increase the burden on Mason's heart to assist Jordan in any way he could. He was sure that if it was God's will, which he believed it was, God would make a way for them to cross paths again.

As they arrived, they saw that there were two police vehicles parked directly in front of the church. Although police helped out directing traffic before and after service, it was unusual to see their vehicles in plain view. Mason got the uncomfortable feeling that something very bad had happened.

"I wonder what's goin' on," Tyler said curiously, obviously coming to the same conclusions Mason had about the scene.

"I don't know, but I hope it's nothing serious," Mason replied with concern in his voice.

They parked their car and began to walk toward the main sanctuary. Mason had been attending this church basically his entire life. His father and his uncle attended church here, so when Mason went to live with his uncle, he naturally continued to go to the same church. He had grown up with a lot of the people here, and that made it all the more encouraging when he came.

The main sanctuary was a large stadium-type setup. It was set up to hold about twenty-five hundred people and was relatively new. They had four different services for people to attend—two on Saturday and two on Sunday—so all five thousand-plus members could attend. Mason had been there when the church was having its services out of a local high school when there were only about two hundred members. It had definitely grown since then, and because of the large membership, they were able to open a wide variety of new ministry opportunities. However, at times, Mason did miss the smaller version of his church. Back then everyone knew everyone else. Now he always saw many faces he didn't recognize, but he was happy it had grown so large just the same.

"Got to go, hon, I will see you in service." After giving him a peck on the cheek, Tyler walked toward a different entrance of the building, labeled "Infants—2."

Tyler volunteered in the nursery every Sunday during the first service, and they would attend the second service together. Mason watched as she walked away, knowing she would have a fulfilling day. She loved babies and was eager to have one of her own. They had been trying for a year and it hadn't happened yet, but Mason was sure it would happen in God's good time.

Mason also served in the church in the first service of the day. He helped run the sound board in the tech booth of the church for the fourth—through sixth-grade classes. They had their own building opposite of the main sanctuary. Mason started in that direction when he felt a hand come across his shoulder. As he turned, he saw the warm, bubbly face of Uncle Joe.

"Hi, son. How are you this morning?" his uncle said warmly as he gave Mason a big hug.

"Great. In fact, I can't imagine a time I felt more exhilarated," Mason returned.

His uncle's eyebrows rose in a questioning look as Mason relayed to him his amazing story that had taken place the day before. They walked toward the kids' building as they spoke. Mason's uncle served there too as a teacher. They had just about made it to the entrance when Mason had finished telling his story.

"Jordan really made me think, Uncle Joe . . . about all I had when I was growing up and all he didn't have. I know I wasn't always the easiest kid to deal with, but yesterday's events really made me see all you had done to raise me up and help me be the man God wanted me to be. I don't know what else to say but thank you."

His uncle's bottom lip quivered a bit, and his eyes began to tear up as he responded.

"No thanks necessary. Seeing you grow into the man you have become is thanks enough. I am very proud of you, and your mother and father would be too," he stammered, trying to hold back the tears.

With that said, they embraced for a brief moment before entering the building.

The first service had gone smoothly, and Mason had completed his part and went out front to meet Tyler to go to the main service. When he saw her coming, he could see she was eager to tell him something.

"Well, I found out why the cops were here," Tyler stated flatly.

"What happened?" Mason replied.

"Last night, after the second service, a mother left her ten-year-old son outside while she used the restroom. When she came out, he was gone. Someone took him."

"*What!*" Mason shouted. *How could something like that happen at a church?* Mason thought.

"Yep. The police are here doing some follow up with some of the staff who were here last night. I spoke to one of the other girls in the nursery, and she said that the only thing anyone saw was a woman wearing a hat and sunglasses and who had long black hair walking away holding the boy's hand.

Mason was baffled, but after thinking for a moment, he realized it really wouldn't be that difficult. *After all, you have a lot of people huddled in their groups talking, plus I bet many of them didn't know the little boy or his mother personally. Even if they did, they probably wouldn't think much of seeing the boy walking off with someone they didn't recognize. They probably would have assumed that it was a friend or relative. Either way, when church lets out, there is basically a huge mob of people walking to their cars. How many of them are just faces in the crowd?*

"That's tragic. Was it anyone we know?" Mason questioned.

"Grace Umbers and her son, Jimmy. I don't know her personally, but I have seen her and her son around campus many times," Tyler returned.

"I will have to call her; she will undoubtedly want any additional help finding her son. Maybe I can do some investigation pro-bono. It's the least I can do," Mason said as Tyler nodded in agreement.

As they entered the service, Mason and Tyler were both filled with grief for the family who had their child stolen from them. Mason entertained the thought for a moment that perhaps this was connected with his case and the others he was researching, but because the modus operandi was so different, he didn't give it a second thought.

The service that day was very uplifting, yet sad at the same time. The pastor had taken a special time of prayer for the boy and his family. This seemed to put the congregation in a somber mood, especially those who had children. Mason, however, took it as a challenge, and it renewed his vigilance both in his career choice and his resolve to solve his own cases.

He promised himself to give Mrs. Umbers a call and offer his assistance, but with so much time gone by, the odds were slim that anyone would find the boy unharmed or at all, for that matter.

After arriving home, Mason immediately proceeded to his study and left a message on Mrs. Umber's answering machine. He was sure that it would be jam-packed full of condolences and offers of help, and he wanted to leave her his contact information before her answering machine ran out of space. Mason recalled his uncle going through this on the morning after his parents were killed. That faint thought brought a sting back to his heart, but he focused all his emotion toward the goal of finding the killers responsible for their deaths.

The rest of the night was uneventful; Mason reviewed the statements he had taken from Jordan once again to make sure he hadn't missed something. He also called the Graftons and informed them that while he was still following up on some leads, he did not have any tangible information on the progress of their case. He hated those calls. It seemed as though he had made more of those than he did on ones that were considered positive, when in fact most of the cases that had an actual outcome were the grim findings of a child's dead body. While it provided closure for the case and for the families he had been hired by, Mason never considered these closures a success. Oddly enough, though, in the few cases he had collected over the years that he felt matched his own, never once had a body been found—not once. If they were in fact linked, and Mason believed they were, where were they? Yet another question that would continue to haunt him unanswered.

Mason was well underway the next day. There was no sleeping in for him, especially after the incident at his own church. He was more intent than ever to find out what was going on with the cases he was investigating. The first stop on his list was Ray's Pawn Shop. Mason dressed himself a little more appropriately this time, throwing on an old pair of jeans, sneakers, and a T-shirt. He was very hopeful he could find the equipment Jordan had sold there. As he pulled into the parking lot, he could tell that the establishment was clearly a place a thief would seek out to sell stolen goods. There were bars on the windows; even the door had bars behind it. Also, in front of the store windows were cement pylons. Mason assumed these were there to prevent someone from ramming through the front of the store to burglarize it.

As he walked in, he saw a glass showcase to the left with all kinds of jewelry, electronics, and even some revolvers. He also smelled the foul odor of a cigar and noticed the whole place was covered with a thick layer of smoke. Toward the back was a door with a cage in front of it. Mason assumed this was the cashier's booth, again meant to protect the cashier in case of an attempted robbery. On the right side were a few aisles with miscellaneous goods and racks on the wall holding guitars and other musical instruments.

As he scanned the store and slowly made his way down the right side, where he assumed the audio items would be, he realized that even his best attempts to blend in were thwarted. Three men were speaking when he entered the store, and now all of them were watching Mason as if they had seen a UFO. One of them was behind the glass showcase counter, and it was clear he was the gent who owned the place. He was short, a little on the heavy side, and white, with black, slicked-back hair. He had a small mustache, sunglasses, and was holding a thick cigar between his yellow, stained teeth. Obviously the last was the source of the smog-like environment in the store. As Mason browsed, he stared at the men for a moment, letting them know he was aware of their ogling. The men all turned inward and continued their conversation. He could overhear most of it as he was strolling down the main aisle, looking for the stereo receiver Jordan had described to him.

"Ray!" one of the men shouted. "You got to be crazy if you think I'll take less than a hundred for this! This is a fine piece of jewelry; it's worth at least that," the man pleaded.

The man behind the counter shifted the large cigar to the right side of his mouth as he spoke.

"Yeah, you're right, it's a fine piece of jewelry—so fine that I bet it could sell mighty quickly to the real owner."

With that the two men looked at one another in shock, and then they caved in.

"All right, all right, fifty, but you're killing me, Ray, just killing me!" the man said resentfully.

A sly smile crossed the owner's face as he greedily swiped the piece of jewelry and quickly shelled out fifty dollars on the counter. The men grabbed the money as if they already knew where it was going to be spent. With that pleasantry dispensed, the owner, who was named Ray, Mason had deduced, now focused his attention on him.

Taking the cigar out of his mouth with his thick, stubby, ring-covered fingers, he questioned Mason about his interest.

"Now what do you want?" the owner said indignantly. "Look, I'm all out of Barry Manilow albums, so don't waste my time," he said, chuckling.

"I'm looking for a stereo receiver . . . one that a friend of mine pawned in here a few weeks ago," Mason inquired.

The owner shifted uncomfortably as Mason spoke, shoving the cigar back in his mouth.

"Look, I buy and sell to whoever comes in here. There's no way for me to know if it's stolen or not, so don't even go there with me," the man barked.

"It's not like that at all . . ." Mason started. "He was a kid, about fifteen, his name was Jordan. He brought in a stereo receiver, and when he told me about it, it sounded just like what I've been looking for," Mason said, while inwardly he laughed to himself because the statement he had just made was true, but not because he was interested in music.

The owner again had a look of anxiety as Mason mentioned Jordan's name. He had obviously encountered Jordan before. He looked at Mason for a long second and then proceeded down the aisle Mason was already on. At the end of it, stacked on some shelves were a bunch of stereo receivers.

"This is all I got. If your friend brought it here and it's still here, this is where it would be." With that said, the man walked past Mason and went back behind the counter, looking to display the new jewelry he had just recently acquired.

"Thank you," Mason returned sarcastically.

As he scanned the shelf, Mason recalled the make and model of the stereo receiver Jordan had described. He hoped it was still here. It was the only real lead he had. He was also sure that the owner, Ray, wouldn't be forthcoming on to whom he sold it if it was gone. Suddenly, Mason's eyes caught the sight of the very make and model receiver he was looking for. Carefully grabbing it off the shelf, he took it to the front desk to pay for it. As he set it on the counter, he received a smirk from the owner.

"How much?" Mason asked.

The man took a long drag off of his cigar and then exhaled the smoke right in Mason's face as he answered the question.

"Two hundred dollars," he stated flatly, chewing the end of the cigar as he spoke.

"Two hundred dollars!" Mason shouted. You could purchase a brand new one for a fraction more.

The owner didn't seem interested in Mason's excitement and continued to arrange jewelry in the showcase.

"I'll give you one hundred dollars," Mason said.

"One fifty . . . and that, my friend, is as low as I go," the owner retorted.

Mason knew he was going to get a berating for this when Tyler found out, but he needed this. There was no telling where this one clue could lead him.

"All right, I'll take it," Mason said, disgusted with the pleased grin on the owner's face.

He took up the receiver in his arms and headed for the door, eager to leave the smoke-filled store he had just been robbed from.

"It was nice doing business with ya!" the man shouted in jest after Mason. "Tell Jordan I said to keep 'em coming," he said as he continued to laugh out loud.

At least that last statement confirmed this was the right receiver, Mason thought.

Mason's next stop was the police station. Whatever prints might be left on the item, they might be able to lift and connect to a suspect. At the very least he was sure that any stolen items notated in the reports would link up to the receiver.

Looking at the receiver in the passenger seat, he shook his head again as he drove away amazed at what he had just paid for a possible piece of evidence in a murder/kidnapping case.

Pulling up to the local precinct he had visited so many times, he rousted up the receiver in his hands and strolled toward the entrance. He knew a few of the detectives by name and was sure he wouldn't have too much trouble getting them to take a look at it. As he walked in the double doors, there was a raised counter that closed off this section to the rest of the station. In the middle sat the stereotypical police officer. You could even see the crumbs from the last donut he ate spread across his uniform.

"State your business," the cop said plainly.

"Can you tell Detective Deturo that Mason Krane is here to see him?"

"Just a second," the police officer returned.

Mason scanned the room as the desk sergeant called for the detective he had asked for. Paul Deturo had been on the force about twenty-five years. He was an acquaintance of Mason's uncle and always offered his assistance in Mason's cases.

"Go on through," the police officer said as he waved Mason by.

Mason waited at the door until it unlocked upon a buzzing sound. Mason immediately took the stairs to the second floor where the homicide division resided. Strolling past various officers and perpetrators as he went, he finally closed in on the office of Detective Paul Deturo.

Paul was one of the few officers Mason had a decent relationship with. He didn't know him that well, except that he had moved to this precinct from New York about fifteen years before. He was in his late forties with grayish-brown hair, brown eyes, a long face, and a short, stubby nose. His most astonishing feature was his size and height. He was over six feet, four inches tall and was about 250 pounds, Mason guessed. Mason always teased him that if he wasn't so close to retirement, he could start playing ball for the New York Knicks.

Paul, seeing that Mason was carrying the receiver, rushed to open the door for him.

"Thanks, but my birthday's not for another couple months," Paul said with a smile.

Mason returned the gesture and placed the receiver in one of two chairs in front of Paul's desk.

"So what can I do for you today, Mason?" Paul asked.

"Well, as bizarre as this may sound, I believe I have a lead on the murder of the Graftons' babysitter," Mason answered. Seeing the doubtful look sweep over Paul's face, Mason quickly continued.

"I know, I know, leave the homicides up to the police, but this was different, Paul," Mason stated as Paul gave him a sidelong glance while folding his arms across his chest.

"Okay, go ahead," Paul said after pausing a moment.

"I think this receiver may be one of the items stolen from the Grafton house. If we can lift some prints off of it and put it through the computer, maybe we'll get lucky and get a hit," Mason urged.

Paul leaned back in his chair for a moment, staring at the receiver before he spoke.

"All right, give me a second. Let me pull the file on the case. As I recall, Mr. Grafton was able to give us some serial number information on all the stolen goods. He had some warranties on some of the stolen items," Paul continued as he was looking through files in the file cabinet next to his desk.

"Ahh . . . here we go," he said, pulling a file from the file cabinet.

As he opened the file on his desk, he flipped the pages looking for the section on stolen property. Stopping a moment and looking up at the receiver, he looked at Mason.

"Well, it's the same make and model as the one the Graftons reported missing. Let's see if the serial number matches," Paul continued as Mason flipped the unit over, easily locating the serial number location.

"363921362-44J," Paul finished, looking at Mason for confirmation.

There was no need for Mason to say anything; the look on his face said it all. The receiver's serial number was a spot on match to the one reported missing from the Graftons' home.

"We better get this over to forensics stat," Paul stated.

"Great! Can you let me know what you find out?" Mason inquired anxiously.

"As soon as I know something, I'll give you a call. I will put this through high priority. Shouldn't take more than a day or so," Paul returned with a smile.

"Great, thanks for your help," Mason said, standing and giving Paul a firm handshake.

That said, Mason walked out of Paul's office and headed toward the stairs. Paul watched him go with a look of curiosity on his face and then returned his gaze toward the stereo receiver.

Something told Mason that this was going to be a big break in the case, and he was confident the forensics team would be able to pull prints off the receiver. The question was, would they get a hit on any of them? These crimes didn't go unsolved for so many years because the perpetrators were sloppy, and Jordan did say the man dumping them wore gloves, but it was worth a shot. Leaving fingerprints on stolen evidence sounded too good to be true for a case that was related to others that were over twenty years old.

Mason was five when his parents were killed, and reflecting on what he remembered of the incident, the masked men had to be in their mid-twenties, at the very least. That would mean these guys were still running around in their late forties pulling the same crimes. That theory made little sense to Mason. There had to be another explanation. It only left more questions and less answers, something he was becoming all too familiar with. Now came the hard part: sitting back and waiting for the phone call. He knew Paul fairly well and was sure he would contact him immediately. Still, Mason was waiting on pins and needles and was eager to get home to work out. His back was still bothering him, but it always felt better after moving. He resolved to do his usual regime but at a slower pace. After all, he wasn't getting any younger, and right now he needed something to do to occupy both his mind and the clock.

CHAPTER 5

A day had passed since Mason had dropped off the stereo receiver to Paul. Mason, per usual, hardly slept, and when the phone rang, he picked it up before it could finish its first ring.

"Hello?" Mason stated eagerly, hoping the voice on the other end was that of Detective Deturo.

"Mason, Paul here. We've got something on your receiver. You had better come on down to the station house."

"On my way," he replied excitedly.

You wouldn't think a person who had been struck in the back by a baseball bat a few days ago could move that fast, but Mason was dressed and out the door inside of five minutes. If Paul wanted him down at the station, he knew that something had been found. If the prints came back without any hits, he would have told him over the phone. Mason was usually a very casual driver, but he must have asked God to forgive him ten times before he reached the police station.

Pulling into an empty spot, he jumped out of the car and jogged for the front door. As Mason flew through the entryway and looked up, the desk sergeant waved him through the locked door without a word. Mason waited for the buzz, and when it came, he flung the door open and took the stairs to the second floor two at a time. After getting to the top, he quickly walked through the partitions until he came to Paul's office. Paul, seeing Mason coming, waved him inside. Not bothering to take off his coat or sit down, Mason immediately questioned Paul.

"What did you find?" Mason said in an excited tone.

"Slow down, old buddy, have a seat," Paul returned.

Sit down! Mason thought. He had been waiting for a lead—any kind of lead—for years. This was not the time to be cordial, but he composed himself anyway. He took off his jacket and sat down in one of the chairs in front of Paul's desk. Paul sat down after him with a manila folder in front of him. He opened the folder and glanced at the contents as he spoke.

"We were able to get three different sets of prints, that didn't belong to the Grafton's, off of the receiver . . ." he started.

Mason's eyes widened. He couldn't wait to hear the rest. He listened eagerly as Paul continued.

"And we were able to identify all three owners of those prints. The first set belonged to you . . ." Paul stated flatly.

Mason was about to rebuke that, but after he thought about it. He realized that he had after all bought the receiver and carried it there, so it stood to reason his prints would be on it. He also scolded himself for not handling evidence with more care.

"The second set belonged to a crook of a pawn shop owner named Raymond Delgado. Is this the guy you bought the stereo receiver from?" Paul asked, handing Mason a black-and-white photograph.

"Yeah . . . That's him all right. I forgot to tell you where I got it, but it was his shop . . . Ray's Pawn," Mason answered. Mason was beginning to think there was a mistake. Paul could have shared this worthless information over the phone. He patiently waited for the third identity to be revealed, but then it occurred to him before Paul spoke.

"Now this third one, I think is our guy, his name is—"

"Jordan!" Mason interrupted him.

Paul looked up in surprise.

"You know him?" Paul asked.

"Yes, he is the one who gave me the lead. He told me he had seen some guy throwing this stuff away and that he had taken it to a pawn shop to sell."

"And you believed him?" Paul asked sarcastically.

"I didn't have any reason not to. Why? What do you have on him?" Mason asked.

Paul pulled out a slip of paper from the folder, but Mason was unable to tell what it was from his vantage point. Paul glanced from Mason to the sheet and began to read.

"Mr. Jordan Moore, been in and out of every juvenile facility in the state. Three counts of breaking and entering, four counts of assault, seven misdemeanors for carrying illegal substances, and a partridge in a pear tree," Paul finished with a smirk, handing the rap sheet to Mason.

"This doesn't make any sense; he's just a kid. He may be into some bad stuff, but murder and kidnapping? There's no way Jordan would have been involved in something like that."

"You sound like you know him more closely than just a tip. Anything you want to share?" Paul asked cautiously.

"I helped the kid out of jam and bought him some food, and he gave me the information for free. He even gave me a physical description of the man he saw putting this stuff in a garbage bin," Mason stammered, pulling out his notepad to refer to as he continued.

"The guy he saw was driving a blue, older model Chevy Impala. The man was tan skinned and was of average height and build, with the top of his left ear chopped off . . ." Mason was about to continue, but he didn't want to go into the tattoo. Several on the local police force, including Paul, had heard the story Mason first told when he was five, but nobody ever listened.

"Come on, Mason, do you really believe this bogus story? It was an obvious attempt to get you to feel sorry for him. These kids on the streets are masters of manipulation. It's a survival tactic."

Pausing for a moment and relaxing his tone, Paul continued, "Now, until we can get something more concrete, he is our prime suspect. I have an APB out for him right now. If we pick him up, I'll let you know." Paul could see the astonished look on Mason's face and decided he better give him a reality check. Walking around to sit at the front of his desk, Paul met Mason's eyes as he spoke.

"Look, Mason, these kids, they start out on the streets, start doing drugs, which escalates into burglary and assaults. It's only a matter of time before they graduate to murder . . . I've seen it a thousand times."

Now Mason's blood began to boil. He didn't know how he knew, but he knew Jordan was not involved in the death of anyone, let alone the Graftons' babysitter. He got up quickly from his chair and yanked his coat off the hanger before meeting Paul's gaze.

"I'm telling you, he didn't do it!" Mason stated firmly, his face red with anger.

With that, Mason stormed out of the office, slamming the door behind him. He was full of anger and frustration. Not only did the clues lead nowhere, but now he had helped put an innocent kid in the firing line as the main suspect. After getting into his car, he slammed the door hard before starting it up and heading for home. As he drove, he tried to think of what steps he would take next. He knew in his heart that Jordan had nothing to do with the murder and kidnapping that took place at the Grafton residence, but because of his record and the fact they had prints tying him to a stolen piece of property, Jordan made the perfect scapegoat.

"There must be something I can do," Mason thought out loud.

His mind still reeling. As he pulled into the driveway, he entertained the thought of trying to find Jordan, but where would he look? He knew about the alleyway he had stayed in; maybe he would find him there. Although, even if he did find him, what would he do next? He would have no choice but to turn him in. Anything else would give the appearance of guilt, and Mason could actually be charged with obstruction.

As he walked in the house, he slammed the door so hard behind him, it sent a small candelabra crashing to the floor. Giving it no heed, he continued into the living room, throwing himself down on the couch in a huff. Rubbing his head in an effort to comfort the large headache he now had, Mason closed his eyes and took a deep breath. After getting a grip on himself, he slid off the couch and got on his knees. He didn't know what was going to happen or what he should do, but he knew that God would have all the answers; whether He would reveal those to Mason or not was up to Him.

"Father God, this has been one heck of a day," he started.

"Please forgive my actions of discouragement and anger. I am confused, and I don't know what to do from here. I pray that you would look out for Jordan, Lord, that you would protect him from the evils of this world. He doesn't know you personally, but he is one of your children just the same. May your Holy Spirit be with him and convict his heart to come to know your Son so that, no matter what happens, he will have received the greatest blessing there is . . ." Mason paused before continuing.

"Also, please guide me, Lord. Let your will be known to me, that You may be glorified through this situation. Please give me wisdom, patience, and strength to follow through on Your plan for my life, whatever it may be. In Jesus's name I ask it . . . Amen," he finished.

Mason, although still very concerned, felt as though a weight had been lifted. After thinking about the way things had happened, he realized that he hadn't done anything wrong. He was following what he thought was right, and things just seemed to be turning out badly.

Getting up from the floor, he calmly retrieved a broom and dust pan to clean up the remainders of the crystal keepsake. After completing this humbling task, he decided to relax a bit by heading to his office to read his father's Bible. It was still early in the day and the only productive thing he could think of to do was to get closer to God by reading his Word.

He decided to read the story of Joseph in Genesis. This story always made Mason feel better when he was discouraged or downhearted. Joseph, time and time again, did nothing but what was right, and almost every time he ended up getting in trouble for things he just didn't deserve. He had been thrown into a pit, sold into slavery by his own brothers at the age of seventeen, accused of adultery, and thrown in prison because he wouldn't sleep with his boss's wife. Joseph had a rough time of it, but he stayed faithful to the very end, and God blessed him for it. Mason had never been a slave or in prison, so the story of Joseph made his problems seem insignificant and trite, but it made him realize that sometimes things just don't go the way we think they should go and that God has a plan that encompasses everything, down to the smallest detail, and involves people Mason might find to be insignificant in the grand scheme of things.

The rest of the day was like many others in most respects. He had no leads on his case or the Graftons' and had to accept that he now had to play the waiting game. When Tyler arrived home from work, she knew immediately something was wrong because she noticed there was an adornment on the wall that was missing. Mason filled her in and apologized for his temper, but she saw how close he was to this case. It was more than a job; it was a search for a truth that had eluded him all his life and being so close to some real answers, she knew, had to be very frustrating. They talked late into the evening about each other's days and then headed off to bed, unaware that somewhere there was another conversation taking place of a much darker nature.

The conference room was dark, with walls made of black, reflective stone, and small lights hugged the bottom of the walls, casting an eerie light from the floor. In the center on one side of a room was a large fireplace that showed shadowy reflections of those caught in its light, and although the fire was raging, the room had a chill to it that could not be snuffed away. It had one large, oval-shaped table with chairs surrounding it and black leather sofas up against each wall. In the room currently were two figures, both wearing black robes with hoods over their heads, making the top half of their faces near impossible to see. They were speaking in hushed tones when a third figure opened and walked through the double doors at the front center of the room. He was a tall, middle-aged man with a police badge hanging from his belt. As soon as he entered the room, one of the cloaked figures nodded to the other, and he quickly left the newcomer and the remaining figure in the room, shutting the doors behind him as he left.

"What news do you bring, Detective Deturo?" the cloaked figure asked in a deep, raspy voice, and although his English was very clear, there was a heavy Middle Eastern accent to it.

"It's Krane, my Lord," Paul stated flatly. "He has a serious lead on one of our . . . hits," Paul continued.

The cloaked figure rose slowly before turning around to face the detective. As he did, Paul shifted uncomfortably and swallowed hard as the eyes of the placid face rose to meet his own. At first glance the figure seemed frail, slightly leaning his left hand on a cane as he walked, but somehow the figure emanated immense power that commanded a fearful respect.

"I assume you have made arrangements to deal with this situation?" the figure continued with a hint of agitation in his voice.

"Fortunately, I have a very easy way to deal with the evidence he has brought forward, but while this will deal with the immediate situation, Krane won't be so easily quelled. I would once again like to request—"

He was cut off in mid sentence by the angry voice of the cloaked figure.

"You are not in a position to request anything!" The man growled, moving closer to the detective.

"I have told you before, we will not make a martyr out of this man." Pausing he continued, "For the time being, Krane is not to be harmed. It would only bring unwanted attention to our plight." The figure continued in a more calm tone. "How did Krane come to be in possession of such . . . evidence?"

"Pure chance, my Lord. A young boy was hiding when Jeremiah was getting rid of the stolen property attained from the Grafton residence. He drove to, what I believe he thought was an unoccupied alley and threw the items in a garbage bin there," Paul answered.

The cloaked figure brought his left hand to his face, stroking his beard as if thinking before he spoke.

"This is most unfortunate, but I know of a way we can use this to our advantage—perhaps even put an end to Krane's ridiculous crusade." Turning again to face the detective, his eyes glowed red as he spoke, making Paul literally shake with fear.

"This is what I want you to do . . ." the figure rasped.

CHAPTER 6

Days passed, and still Mason had received no information on the pending case. He could only conclude that they had yet to find Jordan and were still in search of what they considered to be their prime suspect. Mason had decided to drop by the Umbers residence to give his condolences and again offer up his services for their missing son. Over a week had passed since their son had been kidnapped from church. They received Mason openly and told him everything they had told the police. The incident had occurred just as Tyler had described it to him. There were no real witnesses, just a few folks who had seen the boy walking off, hand in hand, with a young woman with long, black hair. There were some who reported she was wearing large sunglasses that concealed a good portion of her facial features, which explained why no one could give a decent description.

The circumstances surrounding the kidnapping still seemed very strange to Mason. All the witnesses had said was that they saw the woman walking with the boy, but no one could recall her or anyone like her attending the service. *Why would someone kidnap a boy from a church?* Mason thought. He surmised that it could be a woman who had lost her son recently and wanted to replace that gap in her life. Mason was sure the police were looking into that theory, but what else would a grown woman do with a little boy? Mason pondered. He didn't even want to entertain the thought that the boy was taken for some sort of sexual exploitation, but it couldn't be ruled out. As he thought more about it, though, he knew that a kidnapping/ molestation case committed by a woman to a young boy was rare. Cases like that were 99 percent of the time grown men preying on youths of both sexes. Mason had dealt with a few cases like this in the past, but the circumstances around the abduction on this one were a complete mystery. Another motive such as ransom or a woman with a mental disorder was more likely.

He stayed for a couple of hours in idle conversation with the Umbers, both Grace and her husband Larry, before returning home. Larry did not usually attend church with his wife and son, but now blamed himself for not being there. Mason could tell that the incident had put a great strain on their marriage, but he prayed they would grow closer together and to God through this tragedy.

After arriving home from the house call, Mason could see the message light blinking on the answering machine. Hitting the play button on the machine, he listened intently.

"You have one new message, from, 11:30 a.m., Wednesday," the machine's voice rattled on, beeping at the end, signifying the start of the message.

"Mason, if you're there, please pick up . . ." It was Tyler's voice on the other end, and with that revelation Mason's face turned to discouragement. He had been eagerly hoping that Jordan or the police station would have called.

"I'm going to be home late tonight. I have to cover for one of the others who called in sick. You will have to fix your own dinner. There's leftovers in the fridge and some frozen pizzas in the freezer. Love you, bye."

The machine ended on that note. There were no more messages. Mason was almost shaking from the rush of adrenalin that hit when he saw the message light blinking. He never was that good at waiting, and he couldn't help but be annoyed that his expectations were not met.

Taking in a long, deep breath and letting out a long sigh, Mason decided to grab a bite to eat and review the case files. Maybe he had missed something, but he doubted it. After all this time, he had every photograph and every piece of literature burned into his memory. As he walked to the fridge to find what leftovers he could scrounge up for lunch, the phone in his office suddenly rang. Mason turned in that direction, thinking it might be just his imagination, and wanted to hear a second ring for confirmation. Sprinting to his office, he picked up the phone before the third ring could finish.

"Krane," he answered excitedly.

"What the heck have you got me into, man?" a young man's voice yelled from the other end.

There was no mistaking the voice; it was Jordan.

"Jordan? Where are you?" Mason asked impatiently.

"Where am I?" Jordan returned sarcastically. "Where do you think I am? I'm keeping my butt hid from the cops you got chasing me. Word on the street is they think I killed somebody. What the hell have you gotten me into?" Jordan questioned angrily.

"It's a long story. Please tell me where you are and we'll get this all straightened out, together," he urged.

"Yeah, I bet you'll straighten it out, by hauling my sorry butt down to jail. What makes you think I'm going to trust you now?" Jordan asked.

Mason decided to take a different approach. He knew Jordan's best chance for getting out of this was to turn himself in immediately.

"Why did you call me then? If you won't let me help you, why bother to let me know anything?" Mason asked, hoping Jordan would have a change of heart.

There was a large silence before Jordan spoke up again.

"All right, meet me at the diner in one hour," Jordan demanded.

"I'll be there," Mason returned just before the phone went dead.

Mason forgot all about his appetite, grabbed his jacket and keys, and headed out the door. He screeched out of the driveway impatiently, wanting to meet with Jordan and explain everything to him. He didn't know what to do once he got there, but he did know that if Jordan didn't turn himself in, Jordan's criminal history would make him guilty in any district attorney's eyes.

Mason thanked God that Jordan had called him and asked for his guidance as he sped to the diner he had bought Jordan lunch at not more than a week before. He still felt responsible for getting Jordan in this jam, and he was going to do everything he could to get him out of it.

Driving as swiftly as possible, it only took him a half hour to get to the diner across town. As he pulled into the parking lot and parked, he looked down at his watch in irritation, as again he was forced to play the waiting game. Mason thought it best to stay in his car for now, knowing Jordan wouldn't want to be seen by anyone who recognized him, such as his favorite waitress in the diner.

Suddenly, out of nowhere, Jordan appeared at Mason's passenger side window, motioning for him to unlock the door. As he did, Jordan quickly got in, ducked down, and barked directions.

"Drive, I don't care where, just as long as it's somewhere quiet."

Mason didn't need to be told twice, with a teenager down in his front seat; he eagerly left the parking lot. Though morbid, Mason decided to take Jordan to the cemetery where his parents' and brother's grave markers were. After all, it was very quiet, and there were usually very few people there.

When they arrived at the cemetery, Mason parked next to a large oak, not far from where his family was laid to rest. After placing the car in park and shutting off the engine, he turned to Jordan, who he could tell was eager for an explanation. Jordan slowly poked his head up, and Mason could see he was slightly surprised by the scenery.

"You know that stuff you took to Ray's to pawn?" Mason asked.

"Yeah, what about it? I didn't steal it, if that's what you're thinking," Jordan said, back tracking quickly while frantically looking around.

"No, no, no, that's not it at all," Mason said calmly as he shook his head and continued. "I was able to find the stereo receiver. I bought it and took it to the police to have the fingerprints pulled off of it."

"Why?" Jordan asked.

"Because I believed those items you sold were items that were taken from a house where a girl was murdered and a boy kidnapped," Mason stated as he saw Jordan's eyes widen in disbelief.

"I didn't have anything to do with no murder!" Jordan yelled.

"I know that," Mason stated calmly, "But whoever did made sure their fingerprints weren't on it." He paused before continuing. "I believe the man you saw throwing that stuff away had something to do with this."

"Why didn't you tell the cops that then, man? Why are they looking for me?" Jordan said in frustration.

"I did," Mason said flatly. "But . . . your prints were the only ones that could not be easily explained, and you have a criminal history that red flagged as soon as they pulled your prints from the receiver. That makes you a prime candidate as the fall guy for the crime," Mason said cautiously.

"Maybe, but I never hurt nobody! I never committed murder!" Jordan defended.

Mason watched as the teenager's eyes welled up with tears. Jordan bowed his head and let out a deep sigh before looking up and continuing. "There ain't nothing left for me to do here then . . . I better get up outta here," Jordan said with conviction.

This was exactly the reaction he was hoping Jordan wouldn't take.

"Jordan, I know that feels like the right thing to do, but it's not. You need to turn yourself in; anything else and they will hunt you down. We are not talking about some stolen candy bars or television sets; we're talking about murder and kidnapping. They will have all kinds of government agencies hunting for you . . ." Mason could see that Jordan was becoming more upset as more tears ran down the young man's face.

"So what am I supposed to do? Go to jail? Spend the rest of my life in a cage for something I didn't do?" Jordan sobbed.

"It's not like that, Jordan; the evidence is circumstantial at best. Plus you're a minor," Mason said, trying to get Jordan to listen. "Let me take you in, and I promise I will do everything—everything—within my power to get you out of there. Deal?" Mason asked, holding his right hand up for a high five.

Jordan looked deep into Mason's eyes, searching for sincerity, and then glanced at Mason's hand and smiled as he slapped his hand into the fold of Mason's.

"All right. Let's do it, but first I need to do something . . ." Jordan's face hung low with shame as he pulled a bag of marijuana from his pocket as he continued. "If I walk in there with this, they will nail me with something else; I know I will be searched," Jordan stated plainly.

Mason was about to respond harshly upon seeing the illegal drugs, but this time he thought before speaking.

"Give it to me," Mason requested in an even tone as Jordan handed him the bag.

"What are you going to do with it?" Jordan asked.

"Get rid of it. If it's gone, there is nothing to charge you with, right?" Mason stated as he exited the vehicle. Once outside, he started to smash the contents of the bag by placing it under his foot. Once satisfied, he spread the contents over a wide area of grass and threw the empty, clear baggie in the nearest trash can. Once done with the task, he returned to the vehicle, finding a look of disbelief on the teen's face.

"I thought you would turn that in or something," Jordan said.

"Why? What possible good could come from that? You came to the conclusion on your own that you shouldn't have it on you, right? As far as I'm concerned, nobody else needs to know about it. You did the right thing, Jordan, and I told you I will help you as long as you're willing to help yourself," Mason returned sincerely.

"You're all right, dude. Maybe someday I will take you up on your offer," Jordan said jokingly, but Mason could see a hint of honest consideration behind his eyes.

Mason smiled in return and once again felt the urge to help this young man, now more than ever. Jordan was an unpolished stone, a gold nugget that had yet to be found, and Mason felt honored to have been led to help this courageous young man. He was sure God was going to open up the doors to let this happen, but he had no idea how.

Silence ensued as Mason drove Jordan to the police station. Mason knew he was doing the right thing, but his heart still ached for Jordan and the situation he had inadvertently put him in. As he drove, Mason did his best to instruct Jordan on what he should do once they got there. He told him to be honest and forthcoming with any information they wanted as well as the fact that Mason would not leave his side. There were no fingerprints taken in the Grafton house that matched Jordan's. This meant that their evidence was not concrete enough to hold Jordan or charge him with a crime. Knowing that, Mason still knew the best thing Jordan could do was to walk into their custody voluntarily and answer any questions they had as it related to the case.

Pulling into what was now the all-too-familiar parking lot of the police station, Mason shut the car off and took a deep breath before continuing.

"Ready?" Mason asked, looking at the young man next to him.

"As ready as I'll ever be," Jordan returned in an unconfident tone.

As they walked into the station house, the officer behind the elevated desk recognized Mason and waved him through the door. Mason held the door open for Jordan and motioned toward the stairs.

"Second floor," Mason said.

Jordan turned and continued up the stairs, with Mason close behind. As they reached the second floor, Mason guided Jordan to Detective Deturo's office. As they walked toward the see-through door of Paul's office, the detective glanced upward from his paperwork and did a double take as he saw who was approaching. Getting up quickly, he met them at the door to his office. After opening the door, he looked from Jordan to Mason before speaking.

"I would like to take him to one of the interrogation rooms down the hall," Paul stated flatly.

At that, Jordan turned and looked up at Mason in concern. Mason returned his look with one of reassurance, nodding his head as he spoke.

"That'll be fine; he is ready to answer any questions you have and has voluntarily come forward. He also requests that I be present during all questioning," Mason stated firmly, looking into the eyes of the detective as he did so.

"You know that's not permitted," Paul returned.

"Are you charging him with a crime? Is he under arrest at this time? If not, I would at least like to observe during questioning," Mason returned with vigor.

Paul returned a deep sigh before continuing. "Fine, follow me," the detective said with an unenthusiastic sound to his voice.

After leading them down a corridor to a line of rooms, he entered one and held it open, motioning Jordan to have a seat in the room and motioning Mason to the observation room next door before closing the door and seating himself. The room couldn't be more than ten feet by ten feet, with a small table and four chairs in the center and a large mirror that Mason was listening in from. After sitting down at the table, Paul opened a manila folder. He then pulled out a pen and clicked the top of it before he looked up at the teenage boy.

"I am assuming Mason told you why you're here?" Paul asked redundantly.

"Yes. He said my fingerprints showed up on some stolen property," Jordan stated with fear in his voice.

"Where did you get it?" Paul asked as he stared into the young man's eyes.

From there, Jordan relayed the exact same story he had told Mason, down to the finest detail. The questioning lasted for over an hour, but it was obvious to Mason that any inconsistencies the detective hoped to find in Jordan's story were thwarted by his honesty. As they wrapped up, Paul motioned Mason to enter the interrogation room and gave both of them some news they didn't expect.

"Well, that's all I have, but we are going to give you over to the state for custody until this mess can be cleaned up and you can be placed in foster care."

"What? Man, I'm not going to no foster place or orphanage," Jordan retorted with anger in his voice.

"Jordan," Paul stated.

"You have no legal guardian at the moment, right? No permanent address or phone number, and you're under the age of eighteen. That being said, we have no choice but to put you in the custody of the state," Paul explained.

"Place him in my custody," Mason stated quickly as both the detective and Jordan looked up at him in astonishment. Waving off what he knew were going to be Paul's objections, he continued, "I know what you're going to say, but I don't care. I will take full responsibility for the boy and ensure he is present for any further questions."

He was not about to let Jordan slip through the cracks of a sometimes-unreliable state youth care system. He genuinely cared about Jordan, and although he was making this snap decision without the approval of Tyler, he knew in his heart it was the right thing to do.

Paul sucked in a deep breath, ready to explode with objections, but seeing Mason's face, he knew there would be no point in trying to convince him otherwise.

"Fine," Paul stated. "Sign the temporary custody papers on your way out, but if he misses any subpoena for his presence, you will be held to the full letter of the law," Paul said, pointing the manila folder that was in his hand at Mason as he spoke.

With that, Paul held the door open as they left, giving one last word to Mason as he strolled past.

"I hope you know what you're doing," Paul said.

Mason patted him on the side of his shoulder as he passed him, as if indicating the detective shouldn't worry.

Jordan kept at Mason's heels, going downstairs, and sat quietly as Mason signed the necessary paperwork that gave him temporary legal custody of the troubled teen. As Mason was filling out the necessary documents, he smiled to himself as he thought it strange that his job was to return children back to their homes and not provide one. When finished, they both walked out to Mason's car, but before entering, Jordan leaned over the roof of the car from the passenger side.

"Why did you do that in there, man?" Jordan asked suspiciously.

"Because I know you didn't do it, and I want to fulfill my promise to you to do everything to prove it," Mason returned as they both entered the vehicle.

Buckling his seatbelt and motioning Jordan to do the same, a question arose in his mind. "Jordan?" Mason said hesitantly. "Where's your mother?"

Jordan lowered his head in what appeared to be shame and embarrassment.

"I . . . I don't know." He paused before continuing. "About two years ago, we were shacked up in a motel. Then, she went out one night to bring back a John, like she usually did. When she didn't come back after a week, I knew she was either dead or skipped town. I never saw her or heard from her again," Jordan finished, still holding his head low.

"And your father?" Mason pressed. "Has he always been gone?"

Jordan smirked as he replied. "I'm sure he took off the moment he knew my mother was pregnant, but for all I know, she didn't even know who my dad was. She never talked about it, and I never thought to ask," Jordan replied.

Mason could tell the young man was about to break down and decided that pressing him any further for any personal information was not going to bring anything productive. Reaching down and holding Jordan's chin to face himself, Mason did what he could to raise his spirits.

"You know all that stuff?" Mason asked rhetorically, shaking his head. "It's not your fault. Someday I believe you'll understand that, but I know it's hard to see past the pain right now," Mason finished.

Letting out a deep sigh, Mason quickly changed the subject. He didn't want to make Jordan too uncomfortable and knew that building a relationship with him would take time. Just because he was a part of Jordan's life now didn't mean Jordan would turn over a new leaf. Mason knew there would be struggles ahead, but he also took comfort in the fact that God was supporting him every step of the way.

"Well, we better get home to meet the missus," Mason stated in jest as he smirked at Jordan.

Jordan looked at Mason with uncertainty, not knowing where he was going or who he would meet. Mason could see the fear in him; it wasn't a fear of going to jail, being beaten up, or any physical abuse. Jordan was afraid of trusting anyone, putting his life in another's hand. All life had taught him was to look out for himself, and now he was being put into a position where he had to trust someone he had just met. He didn't want to be let down again or let someone else down either.

As they pulled out of the parking lot, there was silence between them. Jordan looked out the window as they drove through Mason's neighborhood. Jordan looked as if he had just entered another country and was clearly anxious on the unfamiliar surroundings. There were no slums in this neighborhood, no liquor stores on each corner or drug dealers visible walking down the street. Instead, Jordan saw well-kept front yards with green grass and large trees and driveways filled with vehicles no less than five years old. To Jordan, it was literally like stepping through a magical mirror and ending up in another world. As they pulled into the driveway, Mason turned to Jordan as he unbuckled his seatbelt.

"Do you have any clothes or any belongings that we need to get? We can stop by your . . . place and pick up whatever you need," Mason asked cautiously.

"Naaa. What I got is what I got," Jordan returned flatly as he eyed the two-story house in front of him.

"Well, tomorrow, we'll get you some change of clothes, sound good?" Mason queried.

"Whatever you say, man," Jordan replied, shrugging his shoulders as he viewed his surroundings. "This you're pad?" Jordan asked in awe.

"Yep, let me show you around," Mason replied.

As they entered the house through the front door, Mason instructed Jordan to hang up his jacket in the closet right next to the front door. He showed him the living room, his office, the kitchen, and the downstairs bathroom. Next, he took him upstairs and showed him the master bedroom, guest room, guest bathroom, and a storage room, which Mason explained they hoped to turn it into a nursery someday. The guest room was ten feet by ten feet with a bed, a bookshelf, and a small night table. Mason almost blurted out an apology for the plainness of it but then realized Jordan had probably never slept in a room like this in all his life, especially if a vacant alley was one of his best places.

"All right, the boring part of the tour is over," Mason stated with a mischievous grin on his face.

Jordan followed Mason downstairs and down another flight of stairs to the basement, which Mason had turned into a makeshift gym. Seeing Jordan's obvious amazement at the facilities, Mason couldn't help to take advantage of the opportunity.

"You know, I've been looking for a sparring partner . . . I could show you a few things in return?" Mason propositioned.

Jordan, still turning in circles, flooded by the imagery of the workout gear, gave a half-dazed response.

"Sure, man, anything you say."

Then Jordan's eyes focused on the wooden dummy, and Mason could see the question coming before it was asked.

"What the heck is that?" Jordan asked, pointing at the wooden dummy.

"It's a wooden doll called a Choy Li Fut. It's used in Kung Fu for drills to simulate another opponent. I guess you could call it the Chinese version of a punching bag," Mason further explained with a smile.

"Oh yeah, I saw one of those in a movie with Bruce Lee. He was doing all kinds of stuff to that thing." Turning to face Mason, Jordan continued to ask questions. "So can you do that stuff, man? Are you a Bruce Lee wannabe?" Jordan asked with a teasing smile on his face.

With that Mason stretched his arms quickly and rotated his neck in preparation for a brief demonstration. Standing in front of the wooden dummy, Mason explained the purpose of each wooden appendage.

"This arm represents your opponent's left hand, this one the right," Mason stated pointing to each wooden arm accordingly.

"This arm in the center, that moves up and down, represents the head. The post in the middle represents the head in a stationary position and the torso," Mason finished.

"So how does it work?" Jordan asked, eagerly curious.

"Well, if your opponent throws a punch with his left, you would block it like this." Mason threw a heavy slide blow with his right that made the wood grunt.

"Then I might pull down his head and kick him in the midsection like this." Mason pulled the middle lever down hard. Then spun around rapidly, landing a midsection blow to the middle pad.

"That's cool, man. Show me some more," Jordan pleaded with excitement.

"Okay . . ." Mason thought a moment. "If possible, you should never defend or attack randomly. Every action has a counter action, and thus a plan is formed on your attack. These patterns of blocks, punches, and counters are called forms. If you practice them long enough, they will happen automatically in situations where you are forced to use this skill. It's kind of like a soldier's training kicking in when he is in the middle of combat. Understand?" Mason asked.

"Sure," Jordan replied.

"Now this pattern is very basic, but if used properly and done with enough speed and accuracy, it can outdo your opponent. It starts with a block with your right hand . . ." Mason spoke as he illustrated. "Then it goes to a block with your left hand. Then, pulling your opponent's head down, you strike three blows. First one with your right hand to the gut, second one with left hand to the gut, and the third with a straight blow to the face. Each strike should be a setup for the next." Mason did the illustrations at a very slow speed so Jordan was sure to see the logic in the methodology.

"You practice that over and over and over until you do it exactly the same, with the right movements every time. This programs your body to react in a situation when you see a punch coming."

With that said, Mason turned and ran through the combination three times with such speed and force, Jordan's eyes were bulging in amazement.

"Oh man! That kicked some major aa . . . uh, that was cool." Jordan fumbled for the words.

"Your turn," Mason said, motioning Jordan to take position in front of the wooden dummy.

With that Jordan jumped in front of the wooden dummy and began to learn the basic routine on the doll. Mason walked him through each step, honing his every movement, while teaching him to shift his balance when necessary and how to throw a punch correctly. Before they both knew it, an hour and a half had passed and only the sound of a door opening from upstairs broke their stride.

Hearing the door, Mason told Jordan to continue on the steps he had shown him. Mason wanted to explain things to his wife privately instead of springing her with the news that they had a new house guest. He rushed upstairs and met her coming into the kitchen. His wife looked at him with a smile and then seemed to try to look past him, obviously hearing there was someone else in the house.

"Who's your workout partner?" she asked nonchalantly.

Mason closed the door to the basement stairs before he answered that question. He anticipated Tyler's reaction would, at least at first, be less than pleasant and he didn't want that to affect Jordan.

"Well, you know the kid I was telling you about, Jordan?" Mason asked cautiously.

His wife was in the process of cutting up some chicken on a cutting board but stopped in mid slice, turning to stare at him with a look of dismay on her face.

"Mason! How could you bring him here without talking to me first! When we talked about this the other night, I thought it was clear that I needed more time to think on it. What—"

Before she could continue, Mason interrupted her in midsentence, waving his hands in a downward motion, indicating that he wanted her to lower her voice.

"It's complicated, hon, but to make a long story short, I got him to turn himself in. I know he didn't do this; the pieces don't fit. After questioning him, they were going to put him in the custody of the state. I couldn't let that happen—not after he trusted me. So I signed some papers making me his temporary legal guardian. I'm sorry I didn't have time to explain this to you beforehand, but I knew it was the right thing to do, and I really need your help with him. He's a great kid and has a lot of potential, but he's in a place of instability and one push in the wrong direction will send him back to the streets. We have an opportunity here to reach out to him and to give him something he's never had: a chance at a real life. I know this is way out of your comfort zone, and I know how wary you are of taking in someone straight off the streets, especially with a past like his, but once you meet him, I know you'll want to do the same for him," Mason stated in a pleading tone.

Tyler took in a deep breath and turned her head, contemplating what she thought was the right course of action. Seconds passed, and she finally returned her gaze to Mason's.

"All right, temporarily we'll give it shot and use this time to test the waters. But I want you to promise me that if we do this and I am not comfortable, that we put him in the state's system," Tyler stated firmly.

Somehow Mason knew that getting temporary custody of Jordan was the right thing to do, and because of that, he knew God would touch Tyler's heart in the same way, if only temporarily. Mason still felt led to be a big part of this young man's life, but as Tyler had stated, if it wasn't a good fit, he was sure God would let them both know.

A smile brewing on his face, he pulled his wife toward himself and gave her a rather long hug while speaking softly in her ear.

"Deal. Thanks, hon, I know it was hard for you, and I appreciate you giving him a chance," Mason said as he finished his embrace and took her by the hand. "Come on, I will introduce you to him," Mason said with excitement.

With Tyler in tow, Mason rushed downstairs, eager to introduce his wife to Jordan. When they got to the bottom and looked across the room, they watched as Jordan repeatedly did the combination to the wooden dummy with accuracy, precision, and even quite a bit of speed. Mason was impressed and leaned over to whisper in Tyler's ear.

"He is a quick learner too," he said. "Jordan," Mason shouted over the thumps to the wooden dummy.

Jordan turned around, and seeing Tyler, began to walk toward them awkwardly as Mason spoke.

"Jordan, this is my wife Tyler." Turning toward his wife he continued with a grin, "Hon, this is Jordan Moore."

Holding out her hand, Tyler did her best not to look uncomfortable or frightened of the young man. "Nice to meet you Jordan. I've heard a lot about you," she said, shaking the young man's hand.

"Uhhh, nice to meet you too. This is quite a crib or uh, place you got here," Jordan returned awkwardly.

"Well, I assume Mason gave you the tour. Make yourself at home, and if you need anything, let me know," Tyler offered.

"Will do . . . Thanks, ma'am," Jordan replied, again seeming unfamiliar and almost uncomfortable with being treated with such dignity.

"Call me Ty, please, everyone else does," Tyler replied informally.

Pausing a moment, Tyler broke the awkward silence that had formed. "Well, what do you say we all get washed up and have some dinner?" she suggested.

Mason and Jordan both nodded their heads in agreement as they all turned and headed upstairs for dinner.

At this time of night, the cancer wing was silent, with the exception of the steady, quiet rumble of respirators and the frequent beeps of machines used to monitor blood pressure and pulse of their patients. They had a nickname for this side of the wing, though many would deny knowing it. It was called "Death's Doorway." The name had evolved since the patients in this particular section were given a 5 or less percent chance of living more than a month. Many here were simply waiting for death to come and relieve them of their suffering. Others would put on a courageous front and fight until the very end. Some would fight so hard they would make it into the local newspaper for their seemingly undaunted attitudes and feats. Still, there were those who were caught in between. They were well enough to stay awake at night yet sick enough to know they had no hope of being cured.

One such individual was Ira Deets. Before emphysema had ravaged his body, he had been an accountant, and a very successful one at that. In his younger years, he was quite a squash player, but now, being in his early sixties, he could only claim to be good at crossword puzzles and the occasional game of chess. He was lucky enough to have his own room at the hospital, but after all, he was extremely wealthy, and even in a hospital, there was a difference between the type of care one with money gets versus those who have zilch.

In the end, though, it made no difference. Death was still going to come for him, and not a day passed that he didn't think about it. He continuously cycled through the days of his life and how he had spent them. Thinking heavily on his double existence, he felt cheated of certain promises he felt he had earned. His bed was next to the window, and he pulled back the shutter to see the light from the almost-full moon shine brightly. He glanced down for an instant at the scar that had remained on his right wrist from the tattoo removal. The Sons had insisted he get it removed since his illness would allow too many individuals to see it, and they were taking no chances in maintaining discreetness. This day and age, most branded themselves with the mark in places that were not easily visible, such as the chest and back, and most of the women had theirs placed on the back of their neck, where it was covered by their hair. As he glanced back up at the motionless orb, he thought about the visitor who had come earlier that day.

It had been just after they had brought him a tasteless lunch of a banana, rice pudding, applesauce, and toast. This was often referred to as the BRAT diet, but Ira didn't see the correlation. It was when he was slurping the last of his pudding that the figure walked into his room, nearly making Ira choke on what he was about to swallow.

"Thestos!" Ira gasped in exasperated fear.

The figure smiled back coldly as he turned and shut the door behind him. Seeing this, Ira swallowed the huge lump that had suddenly formed in his throat. The man was dressed in a nice blue suit with a white buttoned shirt and a red necktie. He looked to be in his early thirties, thirty-five at the oldest. By his skin color and other features, you would assume that he was of Mexican descent. He had dark brown skin with short, slicked-back hair, a mustache, and large brown eyes. He was actually Greek, but only those who knew him personally would know that. After shutting the door, he turned and scanned the room before his gaze settled on Ira.

"Outstanding accommodations, Deets. I shall have to remember to recommend it to our comrades, should the need arise," he said with sarcasm in his voice.

"Why have you come? What . . . What do you want of me?" Ira sputtered out in fear.

"You know why I'm here. Just a subtle reminder of the vows you took," the man said coldly, sending a piercing stare at Ira as he spoke.

"Those vows were false! I never received my reward. I never received what I was promised. Why should I honor the oath?" Ira returned angrily.

"You received every bit of your reward, old man," he continued in a harsh, demeaning tone. "Your success, your fame, your money, everything you got was just as you were promised! Women, parties, cars, houses, and who knows how many other things our father blessed you with. You now have your part to play and must keep your end of the bargain," Thestos finished.

"But I got sick. Tell them I can do more. If they all ask it of the father, he will raise me up to my former self and I can continue our plight. Please . . . I'm begging you, Thestos," Ira blubbered.

"Sorry, old man," Thestos returned. "Your time has come. I will be by tomorrow to complete your, shall we say, transformation. You have until then to get your affairs in order." The man headed toward the door, and with his hand on the doorknob, he turned and continued, "Oh, and just remember, if you're thinking about saying anything to anyone, your daughter will suffer for weeks before we kill her. Have a nice day, pops." With that, the man gave a fake smile, waved, and left the door open as he strolled out.

Ira blinked as he ended the replay of the visit earlier that day. It had only been the millionth time he had thought about it, and it wouldn't be the last. As he continued to stare at the moon, he began to formulate his own plan. After all these faithful years of service, his murder was how he would be repaid. It was ridiculous; he knew he could still be of use. He was just being cheated, and as he thought more on it, he decided he wouldn't allow it. Although death was inevitable, he would get one good lick in before he went, and he knew exactly how he was going to do it without putting his daughter in harm's way.

CHAPTER 7

Early the next morning, the hospital slowly started to come to life. Nurses were making their morning rounds, and the cafeteria was preparing breakfast. Ira was eager for one of his daily visitors to arrive, and his impatience grew by the minute.

A figure finally entered his room, but Ira was disappointed to see it was the nurse coming in to do her morning check-in routine.

"And how are we this morning, Mr. Deets?" the nurse said cheerfully.

"Fine. Fine. I don't need anything, everything is good," he said with a stutter, eager to satisfy her inquiries and get rid of her.

With that, the nurse checked the machines, scratched some notes on his chart, and told him breakfast would be in soon. As she was leaving, a young man pushing a janitorial cart stopped outside his room. He was dressed in a blue janitor's outfit with an ID badge clipped to the lapel. He entered Ira's room and was headed for the trash bin when Ira grabbed his attention.

"Manuel!" Ira whispered excitedly.

"Yes, Senor Deets," the young man returned with a slight Mexican accent.

"How would you like to make five hundred bucks?" Ira propositioned, holding a wad of cash in his hand.

Manuel's eyes lit up as he saw the folded stack of hundred-dollar bills in his hand. It turns out that being a janitor was a pretty lucrative career, especially if you worked near rich people who were about to die and didn't want their last meal to be Jell-O.

"Anything you need, Mr. Deets. What'll it be this time?" Manuel returned.

"No food. I want you to take this piece of paper and mail it to Mason Krane; you got that Mason Krane, K-R-A-N-E. He is a private investigator; he's in the phone book. Do it anonymously, and don't tell anyone that I had you do this, got it?" Ira relayed, handing Manuel a slip of paper.

"Uh . . . sure . . . okay . . . whatever you say, Mr. Deets," Manuel said as he grabbed the note and the cash.

As he took it, Ira grabbed the young man's hand. "One more thing: make sure you don't tell anyone. Once you've done it, come back and I will give you another five of those," he said, pointing to the wad of hundreds.

"Si! Anything you say, Mr. Deets," Manuel returned excitedly.

As he left, Ira knew he had a winner. If there was one thing life had taught him, it was that everyone had a price; you only had to find it. With Manuel having returned to confirm the letter was mailed and the nurse having already completed a second checkup, Ira proceeded with the second part of his plan. He got out of bed, headed toward the restroom, shut the door behind him, and locked it.

Mason and Tyler awoke early the next morning, excited about having a new guest in their home. Mason hardly slept a wink and rushed to peek in on Jordan, who was sound asleep, before heading downstairs to his office. Pulling out his files, as he occasionally did, he realized that even though he had made some progress in the case, really he was back where he started. Jordan's witness of the individual dumping the goods into a Dumpster was really the only lead he had left.

As Mason continued to flip through the pages of his notes, he saw that Jordan had described the vehicle the man was driving as a blue Chevy Impala. He wondered how Jordan could be so certain on the make and model of the vehicle. Today, all the sedan-type vehicles looked the same, and that made it difficult not only to distinguish the make but also the exact model of the vehicle. If Jordan was certain it was an Impala, he probably recognized it because it was distinguishable from other vehicles.

Mason recalled going to a car show a couple years back, and they had a '63 Impala on display. Mason realized that the vehicle Jordan must have seen was an older model. Driving down the street, you could see a '60s Chevy Impala from a mile away. He also realized that this was a vehicle often chosen to "trick out" and restore for its unique body look and was also a popular vehicle for gang members or street hustlers to have. Given Jordan's past, Mason concluded that Jordan must have seen one of the later-model Impalas. If this was true, it would narrow the list of vehicles fitting the description. Mason continued to think on this but became aware he was being watched by a motionless figure in the doorway.

"Hey! Good morning, Jordan. How did you sleep?" Mason inquired.

Jordan stood in the doorway of Mason's office with an expressionless look on his face. He looked well rested, but other than that, he showed signs of being very wary of his surroundings. He was almost acting like a stray dog who had never known a warm, dry place to sleep.

"Good," Jordan replied, shrugging his shoulders.

"Come on in, have a seat," Mason said, motioning for Jordan to sit down before he continued speaking. "I was reviewing my notes from our conversation at the diner and I saw that you said the vehicle in the alleyway was a blue Chevy Impala." Mason looked up after making the statement, looking for confirmation from Jordan.

"Yeah," Jordan replied simply.

Mason did not want to question Jordan's integrity, but at the same time, he needed to confirm his suspicions about the vehicle's year.

"Do you know what year it was roughly?" Mason asked cautiously.

"Nope, but it was one of the older ones. A dude I used to hang with had a brother who had one of them," Jordan replied.

"Was the one you saw in good condition, or was it banged up?" Mason queried.

"I don't know, man," Jordan said, shrugging his shoulders. "It looked all right to me, but I wasn't studying the car," Jordan explained.

"If I showed you some pictures of different years of the vehicle, do you think you would be able to roughly identify which one it looks most like?" Mason continued to press.

"Sure. I could do that. I'll do anything to keep from going to jail," Jordan replied without hesitating.

Over the next hour or so, both Mason and Jordan reviewed different models of the vehicle over the Internet. Visiting many hotrod sites, they often commented about how cool some of these cars looked. In the end, Mason had concluded by Jordan's thoughts about which ones looked similar, that the Impala had to be between a '63 and a '65. He knew this and the description Jordan gave of the individual's left ear would serve to be useful to Detective Deturo in tracking down the right individual. By the time they were done, Tyler was already preparing brunch for them.

"Jordan, why don't you go downstairs to work out for a bit while Ty gets some grub for us? You can practice the rotation I showed you yesterday," Mason suggested.

Jordan didn't need to be told twice; he nodded in agreement and quickly left to go work out in the basement. Mason knew that Jordan was very interested in the martial arts, and he knew he could use this as a bridge to build upon.

As soon as Mason heard the basement door shut, he quickly picked up the phone and dialed Detective Deturo.

"Detective Deturo," Paul answered.

"Paul, it's me, Mason. I have some more information on the man Jordan saw dumping the goods into the Dumpster," Mason said.

There was silence and then a heavy sigh before Paul replied.

"Or is it more likely that your friend has had time to think about it and come up with a more descriptive wild goose chase?" Paul queried sarcastically.

Mason had to bite his tongue to keep from blowing up at Paul's insolence, but then he remembered that Paul didn't know what Mason did for sure and that was that Jordan was completely innocent. Placing himself in Paul's shoes, Mason wasn't sure he wouldn't react all that differently.

"Paul, if you could look into this, I think it would really help. I can help with the footwork if you have a shortage of men?" Mason suggested politely.

Paul sighed heavily in disdain before answering.

"That won't be necessary," he said nonchalantly. "What do ya got?" he asked.

Mason began to relay the more detailed description of the car as well as the condition of the vehicle. Jordan said he didn't see any major or minor damage to the car, but then again, it wasn't the car he was focusing on. After Mason relayed the information, he continued his plea for Paul to trust him.

"There can't be that many vehicles in the city that meet those specifications, let alone an owner who has the top part of his left ear chopped off." After a long silence, Mason continued. "Just check it out, that's all I'm asking."

"For you, Mason, I will give it its due, but don't be upset if this turns out to be nothing. I told you, these kids, they'll try anything to get out of deep water," Paul stated frankly.

With that, they both said cordial good-byes with a promise from Paul that he would call Mason, should they find anything. After hanging up the phone, an evil grin pierced Paul's face as he spoke to himself.

"And he takes the bait, hook, line, and sinker," he stated out loud with a sneer.

Mason prayed that the detail he had given would provide a more viable suspect as well as put Jordan in the clear. His line of thinking broke as he could hear his wife talking on the second phone line, which they used as their home phone number. He was so focused on his phone call with Paul, he hadn't even heard it ring, and from the tone of his wife's voice, it didn't sound like good news. Mason didn't want to eavesdrop, so he waited till the conversation had ended before entering the room. He did manage to catch the ending, which indicated his wife had been called into work unexpectedly.

"I'll be there as soon as I can . . . okay . . . good-bye," Tyler finished and hung up the phone.

"What's up?" Mason asked as he entered the room. He could tell immediately that something out of the norm had happened. His wife had a distraught look on her face as she glanced up to meet his eyes.

"There was a man in the cancer wing . . ." She hesitated before continuing. "He was one of the wealthier ones, so naturally he paid extra to have one of the upgraded rooms with his own bathtub and everything. This guy was really sick, given less than a few months to live. Anyway, fifteen minutes after the nurse finished her rounds, they went back to his room to drop off his breakfast. He wasn't in his bed, and as the student nurses left the meal by his bedside, they noticed that the bathroom door was closed and water was seeping through the bottom of the door. They knocked to see if the man was all right, but there was no reply. A nurse was quickly called who tried the door, only to find it locked. Fortunately she had a key. With the student nurses behind her, they opened the door and found the man had slit his wrists in the bathtub. The scene disturbed the nurses so much, they were sent home for the day, which, when you switch people around to cover it, eventually means they have to call someone in. Lucky me, eh?" Tyler finished sarcastically.

"That's horrible, but I don't understand something. Even you have told me of times when you have found patients dead, and although disturbing, I would think it would be something a seasoned nurse could handle," Mason replied, puzzled.

"The suicide is not what spooked them." She hesitated a moment further and shuttered as if an icy, cool breeze had struck her.

"Before he died, he wrote something on the wall with his own blood," Tyler said.

"What did he write?" Mason asked with morbid curiosity.

"Apparently, he wrote the words, 'He Lives' with a crude shape of a snake above it," Tyler finished.

"Wow! That's really spoo—" Mason's mind suddenly flashed back to the library. The serpent was the representation of the god Apep in ancient Egypt. Tyler could see that Mason was obviously intrigued by some of this information.

"What is it, hon?" Tyler asked.

"It's probably nothing, but one of the books I read in the library . . ." Mason started, but trailed off. There was no need for any further explanation. Tyler had heard enough of his weird stories, but she still seemed intensely interested, so Mason reluctantly continued.

"Apep was always represented in ancient Egyptian culture by a serpent." Mason finished, looking at his wife.

"You don't think there's a connection, do you?" Tyler asked in disbelief.

Hesitating a moment before answering, Mason gave a reply he knew would bring himself and his concerned wife some peace even if he wasn't 100 percent sure he believed it. "Naaaah. Lately I have been trying to stretch things into verifiable facts. I'm sure it's nothing. Anyway, if I get curious I can always get Uncle Joe or Paul to give me a look see on the photos," Mason said nonchalantly, but he could tell Tyler wasn't buying it.

"Well, I have got to go. I fixed some sandwiches for you guys, but you will probably have to fend for yourselves for dinner," she said while walking toward the stairs leading toward the upstairs bedrooms.

"Hey, that's why I've got the pizza guy on speed dial," Mason replied with a smile on his face and getting one in return from his wife.

While he could hear talking going on upstairs, Jordan was busy running the repetitions Mason had showed him the night before. Stopping to rest for a moment, he noticed a cabinet in the far right of the makeshift gym. Glancing to ensure the coast was clear, he walked over to it. It was black, about seven feet tall, and had two doors that opened up. Jordan slowly opened the doors, and they creaked as they opened. His mouth dropped in awe at what he saw before him.

Both the inside of the cabinet and the inside of the cabinet doors were covered in red felt. Among the soft felt were different mounts, each containing a different weapon. On the inside of the left cabinet door were knives—not just regular knives, some of them looked as if they were meant to be thrown. On the inside of the right-hand door were a couple of guns. There were a couple of 9mm hand guns, a .45 revolver, and a 12-gauge shotgun. The center was occupied by two weapons, one hanging vertically at the top and the other horizontally on the bottom. The one hanging vertically was a sword, currently sheathed in a leather scabbard. The other appeared to be a smaller version of the first.

Jordan was amazed. He had never seen such an arsenal. *Is this guy preparing for World War III or what?* he thought to himself. Slowly, he pulled down the larger sword from the mount. Gripping the handle, he slowly slid the sword from its scabbard. The blade gleamed from the light in the room, and Jordan could tell this sword was not made for decoration but for actual use. Slowly dropping to his knees to place the scabbard on the ground, he grabbed the hilt of the blade with both hands and held it firmly in front of him. Then, making a quick slashing motion from left to right, he pretended a mock battle with an unseen foe. His last motion was a forward thrust, sending his imaginary opponent to the graveyard.

"You're doing that all wrong, you know?" a voice boomed from the entry way.

Jordan was so startled he dropped the sword to the ground in shock. Then, seeing it was Mason, he tried to make a calm retreat.

"Hey, man, uh. Sorry about that, I was just checking it out," Jordan said, trying to blow it off.

As Mason approached, Jordan slowly backed up, keeping an even distance between himself and Mason. As Mason strode, he never blinked and never let his straight-faced gaze stray from Jordan's. Mason reached for the sword. Bending down, he picked up the blade and twirled it in a circular motion, again without unlocking his stare, and finally spoke.

"You know, in the days of the Samurai warriors, the only reason a sword would leave its scabbard was to taste blood. If it was not used in battle once taken out, the owner was considered a coward and a fool and even sometimes would impale himself on his own weapon to reconcile his shame," Mason continued, seeing that Jordan was now visibly shaken. "Lucky for you, you just happen to be staying with a fool who forgot to lock his safe," he finished with a sarcastic smile.

As Mason turned to replace the sword to its scabbard and to shut and lock the weapons' safe, he could hear Jordan let out a sigh of relief from behind him. Smiling to himself Mason turned to face the young man.

"Rule number one, Jordan, is don't touch any of this unless I give you explicit instructions to do so, you got me?" Mason stated firmly. "I am the one to blame here, but these are dangerous weapons, and I would not want you to hurt yourself," Mason finished.

Immediately Jordan's calm demeanor returned. "Hurt myself! Hurt myself?" Jordan said with sarcasm. "Maybe you forgot who saved your butt the other day with a switchblade," Jordan stated, obviously feeling his ego had been violated.

"Just the same," Mason continued. "Stay away from these unless you ask me first. Deal?" Mason said with conviction.

"Sure, man, whatever you say," Jordan stated, obviously blowing off the incident.

"If you want to learn how to use a sword, I can show you, but we will use these," he said, gesturing toward some wicker swords, obviously meant for practice. "However, you already have the best two weapons at your disposal: your mind and your body," Mason said.

"Man, that's just mumbo jumbo. Guns, knives, all of those work way better than throwing any punches or kicks," Jordan stated flatly.

"You're right, except for one major exception: those can all be taken away. Nobody can take away what you've learned." Mason paused, as if thinking, and then nodded to himself in conviction. He reopened the weapons cabinet and pulled out a 9mm Beretta. After looking over the weapon carefully, he turned and offered it to Jordan.

"Try to shoot me," he said flatly

Jordan was shocked and didn't know what to do or say. He certainly wasn't about to take practice shot at his new friend.

But seeing his apprehensiveness, Mason spoke up. "Don't worry, it's not real. Its weight and reaction are meant to mimic a real gun for exactly this kind of drill. It shoots plastic pellets that give a little sting, but that's about it," he said in reassurance, again offering Jordan the gun.

Jordan reluctantly accepted but had it pointed at the ground.

"Don't worry, you can't hurt me, even if you do manage to get a shot off," Mason said with an arrogant smirk.

"All right, what do you want me to do?" Jordan asked.

"Let's pretend it's a robbery. You have the gun pointed at me, and I have my hands in the air," Mason stated as he showed Jordan how he should hold the gun. "Whenever you think you're ready," Mason stated.

Jordan waited for a few seconds and could see Mason studying him. Finally he decided to shoot, aiming for the upper chest, but before he could, Mason grabbed the top of the gun and pulled it toward him. Then, turning his body, he turned the gun 180 degrees, rapidly making it impossible for Jordan to hold on to the weapon any longer.

"There you see I now have my mind, my body, and a gun. You, however, have lost the only weapon you could use," Mason stated in a training tone.

Jordan smirked. "Yeah, but I am sure I could hit you now because I know what you're going to try to do."

"Okay, let's try it again," he said, handing it back to Jordan. "Anytime," Mason said.

Jordan went to pull the trigger and was thinking he had him this time, but by the time the trigger had been pulled, Mason had already pulled the gun and started to rotate it, so when the gun fired the plastic pellet, it missed Mason by matter of inches because of his reaction.

"That's unreal, man. How did you know when to move?" Jordan asked.

"Three things make it successful. First, you must study every aspect of your opponent—how his eyes move, his mannerisms, clues to what he is about to do, say, or move. It's kind of like playing defense in football and knowing when the quarterback is going to hike the ball based on his body language. Second, you must wait for the perfect opportunity when you know your speed will be faster than the mannerisms you have studied so that your timing is perfect."

"I can learn to do those two no problem. What's the third?" Jordan asked.

Mason's face became very straight and serious.

"The third is that you must be prepared to die should you fail," he stated flatly.

Jordan just stared at him for a moment in disbelief before Mason continued. "But that's why we practice, and that's why we never try anything like this unless you're positive there is no other option. In my experience, it is far better to give people what they want as soon as possible. They will most likely take it and leave quickly to avoid any attention to themselves.

"But you can't just let them jack your stuff like that," Jordan said.

Mason put his hand on Jordan's shoulder as he spoke.

"There is no material thing in this world worth a life, and it's also nothing God can't replace. Understand?"

"So how do you know when to use it? Jordan asked.

"When you know your only other option is death itself . . ." he stated glumly. "All right, enough of the teaching. Let's go get some grub," Mason stated lightheartedly.

With Jordan in tow, they headed upstairs to get some food. Mason continued to pray they would find the vehicle Jordan had described, but as he covered the last of the steps from the basement, something heavier weighed on his mind. Now that he had Jordan here, how was he going to help him? How would he go about building a relationship with him and hopefully bring him to a point where Christ could work on his heart? They had church tomorrow, and he intended to take Jordan with him. He really didn't have a choice in the matter anyway, because Jordan had been released to his custody, but he didn't want Jordan to get spooked. Hopefully things would work out tomorrow in such a way that Jordan didn't feel too uncomfortable.

The library was at its busiest time of day, but this would not deter the well-dressed man from getting where he needed to go. After all, his group had gone undetected for centuries; they weren't about to make a mistake on how or where they would gather. They had done a lot of remodeling over the years, and the entrances to the temple were very well hidden and guarded. There was no possibility of the entrances being accidentally discovered. They were all under twenty-four-hour surveillance by small video cameras and would not open unless the guards saw you and knew who you were. Even if you were recognized, you had to show a secret sign to gain entrance.

After parking his restored blue 1965 Chevy Impala, he walked to the entrance of the building. As he shuffled past the reception desk at the library, he gave the librarian a quick smile and a wink. She acknowledged him by slowly dipping her head, as if showing him a sign of respect. As he walked toward the back of the library, he headed straight for the men's bathroom. Once inside, he headed to the last stall, which was the widest. This was due to the city codes, which required a handicap stall that would accommodate a wheelchair. This served as the perfect cover for an entrance.

After closing the door behind him, he stood directly in front of the wall, with the toilet to his immediate right. Looking straight forward, he unbuttoned and pulled open his shirt to flash a symbol that had been burned into his flesh. It was a small but a very distinguishable sign of a snake wrapped around a pyramid. A light jutted out from an unseen source and highlighted the mark. It seemed to glow for a moment, just like those stamps they give you to reenter an amusement park. After completing this, he buttoned up his shirt and patiently waited. The guards monitoring the entrance would ensure the bathroom was empty and then lock the bathroom door automatically while the secret entrance was opened. The dead silence in the bathroom was broken by a small click coming from the entrance to the bathroom door. A few seconds later, a five-foot by four-foot section of the wall slid backward and to the side, revealing a passageway. Once the man entered through the doorway, the wall silently slid back into place.

As he walked down the dark passageway, which was lit only by small torches every ten to fifteen feet, he came to what looked like an office with windows on every side. Inside he could see several figures monitoring video screens and other technical devices. They were all dressed in black, loose-fitting bodysuits and were well armed. Most of them had semi-automatic rifles slung across their backs as well as a sidearms at their waists. One of the gentlemen sitting at a desk next to the window glanced up and waved to the man to continue on. This was the second phase of security against unwanted entry into the temple. There was another hidden door at the end of the passageway. It only opened upon a coded entry from within the miniature guard post he had passed. If the first portion of the entry was ever compromised, within seconds those guarding the second entry point would commit suicide, and the equipment within would be destroyed. This way nobody would know of the second entrance, but as careful as they were, this was highly unlikely. They had existed for thousands of years without detection, and they hadn't pulled it off by being foolish.

As the wall slid back, the man stepped into what looked like a four-foot by four-foot room. When the door shut behind him, the small room was lit up by lights overhead and large, numbered buttons on the side closest to the door. It was an elevator that had four levels, but they were all down instead of up. The man pushed the number two button, and the elevator began to descend. Like a normal elevator, there was an indicator at the top that displayed the current floor. Also, in the top right-hand corner was a small video camera. There wasn't a space in this facility that wasn't under surveillance, but even those inside didn't know where all the cameras were or how closely they were being watched.

A small tone rang out as the elevator halted at the second level of the facility. The door slowly opened, and the man stepped off to see what appeared to be a concierge desk, like that of a resort. To the right and left of this large waiting area were large double doors that were currently shut. There were also a few small couches and chairs available, obviously there for those waiting. The man carefully stepped off the elevator and proceeded to the desk. The room was painted with dark gray stripes, and halfway to the ceiling on the wall were lights that pointed upward. Above the desk was a large, circular insignia on which there was a snake coiled around a pyramid and the words *Sennew Sas Ne Apep* etched around the design. Shining from behind the symbol was a bright light, giving a highlighted presence to the symbol. Between the dark, striped walls and the golden emblem lit in brilliance, the room gave off an aura of power and intimidation.

The man continued to walk until he came to the desk. Then he waited patiently for one of the three women with headsets behind the counter to acknowledge his presence. They were all dressed the same, as if in uniform. They had white, long-sleeved blouses and long, dark gray skirts. One would think they were actually part of the room.

The woman he was standing in front of glanced up from her computer monitor.

"Yes?" she asked in robot-like fashion.

"I am here to see Lord Amahte," the man returned, speaking the last in little more than a whisper.

"Name?" the woman replied without hesitation.

"Jeremiah Stone," the man replied.

"Please have a seat, Mr. Stone; someone will be here shortly to escort you," the woman replied.

Jeremiah turned slowly and cautiously proceeded to the closest couch to sit down. His palms were sweating; he was unsure why he had been called. He had been summoned with urgency, which made him nervous. Not knowing was a difficult place to be for Jeremiah. He was way more comfortable knowing what, when, where, and how. As he sat down, his anxiety continued to grow, and as the second passed, they felt more like hours. He reached into his pocket and pulled out a pack of cigarettes, shaking free one to stick in his mouth, but before he could light it, the double doors on one side of the room opened, and a familiar figure appeared behind them.

"Paul?" he questioned as he rose steadily.

"Jeremiah, my old friend. You know you can't smoke in here. Good to see you again. Come, come, we have much to discuss," Paul returned, all the while ushering Jeremiah to follow him. Jeremiah fell in step with Paul while at the same time repacking his un-smoked cigarette.

As they proceeded down the corridor, Jeremiah couldn't hold down his anxieties any longer.

"What's this all about?" he asked nervously.

"Your services are needed immediately on a mission of the utmost importance. Lord Amahte asked for you personally," Paul returned without turning his head to glance at him.

This made him even more anxious, and sweat started to drip from his forehead as they continued their way down the hall. The hallway was designed to match the lobby. Every thirty to forty feet there were large, black double doors on each side of the long hallway. These rooms were used for various purposes, usually meetings or planning sessions, but he wouldn't be visiting one of these today. He was headed toward the room at the end of the hallway, which was called the sanctuary. It had earned the name because it was where the head priest, Lord Amahte, could always be found, and since he never seemed to sleep, eat or even leave the room, for that matter, all personnel thought it fitting, with Amahte's approval of course.

As they reached the end of the hall, Detective Deturo knocked on the large double doors. Half a second later, the doors swung inward on their own, and the two gentlemen passed through. As soon as they were clear, the doors swung shut, again with no visible assistance. To the left of the entrance was a large fireplace, which was seemingly carved right out of the black, reflective marble of the walls. Toward the back was a large desk with two leather-backed chairs within. To the right of the entrance was a large, black leather sofa. Even with the large fireplace burning away, the room felt like a freezer and made Jeremiah's skin crawl. There were no lamps in the sanctuary. The only light was that of the fireplace, which lit up the walls with large moving shadows. A single chair was behind the desk, and it was turned so the back was facing the two men who entered the room.

"Sit down, gentleman," a deep voice commanded, as if coming from every angle of the room.

Paul and Jeremiah continued forward and sat in the two chairs in front of the imposing desk. Jeremiah was now visibly shaking with fear. His white knuckles clenched each other, and sweat began to bead across his forehead as his heart began to race.

"There is no reason for you to be alarmed, Mr. Stone," the voiced boomed again.

The chair slowly turned, but it was as if phantoms were doing all the work; the figure within it never moved. The chair came to a rest as its owner was now face to face with the two men. He was not a very large figure, but he was very imposing nonetheless. The figure's elbows were on each arm of the chair, and with his arms both leaning forward, his fingers touched to form a perfect triangle. His skin was pale and seemed to glow compared to what portions the dark robe he wore didn't cover. A hood covered his head, and the shadow hid the top half of his face, but Jeremiah could feel the cold stare of those eyes on him, and it made him shiver as he spoke.

"My Lord . . . uhh . . . I have come as you requested. What would you have of me?" Jeremiah sputtered out.

"You did well on the Grafton job," the figure returned.

"Th . . . Thank you, Lord," Jeremiah managed to spit out.

"I wasn't finished . . ." the figure said with a deep, powerful tone.

"My apologies . . . My Lord, please forgive your humble servant," Jeremiah stated, bowing his head constantly, unable to look into the unseen eyes of his master.

"As I said, you did well, but you failed miserably on getting rid of the evidence," the figure said, raising his voice slightly.

"I . . . I . . . don't understand. I got rid of it. It's gone. I swear it!" Jeremiah whimpered.

"Gone. Gone, you say." The figure's voice rose as he stood up and continued, "Then maybe you can explain why the police have one of the items that was taken from the Grafton house, or perhaps you would like to explain why the police have an eyewitness seeing you dumping the goods into a Dumpster?" Now the figure was yelling and was pacing behind the desk like a rabid wolf eager to get to its prey.

"I . . . I thought it was empty. There was no one around . . . I . . ."

"Your petty foolishness has put us all at risk." The figure cut him off, but his tone softened as he continued. "However, these things do happen, and now I will need your help to put them straight again."

"Anything . . . I will do anything you ask, Lord," Jeremiah squealed as he fell to his knees in tears.

"I am glad to hear you say that," the figure replied, pausing a moment as he faced the wall and brought his hand up to stroke his small beard. Then he turned suddenly, pointing a crooked finger at the man now weeping on the floor.

"Because your death is what I require!" the figure growled as he pulled back his hood to reveal evil red eyes, glowing in fury.

"No . . . please . . . I beg you . . ." the man whimpered.

As he continued to plead for his life, Jeremiah slowly started to rise up off of his seat into the air. Terrified and screaming, the head of the blubbering man suddenly shifted to the right unnaturally, making a large crunch as if a baseball slugger had just cracked a bat hitting a home run. With that the shrieking screams ceased immediately, and the body fell limp to the floor. Paul turned to see the body lying limp on the floor behind him and swallowed down his own fear. Paul turned his head back to the figure behind the desk, who now had his face and eyes covered with the hood once again. The chair started to turn again as it almost made it back to place it had been when the two men entered, the voice boomed again.

"You know what to do, Detective. Now go, and do not fail me . . . Failure, as you can see, is not acceptable," the voice said in an even tone

Mason didn't sleep well through the night—nothing new for him lately. He was consumed by many thoughts that troubled him. He was frustrated with where the leads had taken him thus far, but more than anything else, he was worried about Jordan. Today they would be going to church, and Mason knew this would be a difficult and uncomfortable experience for him. He had explained to him the night before that they would be going and he had to come because, from a legal standpoint, Mason was his legal guardian. Jordan took the news with a grain of salt, promising not to go anywhere if he could stay at the house, but Mason refused, much to Jordan's dismay. He was eager to get the day started and hoped and prayed that Jordan would be touched somehow by what he heard and saw today.

Mason finished getting dressed and headed out of his bedroom down the hall to Jordan's room. The door was shut, and Mason rapped gently on the door.

"Jordan," he called. "Jordan! Up and at 'em, big guy, we don't want to be late." There was no reply.

Mason slowly opened the door while knocking, not wanting to intrude on the boy's privacy. "Jordan?" Mason asked again.

Scanning the room, he realized it was empty. The bed was made, and a piece of paper lay on the bed. Mason rushed to seize the note, knowing automatically that Jordan had gone. He picked up the folded piece of paper and read it slowly.

Mason,

I really appreciate everything you did for me, but I gotta go. This place, it's not for me, and I know the cops are just waiting to pin that murder on me. There's no way I'm going to jail for something I didn't do. I'm sorry if this gets you into trouble with the police, but it's for the best.

Tell Tyler I really like her cooking and that I'm sorry if I was any trouble. She was right about me. I would eventually mess things up, and I would rather do that on the streets than under your roof.

Take care of yourself, and please don't come looking for me,

Jordan

Mason slowly lowered the note and now noticed that the bedroom window was slightly ajar. He deduced from this that Jordan must have left sometime in the night. Tyler suddenly entered the room, and seeing Mason holding the letter and the open window was all she needed to know to conclude that Jordan had run away.

"Where did he go?" she asked.

Mason sighed deeply as he turned and handed her the note. Watching her reaction as she read, Mason responded after he knew that she had finished reading.

"I don't know how, but I have to try to find him," Mason said, holding up a hand to stem the objections he knew Tyler would bring up.

"I know what you're going to say, but I'm responsible for him, and I have to go down to the police station and let Paul know. You had better go on without me. Make sure you let my uncle know what's going on," Mason finished.

"All right," Tyler said but continued as Mason started to leave. "But if you find him, tell him I'm sorry. He's welcome here anytime, no matter what," she said, obviously feeling guilt over Jordan's letter, which pointed to the fact that Jordan had overheard her reaction to his presence.

"I'll do that," Mason returned with a smile.

Grabbing his keys and wallet, Mason headed out the front door. His thoughts were mangled, and he didn't even know where to begin. He wanted to search for Jordan, but he knew the right thing to do was to let Paul know about Jordan's disappearance first. He wasn't looking forward to it either, as he knew Paul would have a field day with the "I told you so's" and the like.

Arriving at the station, he walked in to see Mr. Jelly Donut himself behind the heightened desk, as he always was. Mason was about to request the man buzz him in when the man recognized Mason.

"You're Krane, right?" asked the desk sergeant.

"Yeah . . . that's me," Mason replied with curiosity.

"Detective Deturo left an urgent message for you. He wants you to meet him at this address right away. He said he called your house, but your wife answered and said you had just left," the desk sergeant said.

Mason reached up and grabbed the slip of paper with the address on it.

"What's this all about?" Mason inquired.

"Hey, ask your buddy Deturo. How should I know?" the officer replied.

Mason was confused, and he glanced down at the address written on the paper as he headed back to his car. Why would Paul ask to meet him at some address? Why would he be looking for him to begin with? Then a terrifying thought ran through his mind. What if Paul had found Jordan at this location and something happened? Mason's heart raced, and his foot shoved the gas pedal to the floor, speeding Mason's car out of the parking lot and on its way to the address Paul requested they meet.

Within a block of the location, Mason was passed by a fire truck, with an ambulance in tow. It was a middle-class residential neighborhood, and his fears of Jordan being here calmed a bit, knowing that Jordan wouldn't be in this neck of the woods by nature, unless he was committing a crime. As he drove closer, Mason could see the flashing red and blue lights of several emergency vehicles parked outside a home. As he reached where they were parked, he saw the whole area had been marked off by yellow police tape, and it was then Mason realized this was the address where Paul had asked to meet him.

Mason parked his vehicle across the street quickly, as again he thought something horrible might have happened involving Jordan. Rushing up to the barrier, he was met by two uniformed officers holding their hands up in an effort to stop him.

"Hold on there, where do you think you're going?" one of the officers asked.

"My name is Mason Krane. A Detective Deturo asked me to meet him here," Mason replied.

Mason peered up at the entrance to the location and saw Paul standing in the doorway. Seeing Mason, Paul yelled at the officers watching the lines.

"John! It's okay, he's with me," Paul said.

"All right, go on ahead," the officer said to Mason while raising the yellow tape.

Walking through the front yard, Mason glanced quickly at the outside of the house. It didn't look like it was on fire, but the area smelled as if someone had burnt a turkey. Glancing to his right at the driveway, he stopped in midstride, shocked at what he saw. There in the driveway was a pristine-looking, early-'60s model, blue Chevy

Impala. His mouth dropped and as he turned he saw Paul had met him halfway and was now face to face with him.

"You found him, didn't you?" Mason asked with excitement.

"I think so, but he's not talking," Detective Deturo returned sarcastically.

"What do you mean?" Mason queried again.

Urging Mason to walk toward the house, he told Mason the situation.

"I was following up on that information you gave me, and there were a few addresses that looked deserving of a follow up. I didn't want to give the leads to a beat cop; I didn't want to look like an idiot when they didn't find anything," Paul said with embarrassment. "Well, I got to this joker's house and I saw smoke billowing out one of the windows. So I kicked down the door, and you'll never guess what I found," Paul finished in a sly tone.

"What?" Mason asked.

"Take a look for yourself," Paul said, gesturing as they entered the front door.

As Mason walked through the front door, an image of horror met his eyes. There in the living room chair appeared to be the scorched remains of a human being. Mason recalled his thought of burnt turkey earlier and realized that it was burnt human flesh he had smelled. Between his thought and the smell, Mason started to cough and gag. He tried his best to control his urges, but they got the better of him as he rushed into the kitchen and vomited in the sink. Coughing afterward and running the cold water to sip as he continued to gag, he felt a hand pat him on the back.

"Easy there, big guy," Paul said reassuringly.

Mason turned the water off and wiped his mouth across his sleeve as he looked up at Paul.

"What happened to him?" Mason said, still coughing a bit.

"We're not sure yet, but my guess is suicide," Paul replied evenly.

"Suicide? What makes you think that?" Mason said with skepticism.

"Come here, I've got something else you should see. Uh . . . but first, you through hacking up anything you've eaten in the last few hours?" Paul asked in concern.

Mason's eyes widened because he knew he was in for another shocker by the tone of Paul's voice. But after slowing his breathing and calming himself, he spoke a confident reply.

"I'm good. Let's see it," Mason said.

"Follow me," Paul directed.

They made their way through the home to the master bedroom. There on the perfectly made bed was a small wooden box and a note in front of it. Mason had already read one horrible note today; he was sure this one wasn't going to be any better.

"When I broke in, Mr. Crispy was already well cooked. Using some blankets, I doused him out before I searched the place and found this. Turns out 911 had a call from this house about ten minutes before I walked through the door, reporting a house fire. This guy obviously didn't want the whole house to go up, just him. You'll understand more once you read the note." Paul gestured at it, handing Mason a set of latex gloves.

Slapping the gloves on, Mason opened the note and read the letter aloud.

> I can live with my sickness no longer. The evil that has caused me to take so many lives in such a terrible way is overtaking me. The sorrow I feel for these children is beyond measure, and I can no longer go on living with such pain. Please tell their parents and friends that I am very, very sorry for their loss, though I am sure it will be of little comfort to them now. At least I will be dead, and I am sure they will take solace in that. With that, I will spare details on how terribly they died. I will only say that the repercussions of such unspeakable acts can only be death. I leave behind only that which I kept for myself as a token of my victims. I release them now to be free, as I will purge this world of the horrible monster that lives inside me.
>
> Jeremiah Stone

Mason placed the note back on the bed and glanced hesitantly at the box. It was made of a dark wood, probably pine or maple, and was about twelve inches wide, eighteen inches high, and about four and half inches tall, with a lid on the top that swung upward on hinges attached to the back.

Opening the box slowly, Mason's eyes widened again as he saw what was inside. The bottom of the box was layered with Styrofoam. Sticking into the Styrofoam were small needles that had what appeared to be a human finger on top of each one. There were more than a dozen of them. One glance was enough, and Mason shut the latch on the box quickly, holding his wrist to his mouth to keep from getting sick. Paul spoke as Mason continued to compose himself.

"Evidently he kept these as trophies. Each one has been cleaned and stuffed with cotton to prevent decay. Guess he had a side hobby in taxidermy as well," Paul said in sorrowful tones.

"I need some air," Mason said, heading for the door.

Upon reaching the front yard again, Mason stripped the gloves from his hands and breathed deeply. Paul followed behind him and continued to ask him if he needed any medical assistance. Mason stubbornly refused, and within minutes he had regained his composure.

"I'm sorry for the scene, but given your history on this, I thought you should see for yourself. We are having the . . . trophies sent to the lab to run fingerprints on, but I think it's safe to say that between the information you gave us and what we've been able to compile on the scene, this guy is our killer," Paul said with satisfaction.

Mason looked at him questioningly as he spoke.

"Are you saying this one guy killed all those kids, including the Grafton child and the babysitter?"

"You saw the evidence. You tell me?" Paul said evenly. "Look, Mason, I'm sorry I didn't give your story any credit before, but the truth of the matter is that you solved this case. I know a lot of cops down at the office think you're a crackpot, but they won't after this. You've been working on this case for how long? Ten, twelve years? Take some satisfaction in knowing that you brought this guy to justice. You're going to be a hero. Who knows—maybe you'll even make *The Tonight Show*," Paul finished.

"It can't be him; it just doesn't fit," Mason said, thinking out loud. Looking up again at Paul with skepticism, he continued to question the validity of all he had seen. "What about the symbol the babysitter wrote? And her message, '*They took him*'? What she reported doesn't support the idea that a single person committed these crimes. How do you explain that?" Mason asked.

"Well, the body is burned to the bone. I doubt very seriously that forensics will be able to tell whether this guy had a tattoo or not, but maybe he did. As far as there being more than one killer, the physical evidence just doesn't support it. We have the car, the stereo receiver, Jordan's testimony, the note and the . . . the . . . fingers to prove this is the guy, and there's nothing indicated he had any help. I worked the Grafton scene. That girl had lost nearly three quarters of the blood in her body before writing that note; who knows what she thought she saw?" Paul continued as he could tell nothing he was saying was affecting Mason's thoughts. He leaned in and spoke in hushed tones before continuing.

"You know what the truth is, Mason? The truth is you've been working on this so hard, for so long, you're afraid to let it go. I know your parents died a horrible death; I've read the file." This statement made Mason visibly sober up quickly with anger.

"But that guy is gone. Whoever he was, he's dead, and now this guy's dead too and neither one of them are going to hurt anyone ever again. Let it go," Paul finished as he reached up his hand and patted Mason's shoulder.

"Listen, I have to finish up here. Why don't you go home, relax, and I will fill you in when the tests come back? Then we can arrange for Jordan to come down and identify the car and pictures of the suspect from a lineup," Paul finished, walking back toward the house.

Mason glanced up in embarrassment as he spoke. "He's gone."

"What?" Paul said, shaking his head and smiling. "I told you, man. I saw it coming from a mile away. I guess you're lucky we got a better suspect," he said jokingly. "Don't worry; we're bound to pick him up sooner or later. Take care and give Tyler my best, and don't forget you broke this case," Paul said in a congratulating tone, giving him a pat on the back.

"Then how come I feel like I got knocked out in the first round?" Mason said to himself as he headed back to his car.

Lucky for Mason, the brain has a way of remembering the mechanics of driving. You could drive halfway across the country with your mind completely somewhere else, though it wasn't the safest way to drive. He was lucky he didn't have to react quickly or swerve to avoid a pedestrian, because his mind was deep in thought. He had just been witness to the closure of the many cases he had worked on, but something about it just left a bad taste in his mouth. There were too many questions he just couldn't figure out the answers to. For one, how did one man pull all of these attacks off without leaving a shred of evidence? Also, there was the symbol the babysitter had written. Mason was sure it was the same one that he had seen twenty-five years ago. How were they linked? The babysitter indicated there was more than one person with her message of, "They took him." The only two living eyewitnesses alluded to the fact that there was more than one perpetrator in the attacks. Mason witnessed three individuals on the night his parents were killed, yet all the physical evidence seemed to point to this Jeremiah character.

Arriving at home, Mason felt as if he had been digging a ditch all day. He was emotionally and physically exhausted and needed some time to gather his thoughts. He was sure the answers would come to him, and even if they didn't, he was sure that God had a purpose in all that had happened. Laying back on his living room sofa, he let out a large sigh and flipped on the television. Tyler wouldn't be back from church for another couple hours, and he figured with a morning like this, the best thing he could do was take a few hours to relax. He flipped through the channels until he came to a football game. He was usually an avid sports watcher, but even as he watched, he continued to dwell on the morning's revelations. Though the corpse was burnt to a crisp, Mason could tell by other pictures in the house that the man couldn't have been over forty-five. Taking that into consideration, if Mr. Stone was the one responsible for his parents' death, that would make him fifteen at the time of the crime, which simply wasn't possible. Shaking his head, he knew the best thing he could do at this point was to focus on something else and come back to this later.

With that, he got a soft drink from the fridge, kicked off his shoes, and placed his feet on the coffee table as he leaned back and watched the game. Fortunately for him, though, Mason was never good at relaxing, and as he got in his most comfortable position, he realized his feet were on top of yesterday's mail, which he hadn't opened.

"No time like the present," he said out loud to himself.

As he sorted through the junk, he pulled out a few bills, a magazine, and then a small envelope handwritten with his name and address. There was no return address on the envelope, and Mason was puzzled by what it could be, as it felt as if it actually lacked any content. After ripping opening the envelope, he found a small, folded piece of paper inside. He removed it from the envelope and unfolded it and was shocked at what he read. It had one sentence on it, if you could call it that, and it was obviously written in another language, at least most of it.

Sennew Sas Ne Apep.
They are here.

Mason only recognized one of the foreign words: Apep. Mason again reviewed both sides of the note and the envelope for any hint as to who might have sent this to him, but there was nothing. It was postmarked locally, but other than that, there was no way to determine where the note may have come from. After thinking on it a bit, he concluded it might be a prank. Perhaps it was from someone who may have heard about his premonitions and dreams, but then again, he had never told anyone about Apep except his uncle and Tyler. Neither one of them would do something like this, plus the other words before the word Apep he had never seen before. He had no idea what these additional words meant.

He forgot about the game, which he hadn't been watching anyway, Mason went to his office to do some research of his own on the web. He was sure he could find some kind of translation. After spending a few moments on different sites, he finally found one that had a large range of words and was able to decipher the first part of the message. Putting that together with the last part, Apep, which he had previously defined as an Egyptian god of chaos, Mason was able to rewrite the whole phrase in English. It read, "Second Sons of Apep," but putting it in English didn't bring him any closer to understanding its meaning. Who had sent it, and why? Frustration overwhelmed him, and again he started muttering to himself out loud.

"Great! You would think after this morning, I would have all the answers; instead all I'm left with is more questions. That's unless another letter is going to hit me today with all the answers!" he stated out loud in frustration as he brought his hand up to rub his troubled brow.

Focusing strictly on this note, Mason was able to come up with a reasonable game plan. First he would see if his uncle could get the note fingerprinted and matched up with the identity of the author. He could tell Paul was eager to put this one to bed, and if it turned out to be nothing, he didn't want to frustrate him any longer by asking him to do it. If he was able to determine who wrote the note, he could ask that person for an explanation and eliminate the possibility of somebody playing a prank on him. Second, he would see if there was anyone at the local university or museum who might be antiquated with such a phrase. If it had some kind of meaning, he was sure some curator or historian would have information on what it meant.

Having that plan set, Mason turned his thoughts to Jordan. He recalled Paul's reaction to the news that Jordan had run away. Because Jordan was not a suspect any longer, Paul obviously didn't seem too distraught about him running away. This let Mason off the hook, but only from a legal perspective. He still felt that Jordan's leaving was in some way his fault and that he had failed him. Deep down, Mason knew he had done everything he could, but one thing Mason was never good at was accepting failure. Even though it wasn't his fault, he refused to give the guilt to God. Just as he had done with his parents' death and his brother's kidnapping, he felt the need to grip that guilt tightly, refusing God's grace as an avenue of escape or comfort until he thought he had earned it. He did not feel worthy of it and felt the need to continue to drag the bag of guilt-filled bricks over his shoulder in everything he did. Little did he know how God's plan would intervene into his own.

On Sunday afternoon, Mason's uncle returned with Tyler from church to find out more information about what had gone on. Both were shocked and relieved to hear that the killer who had been preying on these children had been caught. Although Mason's uncle could tell that Mason wasn't about to let it go at that, they spoke about the letter Mason had received, and once again Mason requested that his uncle use his connections to get the letter to forensics to check for fingerprints. He explained how he didn't want to bother Detective Deturo any longer, especially when in his eyes the cases had been solved. Mason's uncle reluctantly agreed to take the note downtown and try to get someone to do this on his or her own time. He also told Mason that it could take some time, as this would be seen as a low priority to whatever case load they had, but he assured him he would do his best.

By then it was dinnertime, and they all agreed that going out would be a good idea. Mason was exhausted, and just listening to him tell the story was enough to wear out Tyler and his uncle. Throughout dinner, their conversation was very light and for the most part nonexistent. Mason was still stewing over the day's events and was eager to get home. He knew a good workout would do him good and help him to rid himself of some built-up frustration. When dinner was over, Mason and Tyler said their good-byes to Uncle Joe, with his uncle promising to get back to Mason with whatever information he could on the note.

Mason brought out what looked like two twenty-five-inch, black, wooden sticks. They were actually called escrima, and with one in each hand, they could be used to inflict heavy damage or block an oncoming attack. Unlike a sword, every part of the rounded surface could be used to hit an attacker, and with two of them, they were like large extensions of your hands, to be used accordingly. Mason found himself hitting his punching bag with precision and power. Evidently he had not forgotten the skills he had learned. After working up a heavy sweat, he viewed the wall clock and realized he had been down there for two hours. After placing the escrima sticks back in the safe and locking it, he went upstairs to take a bath and to get some much-needed rest. He planned on visiting the local museum tomorrow to see if there was someone there who might recognize the Egyptian phrase written on the note.

CHAPTER 8

Mason awoke to hear the sound of water running downstairs and knew that Tyler was in the process of her daily routine before leaving the house for work. Sitting up quickly in bed, he realized that he must have overdone it the night before. His arms, chest, and back all ached from the routine they had been put through. After slowly rising and placing on his robe, he headed downstairs to pray with Tyler and send her off. As he walked downstairs, tying the front of his robe as he went, he realized that these past couple weeks couldn't have been easy for her either, what with that guy committing suicide in the cancer unit and dealing with her own guilt from Jordan's sudden departure. He hadn't heard a peep from her, and he wanted to reassure her and encourage her that everything was going to work out.

As he walked into the kitchen, he saw that Tyler was just about ready to leave. She had finished rinsing off the dishes from her breakfast and was folding the paper bag with her lunch when she saw him coming down. As soon as Mason reached her, he held her hands in his as he tried his best to speak words of encouragement, another thing he had never been good at.

"Hey . . . Looks like you're ready to go," he said, gesturing toward her packed lunch. "I'm sorry about yesterday if I seemed distant . . . This whole thing has me quite boggled, and I forgot that you've been dealing with a lot of stuff too," Mason said with sincerity. "I want you to know that if you need to talk, I'm here for you and that I don't want you to think you can't share your feelings because you think I might be going through something worse, okay?" he finished with a look of sincerity.

"Thanks, hon. It's been rough. I know you've had a lot on your mind, and with all that happened yesterday, I think we are both reeling. Maybe we can both take the night off, just you and me. You know, go to a movie or something. What do you think?" Tyler said, ending with a wide smile.

"It's a date," Mason replied with a grin of his own.

With that, they prayed and Tyler left for work while Mason headed upstairs to clean up in preparation for his planned visit to the museum. He wasn't sure if he would find anyone who could help him with the strange message, but he knew that there was a reason behind the note and that God had a plan for this investigation. He just didn't know what direction God wished him to take.

As Mason finished getting dressed and finalized his morning routine, his office phone rang. He was just about out the door and thought about letting the machine get it but decided he had better pick it up in case it was something important. Mason turned into his office and rushed to pick up the phone before it automatically went to the answering machine.

"Krane," he answered.

"Mason, it's Paul here. I've got some more news on Mr. Crispy."

Mason detested Paul's continuous badgering of bad humor on the subject. He hated even thinking about the scene that he had walked into, and he knew he would never forget that smell for as long as he lived.

"Give me the scoop," Mason replied, trying to sound humorous as he quickly grabbed a notepad and a pen from his desk. He wanted to catch every detail. There might be more here than meets the eye, and sometimes the slightest detail could open up new avenues.

"His name was Jeremiah Stone; he was a legal consultant at a local firm downtown. There was nothing abnormal about his work habits, but the way he killed himself, he had to have more than a few screws loose. He covered himself in lighter fluid and just sat down in his favorite recliner while burning to death," Paul said.

"Is that possible? Even by force of will, I find it hard to believe this guy just sat there while on fire," Mason questioned.

"True, but the body was so badly burned there was nothing forensics could test to see if he had any drugs in his systems. My guess is he was either loaded or high when he lit himself on fire. Anyway, we got hits on all the fingers . . . uh I mean fingerprints from the victims. They were all children, and one of them was the Grafton child. I'm really sorry about that. I know you were really hoping to find a positive outcome on that case. As you were hired by the family I'm assuming you would like to notify them?" Paul asked and Mason gave a simple nod in return.

"Also, I will fax you a list later today of all the children who were taken. There may be other cases you're working on where this psycho was involved," Paul finished.

"What about the bodies? Any clues as to where the rest of them might be? This guy couldn't just make all those bodies disappear," Mason questioned.

"We are looking into that, canvassing the neighbors and any others who knew this guy, but there were no clues in the house leading to another location. We will keep looking into this, and I will let you know what else I find out," Paul finished.

"Thanks . . . Hey, Paul, thanks for keeping me in the loop on this. I know it's not exactly policy for you guys to do that. It's much appreciated. Also, let me know if you run into Jordan," Mason said.

"No problem, I know you've been working on this a long, long time. As far as Jordan is concerned, I wouldn't count on seeing him again, but I will definitely let you know if we pick him up. You take care—maybe take a long, well-deserved vacation," Paul suggested.

"Thanks, you have a good one . . . See ya," Mason finished, trying to convey by his tone that he acknowledged Paul's suggestion.

Mason hung up the phone, and as he did he ran through the facts he remembered about the scene yesterday. Maybe he was just caught up in this personally, but he couldn't accept that one person was responsible, and the way this guy died seemed awfully suspicious, even convenient. The whole thing made Mason's head hurt. For now, he would concentrate on the note he had received. One thing was for certain: somebody had written it and wanted him to have it, and Mason wanted to know why.

Mason grabbed his keys and headed out to the museum. He wasn't sure about the wisdom behind this line of thinking, but it was a start.

He arrived at the museum a little after ten in the morning. He got out of his car and walked up the steps, remembering taking a field trip here when he was in elementary school. On the outside it looked like a miniature version of the white house without the dome. It had large columns at the top of the staircase to the entryway and clearly had multiple floors. Mason recalled that the person giving the tour when he was a kid said that the exhibits only made up 40 percent of the museum. The other 60 percent was dedicated toward restoration and other archeological and scientific research. Thinking about this, Mason hoped that someone here would be able to answer his questions.

As he entered the building from one of four rotating doors, he saw a reception/security desk in the front. Mason saw one man dressed as a security guard and a woman with a headset in front of a computer terminal behind the desk. As he approached, the woman stopped her activities to greet Mason.

"Can I help you, sir?" the young lady asked.

Mason didn't want to sound like an idiot, but at the same time, he wanted to make sure he spoke to someone who could answer his questions.

"Um . . . Yeah, do you have a tour director I could speak with?" Mason asked politely.

"Sure, just one moment. I will have one of our guides come up front," the young woman finished. With that she punched some buttons on her phone, and her voice was suddenly projected out of the speakers within the museum, calling for the on-duty guide. Then she turned her attention back to Mason.

"It will be just a minute, sir; you can have a seat if you wish," she said, gesturing to the chairs in a waiting area.

Mason nodded in thanks and wandered back to sit in one of the chairs to wait for the tour guide. From the left appeared another young lady dressed in a uniform with a name tag that read "Miya." She approached the desk, and Mason could hear her and the receptionist talking quietly and gesturing at him. When they had finished, the uniformed woman approached Mason.

"Hi, my name is Miya; I am the tour guide on call right now. Is there something I can assist you with?" The young lady offered her hand in greeting as she spoke.

"Hello. My name's Mason Krane. I need to see if someone here might be able to help me with something," he continued awkwardly. "I need to find someone who may be able to assist me by translating this Egyptian phrase into English and any possible meaning behind it," he said, handing the young tour guide a copy of the phrase he had received in the mail.

The young woman took the note and glanced at the phrase in contemplation.

"Not something I would know, but we have an archeologist who specializes in ancient Egyptian culture visiting from Cairo. She is probably your best bet. Let me see if she is available to help you," she finished, returning to the reception desk. He could see her reach behind the desk to grab a phone and do some dialing. When she had finished speaking on the phone, she hung it up and returned back to where Mason was waiting.

"Dr. Kovacs is available. Follow me and I will show you the way to her office," she said, gesturing for Mason to follow her.

As they walked through the museum, it wasn't long before they ventured through a door that said, "Authorized Personnel Only," on the door. They were coded, but the young lady slapped a code in real quick, and the doors opened. She led Mason down a maze of endless corridors and offices. He was taken aback by how much was going on behind the exhibits and made a mental note to take the actual tour one day. After rounding a corner, they came to a hallway full of office doors.

"It's the second door on the right. Go right on in." Seeing Mason's confused look, she answered his question before he could ask it.

"Don't worry, when you're done Dr. Kovacs will give me a ring, and I will show you the way out," she finished with a smile and walked back down the way they had come.

Mason blushed for a moment, embarrassed that he couldn't find his way back, but his attention moved swiftly to the offices in front of him. As he passed the first office, he saw that all of them were the same. The entry doors were framed in wood with a glass panel in the center. The glass portion was blurred so you couldn't see clearly into the room, but it was enough to tell if it was occupied. In the first he saw figures moving around and could hear speaking, but the tones were muffled by the closed door. As he came to the second door, he knocked before opening the door slightly ajar to poke his head in.

"Dr. Kovacs?" Mason said as he halfway entered the room.

"Yes, yes, come in, come in, daylight's burning," an older female voice said with a European accent and a little impatience.

As Mason entered the room, he saw sitting behind a small desk a woman who looked to be in her late sixties. She had short, white hair and a bit of a wrinkly face and was wearing glasses low on her nose. Moving just her eyes up at him, she reminded him of his first-grade teacher, Mrs. Dollar. He had received a crack on the wrist with a ruler more than once from that teacher. He was hoping he would escape this encounter unscathed.

"Have a seat. What can I do for you . . . Mr. Krane, was it?" she said.

"Please, call me Mason," he said, shrugging off the formal title. "I was hoping you could help me translate a message," he said cautiously, not wanting to arouse suspicion. "I received it in the mail and I don't know what it means—that is, except for the last word," Mason said, handing her the copy of the note.

"Well let's see what we have here," she mumbled to herself as she examined the note.

Mason watched her expression and he could tell that she recognized the words. Then, without any warning, he could see her face contort and turn her gaze up to him in discontent.

"So Dr. Feiraday sent you here, eh? Very funny. Well you can tell him that he'll gain no laughter at my expense," she yelled, tossing the note back at Mason. "Oh and when you see him, you can tell him to keep his imaginary stories and folklore to himself. Good day!" she finished, nodding for him to leave, and then returned to her notepad as if he had already left.

"Uh . . . I'm not sure who you think I am, but I don't know a Dr. Feiraday. I'm just here to get this note translated, nothing more," Mason blurted out in confusion.

She glanced up again and looked as if she was going to give him what for, but seeing Mason's expression was enough to stifle her. She shifted in her seat and lowered the glasses from her eyes. The glasses hung around her neck by a cord when not in use.

"My apologies Mr . . . . Uh Mason," she said earnestly. "Some of my lesser colleagues like to play pranks now and again. They know I take my work seriously, maybe too seriously at times," she said with a smile as she continued.

"A lot of people think that the Egyptian culture is mystical and mysterious, but when you've done the research I have, you know that all of that stereotypical thinking is hogwash. There were no aliens from outer space or mythical mummies that would come to life, but there was a culture that revolutionized agricultural and architectural designs for ages to come. Some archeologists like to give notion to the mystical piece and now and again poke fun at my rather obtuse point of view on it, but I can see you're not one of those," she finished with a sigh.

"You're right. I am a private investigator specializing in missing children. This phrase is a possible clue in one of my cases. I'm just looking for some information," Mason replied.

"Someone is pulling your chain then. I guarantee you this has nothing to do with any kind of missing children's case, unless this was meant to throw you off," she replied.

"What does it say?" Mason asked.

"You said you knew what the last word was, so by that I gather that you know that Apep was an Egyptian god, correct?" she asked.

"Yes. The book I looked it up in said he was the god of chaos and often took the form of a serpent in hieroglyphics," Mason replied.

"Very good. I see you have done a bit of research. Well the first part of the phrase, Sennew Sas Ne, means Second Sons of. So your complete translation would be Second Sons of Apep," she said in finality.

This verified Mason's previous research, but he still didn't really know if it meant anything.

"Is that the name of another god who was a son of Apep in Egyptian mythology or something?" Mason replied, venturing a guess.

He could see that Dr. Kovacs was not happy about providing more information around this subject. She took in a deep breath and let out a large sigh, as if going through the motions.

"No, no." she corrected. "In ancient Egypt there was a cult that went by that name, but only for a short time, mind you. I don't get into these kinds of historical goose chases; they are a complete waste of time. The mere fact that anyone gives these kinds of hiccups in the history of the world attention is beyond me," she said sarcastically.

"A cult? I don't understand, what kind of cult? What hiccup?" Mason continued to press.

Again she took in a deep breath before speaking. "Let's put it this way. If I wrote in my journal about a street gang and someone found it four thousand years from now, what possible value could it have?" she questioned and then answered it based off of Mason's reaction. "Exactly, none. Same here—this was some cult that happened to be mentioned once or twice in the ruins of some ancient Egyptian city," she said, clasping her hands in finality.

"I understand your point of view, but without the risk of offending you, is there someone you can point me to who may have more information on the subject?" Mason asked cautiously.

Looking at Mason as if he was treading down the wrong path, she returned her glasses to her face and began to scribble on a blank piece of paper.

"Dr. Ash. He's not a crackpot like the others, but there's no one who can give you more information on this type of thing than him. Here is his address, phone number and e-mail. Give him a ring or just drop by," she said with heavy sarcasm as she handed Mason the information.

Mason scanned the information quickly and stopped dead in his tracks as his eyes widened. "This guy is in Cairo!" Mason said in disbelief.

"Very perceptive, Mr. Krane. Now if you will be so kind, I have work that needs my full attention," she said in an even tone.

Mason was about to ask for more, but he could tell that would only lead to another verbal beating. "Thank you for your time, Dr. Kovacs," Mason said, smiling as he continued. "If I see a Dr. Feiraday, I'll make sure I give him your message," Mason finished with his own bit of sarcasm. It landed him a disturbed glance and nothing more.

With that Mason left the office and headed down the hall. Realizing he had no idea where he was, he asked for help from the first person he saw. They called up the front desk, and the same young lady escorted him out of the museum.

He didn't know quite what to make of this new information. He needed more detail about this "Second Sons of Apep" cult or whatever it was. Too many things seem to line up for this to be a prank or something to throw the cops off. Chuckling to himself, he entertained the thought that perhaps Tyler would be up for a vacation, as Paul had suggested. Either way, he wanted to talk to Dr. Ash to get to the bottom of it.

As he got into his car and proceeded to drive home, he again was perplexed by how every answer he received only led to more questions. Mason was sick of questions and hoped he would be able to resolve this over the phone or e-mail, but after all this time, he was ready for some answers, even if he had to go to Cairo to get them.

When he arrived home, he was greeted by the blinking light on the answering machine. His uncle had called and apparently had already found out some information about the note and the prints that were on it. Eager to find the answers to another question, Mason quickly called his uncle back.

"Uncle Joe? Mason here, I got your voice message. I can't believe that someone found prints on this so quickly," Mason said, starting the dialogue.

"Well, this one even has my eyebrows rising," his uncle replied.

"What do you mean?" Mason queried.

"Well, when I took this down to the station house, I told my buddy down there that this was a low priority. I didn't want them working on this instead of some active cases, you can understand that. Anyway, one of the gentlemen down there said he would stay a bit late to at least get the prints off the note before running a match. The funny thing is when he did this, he recognized one of the prints right away. Don't ask me how, but I guess if you're looking at prints all day, you can see stuff like that. He ran a match in the computer quickly to confirm his suspicions, and he was right. The print belonged to a man name Ira Deets," Uncle Joe said.

"I don't understand. How could forensics identify a print so quickly?" Mason questioned again.

He heard a long pause and a sigh before his uncle replied. "Because they had confirmed the identity of this guy earlier that same day. Turns out he died, and because of the nature of his death, when the body came to the morgue, an autopsy and a fingerprint confirmation was completed," his uncle finished.

"How did he die?" Mason asked.

"He committed suicide by slitting his own wrists in the bathtub," his uncle stated flatly.

Mason shuddered at the thought but still didn't understand why a guy sent him a note before he committed suicide. "This is very strange; I will have to find out who this guy was and what he was up to. Do you know his address? Maybe he left some clues there before he died," Mason said.

"He wasn't at home when he committed suicide. You see, he had terminal cancer and was basically a permanent resident at the hospital. In fact, I'm surprised Tyler didn't mention anything to you about this, but perhaps she didn't hear about it herself," his uncle said.

Mason's eyes widened as he shifted the phone to his other ear so he could write with his other hand. "Uncle Joe, are you telling me this is the same guy who slit his wrists and wrote some kind of message on the wall in his own blood?" Mason asked excitedly.

"So she did tell you about it. Yeah, this is the same guy. Strange, isn't it? I am beginning to think some of your theories are true. Be careful, son. I am not sure what's going on here, but whatever it is, there are strange forces at work," his uncle finished.

"Will do. I am going to go down to the hospital and see if I can find out some more information on this guy. Let me know if you hear anything more . . . and Uncle Joe . . . thanks for your help on this," Mason finished.

They said their good-byes, and before he knew it, Mason was back in his car on his way to Tyler's work. Despite his low comfort level with it, he wanted to see the body of the man who had sent him this note. If this guy had the mark, Mason knew he would be on to something big.

He arrived at the hospital and rushed toward the emergency room, where Tyler worked. He went to the check-in desk and asked for his wife. When she came in, he could see a look of alarm on her face as she rushed up to greet him.

"Hey, are you okay? What are you doing here?" she asked with a heavy note of concern.

Pulling her by her arm to the side of the room, obviously not wanting other people to overhear their conversation, he spoke in hushed tones.

"You know that guy you said killed himself the other day?" Mason asked.

"Yes," Tyler replied.

"Well, Uncle Joe got the prints back on the note that was mailed to me. The man who killed himself is the same guy who wrote that note," Mason finished.

"What?" Tyler said in amazement.

"Yes, it's true. Look, do you know if his body is still here? In the morgue?" Mason asked cautiously.

"I . . . I'm not sure. Why?" she asked in concern.

"I want to get a look at the body. Can you take me down there?" Mason again used a tone of caution.

Tyler sighed deeply before answering his question.

"I could get into a lot of trouble for taking you down there, not to mention he might not even be there," she said, more to herself than Mason. "Wait here, I will be back in a second," she said, walking over to the check-in desk.

Mason could overhear her asking for a break and for her back up to watch things while she was way. When the conversation was finished, Tyler briskly walked back to him and grabbed him by the hand, leading him down the hallway.

"Just promise me that you won't make a big deal down there about this. I know the intern, and he's just out of college. Nice kid. He should let you inspect the body, if it's still here," Tyler finished.

As they made their way through the maze of corridors, stairs, and elevators, they finally came to a pair of double doors with the word "Morgue" on the front. Mason swallowed hard, remembering his encounter with a crispy corpse the other day. He wasn't looking forward to this, but he needed to check the body to see if this guy had the tattoo.

After walking through the double doors, there was a check-in desk to the right. There sitting alone was a young man in his early twenties wearing a lab coat, bobbing his head in rhythm with the music he was listening to through the ear buds he had on. Seeing them walk in, the young, blond-haired man pulled his ear buds out and stood up to greet them.

"Hi, Jimmy," Tyler said to the young man.

"Tyler, what brings you down to the freezer?" the young man replied with a smile.

"Jimmy, I would like you to meet my husband, Mason," she said, introducing him.

"Nice to meet you," Mason said as he shook the young man's hand.

"So what can I do for you today?" the young man asked.

With that, Tyler turned to her husband as she began to leave.

"I will leave you to it," she said, giving Mason a peck on the check before leaving him alone with the young man.

As she left, the young man looked perplexed and shifted his gaze back to his remaining guest, Mason.

"Jimmy, I don't know if Tyler has told you this, but I am a private investigator specializing in lost or missing children. The gentleman who died the other day—the one who committed suicide—has been linked to a disappearance, and I was wondering if it might be possible to examine the body?"

The young man looked at Mason suspiciously for a moment before replying. "Well, we are really not supposed to let anyone back there, but if you just want to look at it, I don't see the harm in that. Follow me," the young man replied.

"Thanks, Jimmy, I will only be a second, I promise," Mason said sincerely.

With that the young man led Mason down the hallway and entered a room that was filled with small metal doors on one side. It almost looked like a wall of ovens, but Mason's stomach churned as that thought ran through his head. Jimmy went to the opposite wall where there were several clipboards hanging in order. After inspecting them, he finally pulled one down off of the hook.

"Here we go . . . uh Mr. Ira Deets, suicide . . . uh 195," he said out loud.

Walking over to the doors, the young man scanned the numbers and then found what he was looking for toward the back. He unlatched the door and slid out a large metal tray. Lying on the tray was a black body bag, obviously bulging with its contents. With this done, he turned to Mason.

"Here ya go. Mr. Ira Deets in the flesh," he said jokingly as he handed Mason a pair of latex gloves. "Is there anything specific you're looking for?" The young man asked.

"Yes. I am looking for a symbol or tattoo. It would look like a pyramid with a serpent coiled around it," Mason finished.

The young man unzipped the bag and threw back the flap, revealing the dead body. The body's color was white as a bone, as if it had been covered in baking powder. Mason had to compose himself before continuing. Jimmy, on the other hand, never flinched or showed any hesitation in the matter. After pulling back the flap, he had returned to scanning the clipboard for information.

"I don't see anything in his chart about a mark or symbol found," he said.

Mason scanned the top half of the body and agreed that he saw nothing that resembled the mark. Maybe he was wrong about this. He didn't think the man had anything on the back side of his body. He was sure that any inspection of the body would have revealed the tattoo in his chart. Sighing deeply in discontent, Mason decided to end this portion of the goose chase here. As he was about to thank the young man for his time, Jimmy spoke up.

"Wait a minute . . . there is something here about a scar on his right wrist," he said.

Mason walked over, flipped over the right hand, and could see that clearly something had happened to the man's wrist, though he couldn't tell what. The young man came up beside him and looked at the scar closely before speaking.

"Ahhh . . . I've seen this before. He used to have a tattoo there. The ligature markings around the wrist show small needle marks. These are the trademark of a tattoo needle," he finished.

Mason's heart began to pound as he looked at the scar on the corpse's wrist.

"Is there any way to tell what the tattoo looked like before he had it removed?" Mason asked.

"Not really, but if I can see the needle marks, I may be able to do a rough outline of what it was," he replied.

Walking over to the only desk in the room, the young man opened one of the drawers and pulled out what looked like a head band. Attached to the headband was a large magnifying glass and flashlight. Looping it over his head, he grabbed a marker from the side wall and walked back to the body.

"Hey, I don't want you to get in trouble for this by marking up the body," Mason said, fearing retribution for the young man's assistance.

"No problem, the markings come off with rubbing alcohol. Do me a favor and shut off the lights," he instructed, shrugging off Mason's concerns.

Mason walked over to the entrance of the room and shut off the lights. The only light in the room now came from the flashlight attached to the band around the young man's hand. Pulling down the magnifying glass and leaning in close to the body, he could see from the far end of the room that the young man was marking the body in small, patient strokes. Mason had not moved from the light switch and found for some strange reason he was afraid to walk toward the body and see how the outline was taking form—not because he thought it would be something else but because he already knew that it would match his suspicions. The premonition of knowing frightened him a bit, as he once again felt there was a great evil at work here. Shaking himself free from his trance, he could see that Jimmy was almost done.

"How's it coming?" Mason called, still standing next to the light switch.

The young man stood up straight and pushed back the lens before answering.

"Come see for yourself. Turn the lights on," he instructed.

Mason flipped the switch and began what seemed a massive trek across the room to the body. As he approached, the young man was taking off the instrument from his head and removing his gloves, while at the same time walking over to the desk to place the item away and grab the solution to remove the markings he had made.

Mason finally reached the body and glanced down at the outline that had been made. There was no mistaking it. Though the snake portion was rough, the pyramid outline was very clear, and without thinking about it, Mason suddenly flashed back to the moment in time when he was five and saw the masked man bend down next to the window he was outside of, revealing the tattoo on the right wrist of the man responsible for the death of his parents and the kidnapping of his older brother. Ironic, he thought—the color the young man used to trace the outline of the once-clear tattoo, was red, the same as the original. At that moment Mason knew he was standing in front of the man responsible for the death of his parents. No facts except for the tattoo would confirm this, but he knew it in his heart to be true. As the thought hit him like a four by four, he stumbled back, stopped only by the wall in back of him. Jimmy, seeing his distress, rushed over to him.

"Hey, are you all right?" the young man asked with deep concern.

Mason could hardly contain his emotion but composed himself just long enough to satisfy the young man's concern. "I'm fine . . . thanks for your help. I really appreciate it," Mason said in a flat, robotic tone.

"No problem. I will clean up Mr. Deets. I think you know how to get out of here, right?" the young man said, almost yelling after Mason, who by then had reached the doors to the room.

Mason didn't have the strength left to reply to the young man's question. After leaving the room, he launched into a run, up the stairs, and out onto the main floors, where he was able to find a doorway leading outside. Once outside, he found a spot under a tree and could contain the emotion no longer. He hung his head as his knees hit the ground and wept bitterly, half in joy and half in sadness, at the knowledge of who had killed his parents. At last he could release the burden he had carried for so many years. He didn't realize how much this had affected him until that moment, and the tears flowed as he praised God for this new revelation. No words could express the peace that had suddenly manifested itself, and his heart lifted with renewed vigor in his quest to continue on with his investigation. He always believed this revelation would be the end of his investigation, but now it had become the beginning. Lives were at stake here, and though he had solved a piece of the puzzle, many more people would be in danger if he didn't find out whom or what was responsible for these heinous acts, which were undoubtedly connected.

Before moving forward, there was one thing more he felt he needed to do. Not bothering to check back in with Tyler, he got into his car and drove to the cemetery his parents had been laid to rest in. As he reached the gravestones, he fell to his knees, overcome by tears of anger and joy. At last he could let himself grieve the loss he had suffered those many years ago. Although his parents had long since been dead, he could feel his fathers, earthly and heavenly, looking down on him, proud of their son, and he continued to weep tears of joy in the peace he had found. After placing a rose on each gravestone, he praised God once again and prayed for his guidance and strength in the days ahead. Before rising to his feet to leave, he turned toward his father's grave.

"Thanks, Dad. You may never have been there in the flesh, but you were with me every step of the way . . . Rest." With that, he kissed his hand and touched his parents' gravestones and the marker for his brother since there had never been a body to bury. Rising slowly, he wiped his eyes with a handkerchief as he strolled back to his car.

As he drove, Mason began to go through the all-too-familiar scenario of analyzing every piece of information, and once again he was left with more questions than answers. To begin with, Mason didn't understand why this guy would even send him the note. Mason assumed he had a guilty conscience and just like Judas, let it get the best of him, but there were other possibilities, and he was not quick to put a stamp on any of them. It seemed to him that if this guy wanted to reveal himself as the killer, he would have just said so. Why write an obscure message that had nothing to do with his atonement of past deeds? One thing Mason was sure of: this guy wanted Mason to find out the meaning behind the phrase, but for what purpose he wasn't sure.

Mason continued to stew on everything he had learned and was still convinced that more than one killer was involved in the deaths and disappearances of the children, but he felt as if he was missing a vital piece of information, more than likely something he had overlooked. As he pulled into the driveway of his home, he resolved to give his mind a rest and take some time to relax. The day's events were enough to emotionally drain anyone, and he was no different. He decided to have a hot bath, relax, and wait for Tyler to arrive home from work. He would have a lot to tell her and knew he would need all his strength to share what he had learned today. They had also planned a night out, and he resolved to save this topic of conversation until an appropriate time.

Peeking into his office before heading up stairs, he could see that a fax had come in. He walked over to pick up the only sheet of paper from the tray and saw that it was from Paul. He had sent him the list of names that were identified by the fingers left in the killer's home. Mason pictured the grizzly scene in his head for a moment and swallowed hard in disgust. Scanning the list, he let out a deep sigh when he saw the name he already knew would be on it: David Grafton. Now that he had definite proof, he knew he couldn't wait on informing the parents. They had hired him for the case, and Paul had given him the go ahead to inform them of their son's death.

Mason kneeled on the floor and prayed for God's discernment, wisdom and strength in telling the Grafton's about the death of their son. Rising when he was finished, he turned and headed back out the door. This wasn't something he was going to do over the phone, and though the day had been exhausting for him, he realized that those feelings were insignificant compared to the loss of your one and only child.

After getting back into his car, he pulled out of the driveway, dreading having to tell the Graftons about their son—not only because David Grafton had been murdered, but also because Mason didn't believe that the killer had acted alone, which is exactly what the police would pitch as their theory of the crime. He needed to be very careful in how he communicated what happened and what he knew. He wanted to give the Graftons the sense of peace he was given early today with the knowledge about his parents' killer, but at the same time relay to them that his investigation was still ongoing. He decided in the end it would best to visit them the following morning.

Arriving at home Mason patiently waited for Tyler to arrive home from work. He had a lot to share with her about the day's events and he needed her ear to provide the support and encouragement he needed.

Time zoomed by, and before he knew it, Mason could hear the familiar jingle of keys opening the front door. He greeted Tyler with a kiss and could see that she was eager to see where his conversation went with the young intern from the morgue. Mason sat her down and proceeded to tell her the day's events from the point of her departure. At times, tears dropped from his tired, worn eyes, but he continued until the very end. He gave no notice o the clock as he continued to provide highlight after highlight. Before he knew it, hours had passed and he still hadn't told her about his visit earlier this morning to the museum. Though his body pleaded for rest, he could not stop without relaying the importance of what he had learned today and what he thought was necessary for him to do. Suggesting they order a pizza, which by this time Tyler was all too happy to agree with, he gave her the highlights of his visit with Dr. Kovacs.

"She wasn't too happy with my inquiry, but I could tell that her advice on visiting her fellow collogue were sincere," Mason finished.

"Sounds good. Do you plan on visiting this guy? What was his name? A Dr . . . . ?"

"Ash, Dr. Ash . . . Well, I want to, but there's a small problem with that," Mason stated cautiously.

"What's that?" Tyler asked, lifting a piece of cheese-filled pizza to her mouth.

"He is based in Cairo and all my attempts to get him to return my messages have failed." Mason paused. "I'm going to visit him," he finished with a cautious smile.

Tyler choked on the mouthful of food before swallowing it hard and then raising her objections. "You want to go to go to Egypt? Now?" Tyler shouted in disbelief.

"Hon . . . I know it's crazy, but there's something going on here, and he's the only lead I've got. Look at all that's happened today. Something strange is going on, something way beyond the death of my parents or the death of some kids. There is an evil at work here that is greater than some thug with a sick fetish for young children. I have to find out as much as I can if I am going to find out what's going to try to put an end to it," he said with sincerity.

Tyler looked into his eyes deeply and then turned her head, as if deep in thought, before speaking.

"Mason . . . I have been with you every step of this journey, and when I heard what you told me tonight, I thought that journey was over, but it's clear to me now that it's not. I can't deny that something strange is going on, but you leaving frightens me. I'm really scared something awful is going to happen to you," she said, suddenly rushing over to hold him.

Holding her tightly, Mason responded in quiet loving tones.

"I promise, nothing is going to happen, but this is something I must do. It's my calling," he said, kissing her head gently.

Mason gave an ultimatum that if he didn't hear back from Dr. Ash within 24 hours, he would be leaving for Cairo as soon as possible. They didn't discuss the trip anymore that night, but it was clear that both of them knew it was inevitable. Their relationship had always been based on God's will first, and though difficult to understand at times, it always brought unity in times of tough decisions. This was no exception, and as Mason continued to hold his wife, he wondered what path lay before him, though he knew it was where he had to go. He, like Tyler, was not looking forward to what the trip would bring, information or otherwise. The only thing he did know was that God was pulling on his heart to go in this direction, and as a faithful servant, he would do his best to obey.

It was procedure to ensure that scheduled or regular visits were done through different channels of the temple. With this knowledge in hand, Thestos opted for an alternate route to enter the temple. It was actually a couple miles away from the library, in a warehouse. Once inside, there was a secret passage that led to elevators on the opposite side of the temple elevators at the library. This way was mainly used to bring in "new stock," as they would call it. They would drive the van inside, unload the children and valuables taken, and walk them down a secret passageway to the temple. It was also used to bring in any equipment or supplies needed. It was quiet, discreet, and basically untraceable. The secret entrance was impossible to find, and given that they owned, in one form or another, the whole block, it was unlikely that anyone could find a way in. Even so, like the library, precautionary security measures were taken so unauthorized entry could not be obtained.

Once the warehouse gates were closed, Thestos walked over and lifted up a portion of a steal panel on the floor, which revealed a keypad. Once he finished pressing in the code, the middle of the room became a large platform, which began to descend. Once he was ten feet below the surface, a cover slid over the top, concealing the secret entry. The platform continued to descend but at a slow rate of speed. Thestos detested taking this way, but its lack of speed made it quiet, very quiet.

After what seemed an eternity later, the platform stopped to reveal a large set of double doors on one side for deliveries and a small doorway entrance on the other for simple access to the temple. Taking the doorway, Thestos proceeded down the pathway, passed the guards' station, and went down the path that led to the main reception area. Walking in, he didn't bother checking in at the desk. He merely gave a nod and continued down the right corridor. At the end of the dark hallway was the office he had come to know so well. Unlike many of the others, he was not afraid of Lord Amahte; in fact, he respected him greatly and considered himself one of his high lord's best men. Once he reached the office, he knocked and waited for permission to enter. Lord Amahte's voice was unmistakable as he gave approval to enter. After walking into the sanctuary, he saw that an older gentleman was already seated in one of the chairs in front of the main desk. The man in the chair turned his head, and after recognizing the person who had entered, rose to greet him and shake his hand.

"Thestos! It's been a while. I trust things are well?" the man said.

"Couldn't be better. Everything is on schedule, and the testing is coming along faster than expected. How are your endeavors with the local police department . . . Detective Deturo?" Thestos said, throwing in that last comment in jest.

"Same old same old, but we finally cleaned up some dirty garbage," Paul returned.

"Have we?" a deep voice behind the desk bellowed.

Both men sat and immediately turned their attention to the figure behind the desk.

"Yes, my lord. The crime scene, forensics, everything was set up as you planned it, and if I may say so, it worked perfectly," Paul stated to the dark figure behind the hooded robe.

"What a waste. It's a shame we had to go through all that just to fix Mr. Deet's mistake. If the fool had killed Krane the night he should have, we wouldn't have had to go through so much trouble," the figure stated with a touch of disdain.

"But it seems mistakes made recently by Jeremiah provided a way to end his ridiculous crusade, and with Ira dead, there is no way Krane can connect any of it, but that is why I have asked you both here today." The figure paused a moment before continuing. "If things had worked . . . perfectly did you say, Detective? Then why is Krane poking around the morgue looking at bodies and visiting museums to translate this?"

In angry tones, he threw a piece of paper on the desk in front of them. The paper contained only a single phrase, "Senew Sas Ne Apep." Both Paul and Thestos looked at each other in disbelief but remained silent. There had been many instances where their lord had knowledge of things that seemed impossible for him to know. It definitely left an impression on both of them, leading them to truly believe their lord had supernatural forces at his command.

"It appears that Krane has somehow found another trail. Knowing him, he will continue his ridiculous crusade for information," the figure ended in a disgusted tone.

"I don't know how this happened, I took—" Paul was cut off in mid sentence.

"I am not interested in excuses. I have my own reliable resources that provide this kind of intelligence. I want Krane's bothersome pursuit for the truth to end. He is getting too close, and drastic measures have become necessary. For the next thirty days, I want him followed. If he discovers any information that could compromise our operation, I want him eliminated immediately. I have a suspicion our young friend will be traveling abroad soon. He may find nothing, but if by some chance he should stumble onto something crucial, killing him in a foreign country will be much easier to explain away. I expect the two of you to place your best men on this assignment. I do not want any further mistakes; there have been far too many of those already," he finished, his eyes flashing red for an instant.

"You both know what to do. Leave me now. I must be in prayer to our father," the figure finished.

Paul and Thestos rose from their seats and once outside the door, proceeded to work together to formulate a plan to monitor Krane's activities.

Once they had left the room the figure raised a hand, and though he was facing the wall opposite of the entrance, two large golden bars folded across the door, locking it. From there the figure proceeded to the front of the fireplace and kneeled in front of it, bowing his head. The robe melted away, along with the old, ragged figure of a man. In the figure's place kneeled a young, handsome figure with long black hair, a clean-shaven face, and large, dark gray wings extending from the middle of his back. He seemed almost flawless, except the left side of this face had a large scar that started on his forehead and went straight down through his right eye and ended at the cheek. His eye must have been badly damaged, as its dark, black pupil was in stark contrast to his almost-glowing blue left eye. With his head bowed, this creature began to carry on a conversation with what could only be described as his master.

CHAPTER 9

Mason spent the earlier morning trying to contact Dr. Ash via telephone. He had sent a message to his e-mail address the night before, but got an automatic reply that indicated he was not available. Mason was determined to speak with Dr. Ash sooner rather than later. Even if he was out of his office, he felt the need so great that he would show up on his doorstep and find the man, just for five minutes of his time. It sounded ridiculous, but he felt as if time was against him and he had no intention of waiting much longer, before he would just fly over there. Besides, if a cult was involved, it certainly wouldn't hurt to do some research in its place of origin.

He left soon after 9a.m. in route for the Grafton's. He didn't want to arrive too early as he figured they wouldn't sleep much after what he had to tell them. But, truth be told, Mason wasn't looking forward to this at all. As he pulled up to the curb, he shut off the car and bowed his head once more in prayer. Nothing was more difficult in this line of work then telling someone their child was dead, let alone that they were brutally murdered. What was worse is there was nothing to show of the body but a single finger. Mason could only pray that God would bring them peace and comfort during this difficult time.

After exiting his vehicle, he continued up the walkway and knocked on the front door. He could hear footsteps approaching the door, and his heart pounded as the moment grew closer for him to look eye to eye with David's parents. After the sound of a deadbolt unlocking, the door swung open, and Mason could see it was Teresa Grafton, David's mother, who had answered the door. She glanced at him in recognition and then in concern before speaking.

"Mr. Krane? We weren't expecting you . . . do you have some news?" she asked with deep concern in her voice.

"May I come in for a moment?" Mason replied.

"Of course," she replied, gesturing for him to enter. "Ian is in the sitting room. He hasn't been doing very well, I'm afraid," she said in a hushed, concerned tone.

Mason followed Teresa into the next room and could see Ian, David's father, sitting in a trance like state, watching television. As soon as he saw Mason, he snapped out of it and quickly shut off the television, giving Mason his full attention.

"Mason . . . good to see you, do you have any news?" he said, rising to greet him with a handshake. Mason shook Ian's hand and had a seat on the davenport before speaking.

"There has been a break in the case . . ." Mason said with a heavy sigh.

He could see them reading his body language and knew that they had already guessed their son was dead; it was just a matter of details.

"What's happened? Where's my son?" Teresa yelled as tears started to stream down her face.

"Honey, please let him finish. Please continue," Ian encouraged.

"Some clues I followed up on led me to a stolen piece of property from your residence. That and some other clues led police to the home of the man believed to have taken your son. He . . ." Mason stumbled, composed himself, and continued.

"The police found the suspect in his home, dead. He had killed himself by lighting himself on fire." Mason paused before continuing. "He left a note behind, which indicated he had kidnapped and killed many children." Mason was interrupted at this point.

"I don't understand. Are you telling us our son is dead?" Ian asked with heavy emotion.

Mason bowed his head and then continued.

"The killer also left behind a box. Inside the box were nearly a dozen index fingers, severed at the knuckle and stuffed for preservation. Police used the prints to identify the victims; one of them was David's," Mason finished.

"David's finger? . . . What kind of sick . . ." Ian composed his last comments but was obviously thunderstruck that such a thing was possible. After a moment of silence, Ian turned to Mason again.

"How do we know he's really dead though? Did they find the rest of the body?" he asked fervently, with his wife now clinging to him in grief.

"No. There were no clues as to what was done with the rest of the bodies, but the police will be looking into everything to try to find an answer." Mason figured this would be a good transition into his own thoughts. "I too will be continuing to investigate the murder and will work with you and police on anything I find. They will be arriving soon to give you some more details, but knowing that you hired me for the case, they wanted me to let you know first," Mason said. "I'm really sorry. I wish we could have found this guy sooner. You both have my deepest sympathies and prayers," Mason said as he rose to leave.

After embracing his sobbing wife for what seemed an eternity and shedding a few tears of his own, Ian turned to address Mason.

"Mr. Krane, thank you for everything you have done. I know you did everything you could, and we are grateful that you tracked him down. Perhaps he knew you and the police were onto him. If that's so, there's no telling how many lives have been saved. Please let us know if you hear anything more, and may God bless you and the police in your continued investigations," he said, shaking Mason's hand again.

The couple led Mason to the door and gave him a warm good-bye, promising to let him know about the funeral services. As he walked back to his car, Mason turned to see that Ian and Teresa were still embracing each other in grief in the front door, watching him leave.

As he drove away, Mason could not help but feel as if he had failed them and God. He hated to fail; sometimes he thought it was the only thing he was good at. There was no doubt that his efforts led to the capture of the killer, but even one death was too many for Mason to accept, and he once again refused to give his guilt to God. For some reason he clung to it as if it were the very air that kept him alive, and he refused to let it go.

When he arrived home, it was all he could do to keep from collapsing from emotional exhaustion onto the living room couch. His heart felt as if it had been dropped from the top of the Empire State Building, and while he had plenty of vigor to continue to fight, he needed direction from his heavenly Father to cure his obsession with using guilt to drive his efforts. Checking his messages and his e-mail he was further discouraged by the fact that Dr. Ash had not returned any of his attempts to contact him.

Easing back into the chair in his office, he opened his Bible, the one that had been his father's, and began to read without any particular passages in mind. Interested in his recent thoughts about Egypt, he turned toward the book of Exodus and read the story of Moses and Aaron and the ten plagues brought upon Pharaoh, who eventually released the Israelites. The story had always been one of his favorites from Sunday school because of the many miracles God had performed through Moses.

I guess every child is enthralled by the supernatural, most adults too for that matter, but something about that story always stuck with him, not so much because of the many miracles performed but because of Moses's determination to stand alone before a mighty Pharaoh with only the faith of his God to protect him and the Hebrews. Mason admired how the heroes of the Bible often faced desperate odds yet were always rewarded with victory for their efforts in one way or another. He wondered if, in those same situations, he would have performed the same and often doubted he would have. Some people over the past couple days had referred to his work as heroic, but Mason believed that couldn't be further from the truth. He didn't allow himself an ounce of credit, and it continued to burden his heart that he couldn't find the truth before these kids had been put to death.

When Tyler arrived home that evening, he had yet another emotional load to unload to her as explained his notification of the Grafton's about their son. When he was finished, Tyler did her best to comfort him, but Mason was so drained from the last couple of days of events, he just wanted to get upstairs and fall into a deep sleep.

Mason, with one arduous task out of the way, slept soundly through the night. When he awoke the next morning, he was surprised that he had actually slept in a couple extra hours, something he hadn't done since he was a teenager. Tyler had long since left for work, obviously not wanting to disturb his peaceful slumber.

After throwing on his robe, he went downstairs to his office and contemplated what would be the next step in his investigation. He sat at his desk and scanned its scattered contents to see that he had left all of his notes, including Paul's fax from the day before, strewn about his desk. Sighing heavily, hating an untidy working area, he began to pick up the pieces of paper and stacking them neatly in the corner. When he came to the fax that Paul had sent him, his eyes scanned over it once more to land on David Grafton's name for an instant before continuing to move to the top of the pile, but before he could, something else caught his eye—something familiar. There were more than half a dozen names on the list, David's near the top. The second-to-last one seemed oddly familiar to him, but he couldn't figure out why. He stared at the name for a moment and then turned his head, concentrating. Then, as if struck by lightning, the information came together, and his face burned red with anger. Grasping the fax in his hand so hard the paper crackled, he ran upstairs and changed clothes quickly. He was out the door in less than five minutes, and his heart raced in pure rage as thoughts of betrayal filled his mind.

"Did he think I was stupid?" Mason shouted out loud to himself as he drove quickly.

Tires screeching as he pulled sharply into the parking lot of the police station, he got out of his car and slammed the door. Grasping the fax tightly in his hand, his knuckles white, he was a model of determination, and nothing was going to stand in his way.

He entered the station and looked up at the lazy desk sergeant with a glare before speaking. "Deturo, where is he?" Mason demanded in an even tone.

"He's in the gym; I'll buzz you in, Krane," the man returned, obviously not picking up on Mason's ire.

The door buzzed and Mason flung the door open as he charged down the hallway. When he reached the end of the hallway, there was a door to the right that said "Gym" on it. Mason pushed open the door with a hard shove. He stood in the doorway scanning the room, but he couldn't see Paul anywhere. There were a handful of people in there on various machines and free weights working, out and Mason didn't feel the slightest guilt in interrupting their routine.

"I'm looking for Detective Deturo," Mason said, not quite shouting, but loud enough and deep enough that everyone in the large room halted what they were doing to give him their full attention.

One gentleman at the bench-press sat up, looked right to left, and then spoke.

"I think he went to the sauna," he said, gesturing to the locker room entryway on the opposite side of the room.

Mason continued his trek and made his way to the back of the room where the doors to the locker rooms, saunas, and showers were. As he weaved his way through each of the sauna doors, he still could not find his quarry. Then, from across the hall, he saw Paul standing in front of a locker buttoning up the front of his shirt. Walking toward him Mason looked to ensure the coast was clear before he confronted him. Seeing that he was alone, Mason came up behind Paul, slapped him on the back, and turned him around. When Paul turned, he smiled and then realized that Mason's expression was less then amiable. Mason grabbed him by the collar of his halfway buttoned shirt and slammed him up against the lockers.

"Who are you working for, Deturo? Do you think I'm some kind of an idiot?" Mason yelled, inches away from Paul's face.

Paul was obviously taken back but kept his cool. "Mason, calm down, what are you talking about?" Paul said, his hands up non-defensively.

"Take a look at this," Mason said, letting go with one hand to shove the fax in Paul's face.

"Yeah . . . so what's the problem?" Paul replied.

"The name second from the bottom," Mason said flatly, continuing to keep a sharp, even tone as he stared Paul in the eye.

Paul scanned the parchment and read the name out loud.

"Jim Umbers," Paul replied out loud. "I don't understand. Did you know this kid?" Paul asked.

Mason tore the fax back out of Paul's hand before replying. "This kid was taken from my church, Paul, and I know for a fact at least a dozen witnesses say a woman with long black hair walked off with him. Don't you think it's a little convenient that this kid should show up on your list?" Mason asked.

"Are you saying this kid's print was planted?" Paul asked in sarcasm.

"You tell me. Is police work getting so tough these days that cops are explaining away deaths in the most convenient ways possible? Isn't it interesting that you should find the guy who did this, but before you can question him, he lights himself on fire, not to mention that there isn't one piece of physical evidence connecting Jimmy to this guy accept a finger, but if you knew who was behind it, you could set the whole thing up, couldn't you?" Mason paused before continuing.

"It's amazing that a guy who was on fire could just sit there, even if he meant to kill himself. That is unless, of course, he was already dead. Then he would probably sit pretty still for you, and being as the body was so charred, guess there's not much chance of finding the trademark of a cult behind all of these deaths to begin with, would there be?" Mason's eyes were weaving wildly, like a tiger about to attack.

"Mason, look, I don't know who talked to you or what you think you know, but there's nothing going on. I even—"

"Don't tell me there's nothing going on!" Mason shouted, cutting him off. "I found my parents' killer the day before yesterday. He had the same symbol that Jordan said Mr. Crispy had on his chest. You know what else? This guy sent me a message—not that he killed my parents, but a phrase in Egyptian, 'Senew Sas Ne Apep.' I am sure you already know what that means, but I'll enlighten you anyway. It means the Second Sons of Apep, and it's a cult. Now tell me, Detective Deturo, why, when all these things start to add up, does there suddenly appear a nice, neat, crispy end to the story? I'll tell you why: because you knew I was getting close. Now tell me what's going on or so help me, the Lord himself will be the only one who will be able to save you," Mason finished with a huff.

Paul lowered his hands, looked to the ground, and then looked up at Mason before answering.

"I didn't know you found your parents' killer, I'm . . . I'm truly sorry to hear it, but what you're explaining doesn't make any sense. I don't know how to help you, Mason, you tell me. What can I do to help you know that what I have done and what I've told you is the truth?" Paul asked

Mason looked at him, squarely thinking to himself, and then he realized the connection.

"Strip," Mason said flatly.

"What?" Paul replied, his face contorting.

"You heard me, strip. Every person that's been connected to this thing so far has had a mark somewhere on their body. If you don't have one, then I'll believe you. If you do . . . well you better start talking now," Mason said flatly. He thought this was a very clever tactic. If Paul refused, he was obviously guilty. If he didn't, Mason knew he was sure to find something.

"This is ridiculous," Paul replied.

"I thought you'd say that," Mason said as he moved once again to pin Paul up against the lockers.

"All right . . . all right," Paul said before Mason could touch him.

Mason was taken aback for a second; he thought for sure he would refuse. Now he watched as Paul stripped to his boxers while Mason searched for the symbol, but as embarrassing as it was for the both of them, Mason couldn't leave it at that if he didn't find what he was looking for. Unfortunately it came to Mason searching Paul's entire body—in between his feet and behind his ears. He even rummaged through his hair, to no avail. Backing off, Mason looked at Paul's sarcastic frown before speaking.

"My apologies. It's not you, but I'm telling you, someone here must be in on it. They've known every move I've made, and it's like they've been building the brick walls in front of me," Mason said in low tones.

"Mason, you know sometimes we want answers to questions so bad that we make up our own answers, no matter how outlandish they may sound. You've been under a lot of stress, and now that we've nailed this guy and the fact that you found the guy who killed your parents, you must be reeling. Take my advice, man, go on vacation. Take Tyler to an island and get away. Do something to get this stuff out of your head for good. Take solace in knowing that your efforts brought peace to yourself as well as all the families affected. Your leads have paid off in the past when I thought they were strange, so I will keep my ear to the grindstone and see if there are any flies on the wall. As for you, I hope you can trust me now when I say that I'm on your side," Paul finished, patting Mason on the back.

"Yes, you are. I'm sorry I doubted you. You're right—this whole thing has been driving me nuts. Uh . . . thanks for your time, Paul," Mason said, shaking Paul's hand as he rose to leave.

As Mason was almost to the door, Paul called after him.

"And, Mason . . . don't worry, I won't tell anyone I gave you a lap dance," Paul said with a smirk.

Mason returned the smile with more than embarrassment on his face as he left the locker room. Once out of sight, Paul leaned back against the lockers and let out a large sigh.

"That was close . . . too close," he said to himself.

Mason's face was still flushed as he left the police station, and he felt as if he was being watched. Something stirred inside him that made him believe that all these things were more than coincidences, but at least now he knew he could trust Paul. Still, he was certain there was a leak somewhere in the department—someone close enough to know all the details, who was in a position to set things up to make this one guy the scapegoat for something much bigger. For what, Mason had no clue, but these conclusions, along with the others, continued to bug him as he made his way home.

CHAPTER *10*

Mason, still hearing nothing from Dr. Ash, wasted no time making his travel arrangements and by the next day he was on a plane to Cairo. This trip would be the longest plane flight he had ever taken, but more than that, he felt that this was the beginning of a much greater trip, one that would test his mind, body, and very soul. He brought all his case files with him and reviewed them on the plane. He knew there was a connection somewhere and believed it was starting to come together he was frustrated with a lack of progress. He was so eager to meet with Dr. Ash; he found himself unable to sit still. Mason was able to leave a message with the general answering machine at the museum letting them know he was coming, but he wasn't sure how they would handle his unscheduled arrival. He was set to be in Cairo a week, and he hoped this would be enough time to meet with Dr. Ash and get some answers to as many questions as he could.

Mason continued to rumble through his notes, and the only thing he could connect was that all the victims appeared to be adolescent males. Then his father's last words hit him like a ton of bricks.

"Remember your brother; remember they came for him . . ."

This confirmed, to a degree, what Mason already knew, that these kidnappers were targeting adolescent males, but why?

Why would they need my brother? Why not me? Mason thought.

Mason continued to think in circles and rack his brain on the possible answers. With a large portion of the flight remaining, Mason did his best to take a nap, but the nagging feeling that he was being watched wouldn't go away. He couldn't tell if he was being paranoid, but with all that had happened recently, he found it difficult to shut his eyes for more than ten-minute intervals during the flight.

When the plane finally landed, Mason found himself exhausted. He hadn't slept more than a couple hours the entire flight and couldn't wait to get to his hotel for a hot shower and a good night's sleep. It was mid-afternoon, but he resolved to use the rest of the day to recuperate and would try to meet with Dr. Ash in the morning. He was still unsure how his visit would be taken, but given that he had traveled across the Atlantic to visit him, Mason was hopeful that the good doctor could spare some time.

Mason had written down all of his destinations with the addresses on different index cards. He thought this would be a useful trick in communicating to cab drivers and the like where he needed to go. After flagging down a cab, he showed the driver the card with the name and address of his hotel. The man nodded, and Mason, together with his one bag, got in the back of the vehicle before it sped off to its destination.

Mason watched as the scenery drifted by, but instantly his expectations of what Cairo would look like were obliterated. It was a very modern city; in fact, other than a few major exceptions, it was a lot like your average US metropolis. Most people walking down the street were wearing business casual attire. Mason could see that the city had buses, taxi cabs, of course, and also some sort of rail system for transportation.

As they came over a small horizon, Mason's eyes widened as he saw the pyramids of Giza located just southwest of the city. They almost looked fake for a moment, and although he had seen many pictures of the pyramids, seen them on television, and even done a report on them in the sixth grade, it was much different seeing them face to face. These huge monuments had stood for centuries; it's no wonder why they were so shrouded in mystery.

As they continued through the city, though, Mason saw some things that met his expectations about the Egyptian culture. The people were mainly made up of Arabs, and there were many who walked down the streets clad in cloth garments and who had cloth wrapped around their heads. He saw women who were fully clad in garments that showed only their eyes and hands. There were street vendors selling everything from jewelry to produce. Mason could even hear the Muslim prayers that were done regularly over loudspeakers from the towers. This city, which often was referred to as one of the cradles of civilization, clearly had made its way into the twenty-first century while at the same time holding onto its cultural roots. Here and now, modern and ancient civilizations lived side by side

As they wove through the city streets, the vehicle finally came to rest in front of a small hotel in the city. It wasn't a resort, but after all, Mason wasn't here to sightsee. After grabbing his bag and paying the driver, he headed toward the main entrance. The fact that a vehicle had been following him since he had left the airport totally escaped his attention. It now sat parked across the street opposite the hotel, its occupants watching his every move.

After checking in without any problems, Mason headed up to his room. He was exhausted from the flight and wanted nothing more than a hot bath, a large meal, and a good night's rest before visiting Dr. Ash. As he opened the door to his room, he noticed that his window had a pretty good view of the pyramids. He dropped his bag, walked over to the window, and opened up the curtains to get a better look. His room was on the third floor of the establishment, and from this vantage point, the view of the huge, triangular structures were much better.

As his eyes scanned over the city, he looked down at a small alley that his window overlooked. In the middle of the alley was figure dressed in all-black garments. He was much too far away for Mason to distinguish any facial features, but it was clear that he was looking up in Mason's direction. After hearing the phone ring, Mason turned to see that the red light on the phone was flashing in sequence with the rings. He wasn't sure how to dial home to let Tyler know he had made it to his hotel okay, so he had asked the concierge to connect him directly once he got in his room. He assumed this was the call. As he turned once more to glance at the figure in the street before answering the call, he now saw that the alley was empty, and a chill ran down the back of his spine. After shaking off the jitters, he proceeded to sit on the bed and answer the phone. It was Tyler, and he let her know he was fine and had made the trip without any problems. They didn't talk long; after all, a call from the United States to Egypt was a little more than long distance.

After talking to his wife, Mason took time to get settled in the hotel. By then, the sun was setting, and he decided to order in dinner and go to bed, thinking this would be best course of action to get a good start in the morning.

Awaking early to the wakeup call he had ordered, Mason had breakfast brought to his room before cleaning up and heading out. When he got downstairs, he asked for a cab, and they flagged one down for him without any problems. As Mason hopped into the backseat, the driver turned and asked him where he wanted to go. Mason was a bit surprised that the man knew English, but then again, Cairo was a tourist destination as well. Mason told the driver that he wanted to go to the Museum of Antiquities and showed the driver the index card that had the address on it. The driver obviously knew exactly where it was and didn't even glance at the address Mason provided.

Dr. Ash had an office at the museum, and Mason hoped someone had received his message and sometime in the next week he would be able to schedule some time with him.

As he arrived at the museum, Mason could see that the building looked old, but the grounds were well kept. After paying the cab driver, Mason made his way to entrance of the large building. In front of the main entrance there were large statues, obviously artifacts, made of stone that decorated the grassy, well-kept landscape. As he walked inside, Mason was shocked at the size of the interior. It was a two-story building, but the depth of hallways that held different exhibits looked enormous. He was sure it would take a person several hours, if not the whole day, to see everything. As he approached the receptionist desk upon entry, Mason asked the young lady in front if he could speak with Dr. Ash or his assistant. She dialed someone on the phone and then directed Mason to be seated, stating that someone would be out to see him shortly.

Again, Mason was sitting in the lobby of a museum, but this time he was surrounded by things both modern and ancient from the

Egyptian culture. He found a small pamphlet on the museum itself, and it stated that the building had been built in 1897 and opened as a place for the Museum of Antiquities in 1902. Mason wasn't shocked to learn that the museum also had 107 different halls. He was amazed at how much history must be packed under this one roof and decided to return to look around if time allowed during his stay.

Mason waited about fifteen minutes before he saw a woman approaching him. She had to be in her late thirties. She had black hair and a tan face and was very professionally dressed. Mason assumed this was Dr. Ash's assistant.

"Mr. Krane?" the woman asked with an obvious Egyptian accent that many of the English-speaking people had here.

"Please, call me Mason," he returned, shaking her hand in greeting.

"Nice to meet you. I am Raj Tesh, Dr. Ash's personal assistant. I received your message, but I am afraid that Dr. Ash is out of town at the moment," she stated politely.

Mason's heart sank. He had to speak with Dr. Ash, and he had come all this way.

"Is he going to be back soon? I am here for the week and really need to speak with him," Mason asked in desperation.

"I'm sorry, but he is currently at an offsite dig about four hundred miles south of Cairo and isn't scheduled to be back for another two weeks," she returned in an apologetic tone.

Mason was crushed, and his face must have shown it, for as he was thinking about what he should do next, Dr. Ash's assistant offered up a suggestion.

"There is one option, if you're up for it?" Raj asked.

Mason came out of his shock in a snap.

"Sure. Please tell me more," Mason returned excitedly.

"There is a transport leaving this afternoon to go down to the dig site. They are taking some supplies and some equipment for the ongoing excavations there. I could see if they will let you tag along. Of course, once you got there, you would have to camp with the rest of the team, but if you're that desperate to talk to him, I am sure they will let you go. Just so you know, though, it's no tourist trip. You would be camping out in the desert and wouldn't have the luxuries of a hotel," she said.

"Yes, please, that would be great. I am not much of a resort person anyway," Mason returned with a smile.

"Okay. Let me have your number, and I will give you a call in a few hours to let you know if it's okay and when you need to be here," Raj said.

"Thank you so much. I really appreciate this. It's been very difficult to find someone with the background to answer my questions, so going an extra four hundred miles after crossing the Atlantic will be nothing," Mason said while handing her a card with his hotel phone number and the room he was staying in.

After shaking hands with Raj one last time, Mason left the same way he had come and had no problems finding a cab back to the hotel. He had been camping many times and viewed this as a small sacrifice compared to what he had already been through to get some answers.

He was only at the hotel a few hours before Raj called and told him to be back at the museum by four o'clock. He didn't realize it until he packed his things, but this actually saved him some cash because he wouldn't have to stay in the hotel. By one o'clock, Mason had packed up his belongings and made it back to the museum. He wanted to look around a bit before leaving and meet the group that he would be accompanying to the dig site. Mason figured breaking the ice with all those going would make it a little easier to see him as just a passenger and not a hindrance.

After walking again through the entrance of the museum, Mason immediately let Dr. Ash's assistant, Raj, know that he was there and planned on looking around the museum until it was time to go. He also offered his assistance should they need any help packing up the transport. Raj instantly took advantage of the offer to add an extra helping hand, and although Mason was slightly disappointed he would not get a chance to view the museum, he was thankful that this would give him an opportunity to meet some of those going to the dig site and build some sort of rapport with them. Raj came to the lobby and guided Mason toward the rear of the museum, where the real work took place. She guided him to a loading area, where could see a large truck with a canvassed cargo area in the back. As he approached with Raj, he could see that there were several individuals loading equipment and supplies into the back of the truck. With Mason in tow, Raj approached a gentleman who seemed to be overseeing the operation, holding a clipboard and occasionally giving direction in

Arabic, the native language of this part of the world. Raj spoke to the man first in Arabic, gesturing at Mason before guiding him over to introduce him.

"Mason Krane, this is our supply co-coordinator, Abdul Sanja. He will be the one in charge of the transport to Dr. Ash's site," Raj said, gesturing toward the man.

"Nice to meet you. I can't thank you enough for letting me tag along. If there is anything I can help with, please don't hesitate to ask," Mason said, offering his hand in greeting.

Abdul was definitely what Mason would consider a native to this country. He was dark skinned with black hair, probably in his mid-thirties, and his English had a heavy Arabic slang to it.

"No problem, Mr. Krane. Our journey will be a long and bumpy one, so I hope you are prepared for a hard night's travel." Seeing the confused look on Mason's face, Abdul continued, "We travel at night to keep the vehicles from overheating and to make it a little more comfortable. The desert during the day can get quite hot, making the back of that truck like an oven." He paused before continuing. "You can put your things on the truck and help load those crates and equipment as well. None of my men speak English, but I told them you were coming to help, so they will direct you on what to do," Abdul finished.

Turning around, the man went back to giving directions and marking things down on his clipboard as the workers busied themselves loading the truck. Mason turned to Raj one last time to thank her.

"Thanks again for this suggestion. I won't have any problems at all, but is there something you want me to sign to remove you and the museum from any liability?" Mason asked as he got the feeling that Raj needed something from him.

"As a matter of fact, we do. It's a formality really, and we only need it to—"

Mason waved her off before she could finish. "I completely understand. Just tell me where to sign," he said with a smile.

After signing off on the document, he thanked her once again and then rolled up his sleeves to help load the transport vehicle that would be taking them to the dig site. When they had finished, they ate a quick meal and hopped in the back of the transport to depart. Mason was thankful he was sitting close to Abdul. He was hoping during the lengthy journey he could ask some questions about the work they were doing. It piqued Mason's interest, and he thought it the best way to pass the time during the long drive. They left at dusk, so there was really nothing to see outside, plus the canvassed truck had no windows, so any sightseeing would be thwarted.

About a half hour into the journey, Mason struck up a conversation with Abdul to pass the time away. As it turned out, Dr. Ash was in the middle of an important excavation of a site previously thought not to exist. It was a set of temple ruins that were thought to be used as preparation chambers for a nearby tomb. In the ancient Egyptian culture, even the dead were brought food and offerings. These ruins they had uncovered were thought to be used for exactly that purpose, but there location was far from any main city. This was why, from an archeological point of view, they were such an important find. Mason thought it ironic that on one side of the world so many were dedicated to uncovering the past while he was working so hard to figure out the present.

As he continued to carry on a conversation with Abdul, he was oblivious to the fact that they were being followed by another transport, not more than a couple miles behind. Traffic out here was occasional, but still those who were on Mason's trail wanted to take no risks in being detected. They were on a very serious mission, and one of their main objectives was anonymity.

After a few hours, Mason, along with others on the transport, fell asleep. Although the roar of the transport and the bumpy road presented an obstacle to slumber, it only took minutes for him to drift off.

Suddenly, without warning, there was a large bang, and the vehicle came to a rough halt. Mason and the others awoke with excitement and quickly exited through the back of the transport. Mason stayed with the group, who seemed all too anxious to find out what happened. Abdul soon came around the corner, and raising a hand, he shouted something in Arabic to the rest of the workers, which seemed to calm them down. Then he saw Mason and walked over to explain the situation.

"We have a flat tire on the front of the truck. We have a spare and should be back on the road within the hour," he finished. Then he continued over to the workers and began to give directions.

As he walked around the truck, Mason noticed something immediately; it was as if the earth had been put to sleep. It was quiet—very quiet; you could have heard a pin drop in this desert wasteland. Again he was taken back when he glanced upward at the night sky. It was clear, and he swore he had never seen so many stars in his life. Although he had not thought about it until that moment, he walked a little ways away from the transport, got on his hands and knees, and thanked God for allowing him to see such beauty. Mason, with his current surroundings, suddenly felt very small, yet he knew God was taking in an interest in him, and that thought was overwhelmingly comforting.

Just a few minutes after that, Mason could see a vehicle coming into view of where the transport's tire had blown out. Several of the workers and Abdul himself tried to wave the vehicle to slow down, but the vehicle sped past them quickly, leaving a large cloud of dust from its passing. Abdul and the others were angered by this and shouted what Mason assumed were insults. Mason even thought it was odd the vehicle didn't stop, especially in this kind of environment. If the transport were damaged beyond repair, they would be stuck out here; it's not as if calling a tow truck on your cell phone was an option. This was a matter of survival, and for someone just to drive by uncaringly was more than rude.

Soon the tire had been fixed, and they were back on their way. Abdul commented to Mason that they would be at their destination a little after midnight and that they had a small tent and cot for him to sleep on. Mason was very grateful for the extra lengths they had gone to in order to let him come. He hoped it would not be in vain and promised himself to help wherever he could while he was there. Dr. Ash sounded like he really liked to get into the thick of his work, and Mason hoped that his presence would not be seen as a distraction.

A few hours passed, and the transport's speed reduced dramatically. Once they were at a halt, everyone jumped out of the back and started to unload the gear, Mason included. The camp was shut down by this time, but Mason could see not far from the main camp area that there were large areas marked off by tape and stakes. The camp was basically a large, huddled set of cloth-type tents. Some of them were as large as a small home. Still other tents looked like they could only hold two people at the most. Mason thought the scene looked remarkably like something out of war movie, where an army set up base camp before attacking at dawn.

After the unpacking was completed, Abdul led Mason to a tent he knew to be empty. Apparently these tents had already been set up in expectation of the transport's arrival. Mason thanked him and ducked down to walk into the small tent. Because these tents were more like large blankets in the form of a house, the flooring was the sandy desert. There were wooden cots set up on each side of the tent and a gas lamp hanging from the middle rod. On each cot was a rolled up blanket and a small pillow. Mason set his bag on one cot, lit the lamp, and sat down on the other cot. He changed into some clothes he could sleep in and was thankful for the tent, as he had camped in worse conditions. After taking off his shoes, he almost placed them on the ground, but the notion of desert scorpions suddenly flooded his mind, and he decided to place them on the other cot as well. After shutting off the lamp and saying a quick prayer, he laid back on the cot to go to sleep. He was anxious to meet and speak with Dr. Ash, but the late hour and long trip had worn him out. He shut his eyes and was asleep within minutes.

Mason had always been a light sleeper, so when he heard voices speaking in foreign tongues and other noises, he stirred a bit. Of course, then he remembered that he was a guest here and did not want to take their hospitality for granted. Squinting as the sunlight streamed into his tent, he glanced at his watch to see what time it was. It was six o'clock in the morning, and Mason groaned as he threw off the blankets and forced himself up out of the cot. He rummaged through his bag, picked out some clothes, and began to get dressed, but having the willies the night before about scorpions, he gave each of his boots a good slap to extricate any unwanted guests. Mason did his best to comb his hair and shave, but without a mirror, he wasn't sure of the quality of the job. He felt a bit awkward knowing that as soon as he stepped out of the tent, he would get looks of curiosity. What made things worse was that he didn't know anyone here except Abdul, and he would have to mill around to find him as well.

"Well, everyone's got to eat breakfast," Mason said out loud, trying to boost himself up.

He would try to find the chow line and move on from there. After grabbing his sunglasses, he headed outside his tent in search of a familiar face or food, whichever came first.

As he had suspected, a few of the workers gave him an odd look here and there but then shrugged him off. He recognized a few of the men from the transport and could see a few of them pointing to him while talking to others, probably explaining the reason for his presence. Mason was grateful for that; he hated being the center of attention, and the more he could blend in the better. He could see that everyone was headed in the same direction—a large tent in the center of the camp. He followed the others, and it wasn't long before he saw Abdul. Mason waved at him, and Abdul, seeing him, started toward him.

"Good morning, Mr. Krane. How did you sleep?" Abdul asked.

"Great; the accommodations were more than adequate and much appreciated," Mason returned.

"Good, good," Abdul said, motioning for Mason to follow as he continued.

"Follow me and I will introduce you to Dr. Ash. Then we'll get some food. He is always up at the site while the men eat. He plans out the day's work that way," Abdul finished.

"Sounds great," Mason said as he walked side by side with Abdul.

Together they walked away from the camp to the marked-off place Mason had seen the night before. It was about a hundred yards away from the main camp. It was on a rise, and Mason could see a solitary figure glancing over the area. As the two approached, Mason could see the man clearly now because he was only about ten feet away. He was fair skinned, and Mason assumed that he was not a native of Egypt, especially with the last name Ash. He stood about six feet tall and was very stocky, abolishing Mason's expectation of a short, nerdy archeologist. His brown hair and eyebrows were both thick, and he wore glasses on his clean-shaven face. After seeing the men approach, he glanced at Mason with a questioning look before walking toward them to meet them halfway.

Abdul spoke to Dr. Ash in Arabic, and Mason overheard his name a couple of times. Abdul was probably explaining Mason's presence in the camp. Finally Dr. Ash turned to Mason and introduced himself.

"Mr. Krane, I am Dr. Samuel Ash. Welcome to the desert," he said with a British accent, holding out his hand in greeting.

"Thank you. It's very nice to meet you, and please, call me Mason," Mason returned as he shook Samuel's hand.

"I remember Raj mentioning something about you a week or so ago, but I didn't expect to see you show up here," Dr. Ash said.

"I'm sorry about the interruption, Doctor, but it's a long story, and I need your help," Mason returned politely.

"Well, I will do the best I can. From what I remember Raj told me you had some questions on a particular cult that existed in ancient Egypt." He paused as if in thought before continuing. "We have a lot to accomplish today, but how about you and I meet this evening for dinner and I will do my best to answer any questions you have?" Samuel said.

"That would be great. I really appreciate all you and everyone else has done to help me. Is there anything I can do to help out around here? I'm not a scientist, but I wield a shovel as well as the next man," Mason returned with a smile.

Samuel smiled in return before answering, "Sure, sure. Abdul can give you a few things to do after breakfast, and then we will get together tonight." He then turned to Abdul to discuss a separate subject.

"Abdul, I've been getting some rather strange readings on the ultrasound and would like to concentrate the dig on the southwest corner. Either there is some kind of cave or chamber down there or our equipment is on the fritz again. There shouldn't be anything there, but by some chance there is, I want to find out what it is. Make sure your diggers are careful; I don't want anyone getting caught in a sinkhole." With that said, Dr. Ash nodded to both of them and turned back to survey the dig site.

Mason's curiosity was piqued by all that was going on. He thought about all the poor souls who came over here and spent a fortune to stay in some resort while he got to really experience what Egypt was like. He promised himself not to take a single moment for granted, and it wasn't hard. He enjoyed working outdoors, and the directions Abdul had given were fairly simple. Mason's primary responsibility was to start helping other diggers on a new plot they had discovered. The other men were friendly and showed him what to do and how to do it. He caught on fast and found that, while he had blisters within one hour's work, he couldn't get enough of the people, the culture, and the pure adventure of it all.

Mason even made a few new friends, and although they knew very little English, they were communicating well enough to tell a joke or funny story here and there over lunch or on water breaks. Mason was also amazed with how unified they worked together. It was like watching a colony of ants, each having a specific job that directly contributed to the whole. They even sang songs while they worked, and Mason got a few of the words down on some of them. When the day had come to a close, Mason found that he was very tired, but he felt as if his effort had been a part of something spectacular. He took great pride in knowing he had been a part of the day's activities. At the end, Abdul directed Mason to a makeshift shower where he could clean up before joining Dr. Ash for dinner. Dr. Ash had his own very large tent, which was easily tall enough to walk into without ducking.

By the time Mason had finished cleaning up and changing his clothes, the sun had well past set, and the camp was lit by lights powered by generators. Mason approached Dr. Ash's tent, but thought it would be rude just to walk through the flaps. He raising his voice a little outside of the entrance and called out to him, "Dr. Ash! It's Mason Krane, is this a good time?"

Mason heard the approach of footsteps to the entrance from the opposite side and saw the familiar face of Dr. Ash through the flap he had drawn back.

"Yes, please come in, sit down. I have already had dinner brought for us," Samuel replied.

"Thank you," Mason returned as he walked through the entrance. As he glanced over the scene, Mason could see a table toward the left half of the tent with two hot plates of food, the steam rising from them, obviously still very warm. Mason sat down in the place Samuel had directed him but felt a bit uncomfortable. Mason never felt right about eating a meal without praying first, but he didn't want to offend his most gracious host. Nonetheless, he felt obligated to honor God first and tried to tread as softly as he could.

"Dr. Ash? Be—" Mason was suddenly cut off by his gracious host.

"Please, we are very informal out here. Just call me Samuel, and don't worry, I can see you are a man of faith; please continue," Samuel said in a polite tone.

With that Mason bowed his head and said a short prayer. He did not know if Samuel was a Christian and partook of the prayer with him, but Mason could tell he was not offended by the act.

"Please eat; there will be plenty of time for talk. You must be hungry. I saw you working quite hard out there today," Samuel said.

"It's really great to be out here, and I enjoy being able to assist. Your men are very friendly, and believe it or not, it's an experience I will never forget," Mason said, smiling. Samuel returned the smile before continuing.

"We shall see if you still feel the same way in the morning. Your body has a way of changing your mind a day after a good day's work," he said with a smirk.

Mason returned the smile, and the rest of the meal was quiet for the most part, except for idle chatter about the day's activities and just general knowledge about each other. Mason told Samuel about his job as a private investigator and the case he was investigating that led him here. He even felt comfortable enough to tell Samuel about the death of his parents and the odd dreams he had been having recently about the way he saw his brother murdered. Samuel was shocked at the abductions and was eager to help in any way he could. When they had finished their meals, a man came in and removed all the dirty dishware from the table, replacing it with tea, biscuits, and a fresh, hot pot of coffee. When the man had exited the room, Samuel turned to Mason with a more sincere and serious focus.

"Now then, Mason, what questions can I answer for you?" Samuel began.

Before Mason began, he pulled out his notebook, which contained notes from his case as well as the drawing of the symbol he had found on the babysitter and his parents' killer.

"A Dr. Kovacs gave me your contact information. She told me you would be the only one who could give me sincere and honest information. She seemed to think that my question was some kind of joke, but when she realized it wasn't, she sent me to you." Mason paused and took a deep breath before continuing.

"As I told you before, I'm working on the disappearance, kidnapping, and probably the murder of several children in my hometown. One of the clues that led me to you was this." Mason pulled out the note he had received in the mail and handed it to Samuel.

"Sennew Sas Ne Apep . . ." Samuel read the note as if it was his primary language, but his face and tone held wonder.

"I was hoping you could tell me what it means, not just the words, but if it means anything to you?" Mason asked hopefully.

After glancing at the note for what seemed an eternity, Samuel laid it softly on the table before lowering his glasses to look at Mason. After rocking in his chair a bit, he gave a long sigh before speaking.

"It's a good thing Regina sent you to me. There's a lot of weirdoes out there who would have filled your head with a lot of nonsense. She knew I would give you the facts, at least as I know them," Samuel began.

"Please, any detail or anything you know would be extremely helpful to me," Mason pleaded.

"I don't know if Regina, Dr. Kovacs, translated this for you, but it says, 'Second Sons of Apep,'" he started.

"Does that mean anything to you?" Mason asked again with excitement and hope.

"Yes, though it's a bit of a story. I am glad we stopped digging a little earlier than normal." He paused before continuing. "Let me preface this by telling you that some of what I am going to tell you is rumor and has no scientific proof whatsoever. However, there are some facts to this story . . . I will tell you what I know and leave it up to you to decide what you find valuable. Sound good?" he asked.

"Fine, any information you can provide would be great," Mason returned eagerly.

"Good." He took a deep breath before continuing. "The 'Second Sons of Apep' were an ancient Egyptian cult that existed roughly 1500 BC. You are a Christian, I can tell, so some of this will make sense to you if you paid attention in Sunday school," he said with a smile. "Do you know the story of Moses and the ten plagues of Egypt?" Samuel asked.

Mason was quite familiar with this Old Testament Bible story—how Moses and Aaron came before the pharaoh of Egypt and demanded the release of the Hebrew slaves. When Pharaoh refused, Moses and Aaron unleashed nine plagues on the Egyptians ranging from disease to insect infestation. After the ninth plague, God told Moses that, at midnight, he would pass through the land of Egypt, and those households who did not have the blood of a pure lamb on their doorframes would be subject to the tenth and final plague of Egypt, the plague of death. Any household not covered by the blood of the lamb would find their firstborn son dead.

Because the Israelites were God-fearing people, they listened to Moses and put the blood on their doorframes to keep themselves immune from the plague. Thus the Lord passed over their homes and did not inflict any harm to their firstborn children. This is what started the Passover tradition. The Egyptians, however, did not heed Moses and Aaron, so all the firstborn sons of the Egyptians, including the livestock, died. Pharaoh was so distraught because his firstborn son died that night as well. He told Moses and Aaron to take the Hebrew slaves and leave Egypt. Mason was anxious to hear what this had to do with the Second Sons, though; he couldn't figure what the connection was.

"Yes, I have read the story many times. The children at my church like that one. It's right up there with David and Goliath, but what does that have to do with this?" Mason asked.

"Like I said, Mr. Krane, some of this story is rumor based and has not been proven or disproven. As you will find common throughout history, mankind's insignificant or sometimes embarrassing points are not documented well and are therefore handed down from generation to generation by word of mouth. Such is the case with the history behind the cult of the Second Sons of Apep," Samuel replied

"A cult?" Mason excused himself immediately, not wanting to be rude. "I'm sorry, please continue," Mason said, deciding to try to hold his questions for the end, but Dr. Ash didn't seem to mind and continued.

"Well, as you know, the last plague sent down by God was the plague of death, killing all the firstborn sons of the Egyptians. Not only did Pharaoh's son die but all those who had sons in his household as well, including a group of Pharaoh's top magicians and sorcerers. They, like Pharaoh, agreed that Moses and Aaron should give the slaves their leave immediately, lest more tragedy would strike, but as it all sank in, their fear turned into rage, and an appetite for revenge took its place. With a fire burning in their blood to wreak retribution on the Israelites, the magicians and sorcerers convinced Pharaoh to send out his army of chariots to hunt down the slaves and kill them. You are probably familiar with this story as well. Moses parted the Red Sea and left Pharaoh's army to be obliterated as the walls of water closed in around them when they tried to cross. When the army was destroyed, this squelched any hope of revenge for Pharaoh, but according to legend, the magicians and sorcerers were not so easily thwarted." Samuel stopped for a moment to take a couple drinks of coffee before continuing on.

"One thing you must understand here, Mason, is that there were many Egyptian gods, some viewed as good and others evil. Contrary to popular belief, worship or prayers of any kind to evil gods were seen as despicable, and any individuals thought to be following such gods would be punished immediately, sometimes even put to death.

"Well, when these magicians and sorcerers cried out to their gods, the gods answered with silence, and most of them gave up. But according to folklore, five of these sorcerers were so bent on revenge that they prayed day and night to the darker gods or to any god that would listen to their pleas for vengeance.

"They went without food and water for nearly a week until they all had a vision. The god Apep visited them in a dream state and offered the sorcerers a pact. He would grant them the power to exact revenge for the death of their firstborn sons, but in exchange they would need to dedicate their remaining sons to him to fulfill his plan for exacting revenge on the God of Moses. Apep was the god of chaos and was jealous of all that the god of the Israelites stood for. It is said that Apep would use the blood of the children of the God of Israel to wreak havoc upon the earth.

"The sorcerers agreed to the terms and trained up their second-born sons in the ways of sorcery and worship of the god Apep, thus the name of the cult. What their true agenda was is unknown, but there is some evidence that many children were kidnapped and even sacrificed as an offering to their god. As I said before, though, any people discovered to have taken part in such a thing were usually executed. There were many such cults, just like today; you have cults where the members commit murder, mass suicide, or other such nonsense." Samuel fell silent as he took several continuous sips of coffee, waiting for Mason to respond.

Mason was awestruck. He suddenly realized the clue that had been escaping him all this time, and it was right in front of him. All of the kidnappings were not only male children but firstborn male children, and the ones he knew semi-personally were Christians. He even recalled his father's last words.

"Remember that they came for him . . ."

His mother and father were devout Christians, and Jason, his brother, was their firstborn son. Mason suddenly became aware that Dr. Ash was staring at him with concern.

"My apologies . . . this is quite a revelation," Mason started.

"How so?" Samuel asked.

"What if I was to tell you that I believed this cult was still in existence and was using kidnapped Christian children for their agendas of havoc?" Mason asked cautiously.

Instantly Samuel began to laugh in jest and shake his head in disagreement.

"Such a thing would not be possible," he replied.

"But why?" Mason pressed.

"This cult began over three thousand years ago, if it existed at all. As I said, a lot of these are just stories. Plus, there is no way something like this could go undiscovered this long without a trace of evidence. The ancient gods of Egypt, in today's culture, are little more than a piece of the past and are, for the most part, not even recognized as actual deities," Samuel replied.

"I know this must sound crazy, but I have found evidence that this cult may not only still exist but is still kidnapping children," Mason started.

Mason spent the next hour filling in Dr. Ash on his investigations so far. He told him about how he had received the note with the Egyptian text and the several unsolved cases of kidnapping in his area that were all firstborn sons of Christians. Mason even went as far as to give Samuel a detailed account of that horrible night so many years ago and the nightmares that accompanied it.

After pulling the drawing from his notes, he showed Samuel the symbol of the pyramid with a snake coiled around it. "This is the symbol I saw on the man's wrist, and it was verified by a babysitter found dead at the scene of one of the kidnappings. Do you recognize it?" Mason asked.

Dr. Ash studied it for a moment before returning the paper to Mason.

"I've never seen anything like that, but like I said, few facts are known about the cult of the Second Sons. Couldn't this be a ruse to keep the police from finding the real killer?" Samuel suggested.

Mason sighed deeply before telling him about the suspect they had found burnt to a crisp and the note he left behind.

"If this gentleman was crazy enough to set himself on fire and keep a collection of his victim's fingers, he was certainly crazy enough to pin it on a cult," Samuel concluded.

Mason again sighed deeply. He had found another crucial piece of the puzzle, but again the rational seemed to suggest that he was trying too hard to make the pieces fit.

"Sometimes at night, I dream about the way my brother died." He paused a moment before continuing. "He was brought into a circular chamber lit only by candlelight. In the middle of the room there's a stone altar, which a procession of hooded figures lays him on and then slits his throat. The blood drains into a chalice below sitting in the open mouth of snake. The killer brings it to his lips and smiles, as if he knows I'm watching. I can't get it out of my head; I just can't," Mason finished and hung his head for a moment rubbing his hands through his hair.

Samuel looked at Mason with concern for a moment before standing up to speak.

"You need your rest, Mr. Krane. Whatever mysteries have yet to be solved in your investigation, I pray that some of them were put to rest today. Sometimes we need to let go and then, if need be, get a better grip before carrying on. God has his own way of working things out, and sometimes we need to step back and let him do it," he said with a smile.

Mason got up and returned the comforting smile Samuel had on his face. Samuel asked if he could pray with Mason, and Mason jumped at the opportunity. The whole time he had no idea Samuel was a believer, but Samuel's prayer of guidance and encouragement told Mason more than he needed to know. When they finished, Samuel informed Mason that the transport would be leaving tomorrow in the mid-afternoon. Nodding in acknowledgment, Mason shook Samuel's hand and headed off to bed. It had been a long day, both physically and emotionally, and Mason needed no prodding once he got to his tent. He was asleep as soon as his face hit the pillow on his cot.

After he had entered his tent, those keeping watch on him from the darkness began to approach in stealth, not wanting to be seen.

Mason tossed and turned a bit in the night. He kept seeing his brother over and over in his dreams. Finally he saw his brother's face on the altar again, except this time, his brother turned to face him and said his name loud, as if to grab his attention.

At that, Mason awoke to a very strange sensation around his whole body. His eyelids felt as if something was draped over them and he couldn't open them. He started to reach up with his hand to remove whatever it was, but he halted when heard a familiar voice.

"Don't move!" Samuel said. "Give us a moment more, and we will have them all," he said, after which Mason could hear him giving orders in Arabic to a third party in his tent.

Mason felt as if someone was prodding him here and there over his whole body. He also felt the same sensation of something draped over him on his hands. after rubbing his fingers together slowly, he realized what it was, or at least what it felt like. As a child, Mason remembered playing hide and seek one night with some kids in the neighborhood. It was a cool night, and although the moon was out, it was still difficult to see. Mason had picked what he thought was a particularly good hiding spot in a hollow spot in some bushes. He wasn't there long before he felt his hands and face run through the sticky substance of a spider web. It spooked him so bad he fell out of the bush frantically trying to wipe off all the webbing and any spiders that had hitchhiked.

Remembering this didn't help Mason's situation, and he had to focus to keep himself from panicking. He could hear the concern in Dr. Ash's voice and decided that he had better listen because he didn't believe Samuel would put him in danger. So, waiting patiently, Mason did what he could to remain calm until he was told otherwise.

"Okay, my friend, now get up very slowly," Samuel directed.

Mason did as he was told, and as he got up, he realized that this was far worse than his experience as a child. He was literally covered head to toe in a cocoon. In fact, it was so thick he had trouble sitting up in his cot. With the assistance of Samuel, he began to peel away the layer of silk that had covered him. After removing the webbing from his face and hands, he began to see why he had to remain still. Looking behind him on the cot, he could see the smashed bodies of dozens of quarter-sized spiders and few that were much larger and of a different color.

"What happened to me?" Mason asked, confused.

"I don't know. I've never seen anything like this before, and I doubt anyone else has either. We have the truck pulling around to take you to the nearest hospital. It's imperative that you get immediate medical attention. How many times were you bitten?" Samuel asked.

Mason stood up and continued to remove the webs from the rest of his body. He slept in shorts and T-shirt, which basically meant his whole lower body was covered in the sticky, silk webbing. After feeling around and doing a self-check, Mason found no source of pain and could feel no bites.

"I don't think I have any," Mason returned.

"That's impossible! Are you sure? Even one bite could be serious," Samuel pressed.

"Why what kind of spider is that?" Mason asked.

Mason hadn't noticed this before, but apparently the reason they wanted him to hold still is they needed to get all the live ones off of him. Samuel held up a large glass jar, which was filled with what had to be at least 150 of them.

"The Latin name for these smaller ones is *Loxosceles reclusa*. Here they call them violin spiders, but in the United States they're called brown recluses. These larger ones are six-eyed sand spiders. These guys have the most deadly venom of almost any spider. They don't have antivenin for this spider, and its nickname is *Sicarius hahni* or murder. One bite from this guy will bring down a full-sized rabbit. Which makes it all the more important that we get you some medical attention as soon as possible," Samuel finished, still holding up the jar.

Mason's eyebrows shot to the sky in shock and amazement.

"How did they all get in here?" Mason asked.

"This jar, opened, of course, was at the foot of your bed when I came into your tent this morning. You were covered in them. I thought for a moment you were dead. Are you sure you haven't been bitten? One had to have bitten you. Look at all the ones you killed just rolling in your sleep," Samuel said.

Mason continued to search, and despite any embarrassment, he proceeded to change clothes in an effort to ensure he wasn't bit. After finishing his search, he turned back to Dr. Ash.

"Nope, nothing. I guess the good Lord was looking out for me," Mason concluded.

"Looking out for you? You were covered head to toe and you didn't get bit once? It's a miracle!" Samuel said in amazement.

"Why would that be at the foot of my bed?" Mason asked, gesturing toward the jar.

"Somebody obviously doesn't want you breathing," Samuel returned.

"Now do you believe me?" Mason queried.

"I'm starting to, especially after what I found this morning." Seeing Mason's confused look, he continued.

"Get finished cleaning up, and I'll show you. Oh, and don't worry about these, we'll give them to the fire." He chuckled, again shaking his head in disbelief as he made his way outside.

Though he did his best to hide his fear, Mason was still quite shaken by the incident. This was clearly an attempt to take his life, which made it all the more peculiar. As he finished cleaning up, many questions came to his mind. He must have been followed by someone who didn't want him to know the truth about the cult. Also, why hadn't the spiders attacked him? Was God protecting him in some way? He didn't know. What he did know was that he was on the right track and someone was getting scared of what he might find.

Mason took a deep breath and gathered himself before exiting the tent. As he pushed back the flap and took one step out, he noticed that there had been quite a gathering as the news must have traveled about his miraculous escape. He felt awkward as the workers pointed at him and whispered to each other as he made his way with Dr. Ash toward the dig site.

"Never mind their ogling, Mr. Krane; they're a bit superstitious, that's all. Can't say I blame them after what I saw," Samuel said with a smile, motioning to Mason to follow him. Then he shouted in Arabic to the workers. He must have told them something to the effect of get back to work, because they all broke up and started toward the dig site.

Mason and Samuel continued up a steep slope to the site where he had first met Samuel the day before. He had helped with some of the digging here yesterday and wasn't totally unfamiliar with the layout. Samuel continued to lead Mason to one of the many chambers they had unearthed while digging the day before. In this specific chamber, which looked like a rectangular hole in the ground, there was a small opening at the bottom, which looked like a bottomless pit, void of any light.

"I thought something was wrong with our equipment when we kept getting strange readings, but sure enough, there is another room underneath this chamber," Samuel said, pointing at the spot in the ground.

"I went down there this morning, and there's something you must see," Samuel said, directing Mason to put on the harness nearby to be lowered into the chamber.

Mason had done some wall climbing before, and the harness looked very similar, except this time there was no climbing involved. He wasn't sure about being lowered into an abyss, especially after this morning's fiasco, but after giving his spine a firm kick, he proceeded with the preparations. The hole was wide enough for each of them to be lowered on opposite sides at the same time. Several workers were holding Mason's line, and Samuel had a crew attending to him as well. Before heading down, Samuel handed Mason a hardhat with a flashlight on top of it and a flashlight to carry. After slipping the flashlight into his pocket, Mason nodded to Samuel and his crew that he was ready.

As soon as they began to descend, Mason could see what must have been the ceiling of the room. It was at least ten to fifteen degrees cooler, and the air was musty, as if they had just entered an old cellar. There was nothing unique about the room, and it looked as if it was carved right out of the rock. As they got farther down, Mason could see that the room was quite large in size, at least twice that of the chamber that was built above it. They seemed to be coming down in the center of the room, and it looked as if the walls were forty feet away in every direction. Still, with only his light and Samuel's, it was difficult to see. Mason looked below him and realized that they were coming down on some sort of raised platform. It was about thirty feet below the ceiling, and when they had touched and some slack was let off, Samuel shouted back up to the workers that they could release the rope. Samuel and Mason slipped out of their rigs and climbed down to the floor of the room, breaking out their extra flashlights in the process.

"I thought you should see this," Samuel said as he walked to one wall and began to light some lamps that had been brought down.

At first glance, again Mason saw nothing fascinating about the room. In fact, there wasn't even any writing or drawings on the wall, but as Samuel was about three-quarters of the way around the room, lighting lamps as he went, Mason realized the room was circular. It was then that Mason began to recognize where he was standing.

"I know this place," Mason said out loud, gazing around the room in awe. "I have seen it in my dreams," he continued.

"I know. You told me about it, remember? That's why I came to get you this morning. This chamber is a sacrificial chamber. The fact that there are no writings or glyphs on the wall signifies that this was a place that was to be kept secret," Samuel said.

Glancing back at the risen platform they had landed on, Mason realized what it was. It was an altar, the one he had seen his brother butchered alive on.

"This is where my brother died," Mason said.

"That's not possible," Samuel said cautiously. "No one has stepped foot in this room for over three thousand years." After pausing a moment, Samuel continued, "This place was buried under fifty feet of desert. I think what you saw was an ancient sacrificial rite performed by the Second Sons. You just happened to place your brother's face as the victim. I believe that this was one of the chambers used to spill the blood of innocent children, and I believe that the Second Sons were the cult that did it."

"How can you be so sure that it was them? You said yourself that there were many cults that existed during this time," Mason asked.

"Well, besides the fact that you basically described this room to me in detail yesterday, and this morning's event, there's this," Samuel said, motioning Mason to come closer to the altar.

Mason stepped up to the altar as Samuel took his flashlight and pointed it at the side of the altar's front end. There, carved plain as day, was the symbol of the pyramid surrounded by a coiled snake. Mason gasped in astonishment and returned Samuel's look of deep concern.

"It's the only glyph or symbol in this whole room," Samuel said calmly, standing erect. "I don't know what you've gotten yourself into, my friend, but I pray that God is with you every step of the way," Samuel said sincerely.

"Has anyone else been down here?" Mason asked.

"No. I always check out these types of things first, and once I realized what it was, I gave strict orders that it was not to be entered," Samuel replied.

"Good. I don't know who these people are, but you've seen what they tried to do to me. If they find out what you've discovered, they may try to hurt you, your workers, or something to keep their existence hidden," Mason said urgently.

"Mason, rooms like this have been discovered before. There is no secret about the cult's existence; it's been proven. I believe they just wanted to keep you from finding out more about it. If this cult still exists, as you believe, then they are still trying to do the work of the chaos god Apep. What kind of havoc, besides the sacrificial deaths of children, is in their plot? . . . Only God knows for sure, but if they have truly stayed hidden for this long, you can bet they are involved in something horrific," Samuel finished.

Mason thought for a moment and decided that he would not try to convince Samuel otherwise, but he must leave immediately, before those who sought him would be enticed to stop Samuel as well.

"I must leave immediately, but do me a favor. Try to keep the discovery of the symbol in the chamber off for as long as you can. This way, when I go, they will follow me and hopefully not give you any trouble," Mason said.

"That shouldn't be a problem at all. In fact, I can hold off the discovery of it for a good month or so. From an archeological perspective, it's not what we would call a super-find. It's just a chamber, like hundreds of others uncovered with no glyphs, and to emphasize that point . . ." Samuel didn't finish his sentence; he turned his flashlight back to where the symbol was on the altar and gave a swift, hard kick with his boot. With that, the symbol and the surrounding area of the altar turned into crushed earth.

"I will get the transport to take you back immediately. I suggest you get on a plane and get home as soon as possible. There is no telling what lengths they might go to once they find out you're still alive," Samuel finished.

Mason nodded in agreement as they both began to put the rigs back on to be pulled out of the chamber. Once strapped in, Samuel shouted an order up top, and they were pulled out of the hole. Once up, both Mason and Samuel did their best to act as if there was nothing of worth in the chamber. Mason went to his tent and began packing up his gear. Giving one last look to the cot, still full of dead, crushed spiders, Mason eagerly left the tent and headed toward where the transport was parked, eager to be on his way home.

As Mason threw his bag in the back, he saw Samuel walking toward the vehicle. When he was within arm's distance, he held out his hand.

"I wish you a safe journey back to your country, and God be with you, my friend," he said. "I have alerted the driver to stop for no one, lest you fall into some kind of trap. By now, those who would have you dead will most certainly know their attempt on your life was unsuccessful," he finished.

"Thank you . . . for everything, and may God be with you as well," Mason replied, shaking his hand.

With that, Mason threw his bag in the back as the truck's engine roared to life. As the transport pulled away, Mason contemplated all he had learned and experienced here. He was positive the Sons were responsible for most if not all of the kidnappings now, and who knew how many more children were in danger because of their agenda? Knowing how and why all the children had died sent a shiver down his back, and although he understood the basis for their motivation, he sensed that there was a greater purpose in what they were doing. Samuel had said that the god Apep had struck a bargain with the priests who had lost their firstborn sons, but he could provide no information on what the priest's end of the bargain would be. The only clue Samuel could provide was that Apep wished to wreak chaos on the world through the blood of the firstborn children of God. How and what they would do, Mason didn't know, but with this new information, he was more determined than ever to find out. It was his belief that these terrible crimes would continue until Apep's demands were met. Mason knew that a portion of the agreement had not been completed, which only confirmed his suspicions all along that more lives would be in danger.

CHAPTER *11*

Mason arrived back at the museum in Cairo by mid-afternoon and was eager to return home. He caught a cab straight from the museum to the airport, wasting no time in sightseeing as he had previously planned. Once he arrived, he rescheduled his flight for the next available one to the States. Then he called home but was greeted by the answering machine. Mason left Tyler a brief but detailed message with his flight information and when he would be arriving. He did not say anything about the attempt on his life, knowing this would serve no meaningful purpose at this point in time.

His flight didn't leave for another hour and half, but he spent the entire time at the gate going through his notes over and over again. He knew Paul would never believe him fully about his theory of a three thousand-year-old cult kidnapping Christian firstborn boys to fulfill a promise to an ancient Egyptian god of chaos. Summarized like that, even Mason found it hard to swallow. He needed some hard evidence; otherwise it was pointless to go to the police. Even Paul would need something more solid than a history lesson, and since Mason believed there was a leak somewhere in the police department, he wanted to be absolutely certain of what he shared was undisputable. Besides, whatever he told Paul might end up in the hands of those who, Mason believed, arranged the convenient death of Jeremiah Stone and the explanation for many missing children. He would just have to keep digging, but where to go, he didn't know. After he boarded the plane, he continued to sort through his thoughts. After reviewing the details again, looking for a shred of proof, he finally got frustrated and ended up falling asleep for the duration of the flight.

As the plane touched down, Mason awoke and was hopeful that Tyler had received his message and would be waiting for him at the gate. Tired and worn, he grabbed his bag and headed down the ramp and up toward the main exit, hoping to see his wife's shining face. He didn't realize how much he had missed her until now, and he realized that he hadn't given her the attention she deserved lately. Although his work was important, he wanted desperately to make it up to her and their relationship.

As he approached the gate's exit where expecting relatives were gathered, he didn't see Tyler. As he continued to walk closer and closer, it wasn't until he was standing right in front of him that he recognized his uncle Joe.

"Uncle Joe?" Mason asked, confused. "Where's Tyler?" Mason queried with concern.

"No worries, son," his uncle replied. "Something happened while you were gone."

Mason immediately thought about the attempt on his life and wondered if they had tried the same thing here. Panic stricken by the thought, he began to drill his uncle for information.

"Is she hurt? Where is she? Why didn't she come?" Mason said, almost yelling.

"Easy, easy, Mason. She's fine. She is keeping watch over a friend of yours," Uncle Joe said.

"Who?" Mason replied, the concern in his voice dropping significantly.

"Jordan," his uncle replied. "I guess he called your house the day after you left. He was in real bad shape, almost overdosed on crystal meth. If it hadn't been for Tyler, he would have died.".

Mason was both excited and alarmed to hear the news about Jordan. He had always hoped he would see him again, but these were not the circumstances he was hoping for when he thought about it.

"Jordan was barely able to tell Tyler where he was before he passed out. When she couldn't get him to respond after that, she went to where he had told her and found him passed out not ten feet from a phone booth. She rushed him to the hospital, and they were able to stabilize him. Now he is dealing with a much more difficult problem," his uncle finished.

"What's that?" Mason asked with deep concern.

"He has been going through severe withdrawal from the drugs he took, and Tyler has taken him to a detox clinic. She has barely left his side since he has been in there. She sent me to pick you up because he was having an episode and went into a rage. She was the only person there who could keep him calm and help him fight it, and she didn't want to leave his side," Uncle Joe finished.

"That sounds like Tyler," Mason replied with a hint of pride in his voice. "Well, lead the way," Mason finished with a sigh of concern.

Mason's uncle led him through the maze of the airport out to the parking lot to his awaiting vehicle. As they walked, Mason may have been silent, but his mind was running a mile a minute. All his thoughts about his recent adventure abroad had disappeared and been replaced by a deep concern for the current situation. Mason was split as to how he felt about the whole thing. On one hand, he was very thankful that Jordan had called and that Tyler had responded and helped him, but on the other, he was concerned about his wife's safety and the danger she might be putting herself into. Mason's uncle had brought him to a detox center once, when he was fifteen. His uncle had caught him smoking a joint with some kids from school.

It was a scene he wouldn't forget for the rest of his life. His uncle had him there, explaining that none of the people in here started out as addicts but by giving into the temptation just once. Mason remembered walking down the bleach-white hallways and hearing screams of anguish in the distance or behind closed doors. He was brought to an observation room that was used to monitor patients and their status of recovery.

Mason's uncle made him stay there for two hours watching the monitors that showed the many people reacting to the withdrawal symptoms in horror. One man cursed repeatedly and threw furniture from his room. Others were covered in sweat and curled up into a ball in the corner of their rooms, howling in fear and paranoia at the slightest sound or movement, real or imagined. There was one particular patient Mason remembered—mostly because he couldn't have been much older than Mason at the time—who was slumped over a trash bin in his room and was vomiting uncontrollably. Mason had watched in horror as the young man continued on and on until at last other bodily functions began to lose control as well.

Toward the end, Mason rushed to the men's room and got sick to his stomach for a good five minutes. When he emerged, his uncle glanced at his ghostly white face and decided he had had enough and took him home. Mason had never touched another joint or any other drug since then and had no plans to. It might have been a very harsh way to get the message across, but it worked, and Mason was thankful his uncle had taken action instead of leaving him to figure it out like so many other parents did. What scared Mason the most about that night was the fact that none of those in the facility had someone there with them. They were alone, left to deal with their inner demons without God, without their parents, and without even a friend. Weeks later, one of the kids Mason had been caught smoking the joint with was found dead in his bedroom. He had committed suicide. Apparently left to his own devices, it was the only way he knew how to work out the difficulties in his life.

That memory made Mason realize that, although Tyler might have put herself at risk, she had also made herself an icon of solace for Jordan, and to Mason, there couldn't have been a better example for Jordan. Knowing that he didn't have to face such a terrible ordeal alone probably meant the world to Jordan, and realizing this, Mason wanted nothing more than to be by his side as well.

When they arrived at the facility, it was a little after midnight, but Mason's fatigue had all but disappeared once he found out about Jordan and Tyler. This was not the same place his uncle had brought him when he was younger, but he got the same feeling when he walked into the office. This was supposed to be a place of healing, but the pain and suffering that went on inside deterred you immediately from that fact. Uncle Joe walked up to the reception desk as Mason hung behind, gathering his surroundings.

In the waiting room, Mason saw several somber faces, obviously waiting to hear how their loved ones were faring. Mason took note of the fact that the group was quite diverse in race and financial stature. Drugs may have been a lot of things, but the one thing they weren't were discriminatory. They affected all races, creeds, and income levels. From the wealthiest stockbroker to the hooker on the street, drugs would welcome anyone with open arms. Mason thought it ironic that people, even the church, could at times be more judgmental and bigoted then these very addictive and destructive agents. He felt ashamed at his own life as a Christian and how many times he had shunned those he felt unworthy of his attention. Satan, on the other hand, didn't work that way and would use any means necessary to welcome anyone and everyone into his world.

Mason snapped out of his own thoughts when he saw one of the nurses come around the corner to lead his uncle down a corridor.

Mason's uncle turned toward Mason and motioned for him to follow. As Mason came up alongside his uncle, both in tow to the nurse, his uncle filled him in on the latest.

"The nurse says he is doing a lot better. Apparently he had quite a bout earlier today and if not for Tyler being here to calm him down, the nurse said they would have had to sedate him and keep him bound in his bed," he said as he took a deep breath and continued. "She also said he is past the hump, so to speak, and should be able to go home in a couple of days."

"What home? He hasn't got anything or anybody to go home to," Mason responded calmly with a heavy sigh. "I hope we can convince him to come home with us. I'm sure that Tyler has already made that offer. I pray he decides to take it," Mason finished as the nurse finally stopped before a door leading into one of the rooms.

"It's okay for you to go in now, but please be quiet and don't stay longer than a few minutes. He's sleeping now, and the doctors don't want him disturbed," she said, leaving them in front of the door.

Mason's uncle looked at him expectantly and motioned for him to enter first. After grabbing the door and opening it slowly, he entered the dimly lit room. He could already see a figure sitting in a chair next to the bed. Tyler's back was to him, but she turned upon hearing the door open and got up quickly when she recognized Mason's face. Rushing to him, she gave him a long hug and a kiss without any words. She then moved to greet Mason's uncle, who had filed in silently behind him.

Mason slowly made his way toward the bed and could see Jordan sleeping. Mason immediately noticed that Jordan didn't exhibit the traits of a person comfortably asleep. His body twitched constantly, and his face and hair were dripping with sweat, even though the room was quite cool. His eyes sockets seemed a bit sunken, and his face looked at as if it had been scratched in several areas, probably from his withdrawal-induced fits. Seeing this, Mason's heart was pricked by guilt. He felt that he was somehow responsible for Jordan's condition. As he looked back on his actions, he felt there was more he could have done for Jordan, and he had to stifle back the tears from his eyes while he continued to watch Jordan fitfully sleep. Mason turned to speak to Tyler but was instantly met with her nodding her head in disagreement as she held her finger up to her lips, insisting on silence. Then she pointed toward the door and motioned for both of them to follow.

Once outside the room when the door had shut, she turned toward Mason.

"So how was your trip?" she asked in a half-whisper.

Mason paused a moment because this wasn't a question he could give the usual pat answer to. So much had happened, and it would take more than a few moments to explain everything.

"Eventful . . . very eventful. I will tell you about it later. Too much has happened to explain it here, but I will say that it was full of surprises," he stated with raised eyebrows. "So how is Jordan doing?" Mason asked, changing the subject.

"He's fine now, but earlier he was having quite a time of it," Tyler answered as she looked back at the door to his room. "He had a couple violent outbursts before I got him to settle down. They were actually contemplating putting him in a padded safe room for a while, but I got him to a manageable level, and they changed their mind." She paused a moment before continuing. "He has been going through some counseling here that they offer, and I have been reading and discussing the Bible with him a lot. He acts like he's not interested, but then he asks a lot of questions. His outlook is very encouraging," she finished.

"The nurse said something about him being able to leave soon. Is it okay that he comes home with us?" Mason asked.

"I was hoping you would say that," she said with a smile. "He and I have become quite good friends and I understand now why God laid such a burden on your heart for him. He will be more than welcome this time, and hopefully we can help him make a decision for Christ."

Mason smiled in return and was very thankful that God had used Tyler in such a way. After hearing about this, he knew they had a real chance of helping Jordan not only to get away from the bad elements he had grown so accustomed to but to make a decision to follow after God.

"Well, I have a lot to tell the both of you. Are you guys hungry?" Mason asked.

Both Tyler and Mason's uncle nodded in agreement, not so much because they were hungry but because they could tell that Mason had a story to tell and they couldn't wait to hear it. After Tyler grabbed her purse from the room and checked in with the nurse, they left.

They headed out to a twenty-four-hour diner for some apple pie and conversation. Tyler left a message with the check-in desk to give to Jordan to let him know they would all be back the following day.

Once at the diner, Mason spent the next hour and a half telling his wife and uncle about his experience in Egypt. Eyebrows raised, and looks of concern crossed their faces as he told them about the attempt on his life and the information he had found. Mason could tell by the end of the conversation that both Tyler and Uncle Joe were baffled at what he had found out and what had happened to him. Both Tyler and Uncle Joe had always supported him, but deep down both of them, up until this point, thought that some of his theories were slightly misleading—not because he wasn't a good investigator but because they knew more than anything what Mason was searching for was an answer. After hearing about his latest trip, they both agreed with Mason that there was something big going on here that not even Mason could have imagined. There were too many things that connected, and for the first time, Tyler was afraid for her husband's safety. One thing was for certain: whatever Mason had stumbled onto was something somebody would go to the greatest lengths to keep hidden.

"Mason, why don't you hand this all over to the police? I am sure Paul can do something with this," Tyler said with heavy concern.

"It's not that easy, hon. I am convinced that someone on the department, near Paul, is in on this whole thing. I can't compromise the safety of anymore missing children by taking the chance that information could be leaked." This statement got a raised eyebrow from Uncle Joe, who used to be a police officer.

"Plus, Paul will want proof and beyond what I know to be true in my heart, I have no evidence to hand over to produce a fruitful investigation. That's why it's important that both of you keep this to yourselves as well. If word gets out to these people that I am still working on this, they may try to kill me again or worse yet, one of you. My prayer is that they will assume their attempt on my life has scared me into dropping my investigation." He paused, hanging his head for a moment before continuing.

"For now, let's concentrate on helping Jordan. Even though I have a lot more information and have some idea of what's going on, I don't have the slightest clue where to go next to get the proof I need," he said. "I need some time to think and put together a game plan." He said this last bit more to himself then his audience.

"Okay, just promise me you'll be careful. I don't want to lose you," Tyler said sincerely.

"No way," Mason returned with a smile.

The rest of the conversation was devoted to what they would do in preparation for Jordan. Mason said he would go visit him for a while tomorrow and see how he was doing. Tyler had missed a few days of work, and Mason thought it would be good for Jordan to see another face anyway. Mason was hopeful Jordan, upon release, would come to stay with them again and take advantage of an opportunity to turn his life around.

Four men entered the room timidly, knowing full well that their master would not be pleased. The room was dark, like the rest of the temple, but this room had a single bright light from the ceiling shining down on the middle of the room like a spotlight. There was no furniture in the room, and the only other thing in the room was a shirtless figure sitting in the middle of the light with his arms and legs crossed and his eyes shut. The figure sat there motionless until the doors shut behind the men. Then his eyes opened before he spoke.

"Were my instructions in any way unclear?" He spoke with a deep accent.

"No, sire . . . but there were complications—" The man was loudly interrupted as the figure stood, glaring at the men as he spoke.

"Then why did you fail?" Thestos shouted.

The men were speechless and simply hung their heads in silence.

Walking toward one of the walls, Thestos pulled on a knob that opened up a small drawer. In the drawer were several blades. Grabbing four of them, he turned as he spoke.

"You all know the price for failure, but you're in luck, as I'm in a particularly generous mood," he said in deep tones as he turned and walked toward the men. "Kill me and you live, fail and you . . . well you get the idea." He said the last bit with an evil smirk.

Lightly tossing the blades to the floor in front of the men, he stood in front of them with his arms folded behind his back.

The men looked at each other, and then each kneeled down and picked up one of the blades. Watching him carefully, they scattered around him, planning to attack him from all sides. Knowing Thestos, they understood their only chance of survival was to kill him. He had a reputation for playing with those he was assigned to kill, enjoying every second. As they started to close in on him, he didn't move, only smiled, feeding off the fear that came from them.

One of the men looked at each of the others, then back at Thestos, and screamed as he raised the blade up over his head and ran toward his intended victim. At the same time, one of the men standing directly behind Thestos started to advance in much the same manner. As they approached, Thestos still continued to remain motionless until the last possible moment. As the man with the blade raised over his head was about to come down right on Thestos's chest, he grabbed the hand with the knife, spun, and bowed in one movement. Then, pushing forward, he shoved the blade, still in his attacker's hand, into the man attacking him from behind. The blade pierced the man square in the chest.

Next Thestos pulled the knife free and twisted it from its owner's hand, spun toward another attacker just as he was approaching, and brought the blade across his throat, which brought the man to the floor instantly. The man grabbed his wound, dropped his blade, and made a gurgling sound as he writhed on the floor. Turning, Thestos threw the blade he still held at the man on the opposite side of the room. He was in shock and had yet to move. The blade landed squarely in his abdomen, and the man gasped as he fell to the floor. Thestos then turned to the man who had first attacked him who was still on the floor, realizing that his comrades were dead, all by his own weapon.

"Please, sire, have mercy!" the man pleaded.

Thestos again smiled before responding.

"Oh, but I have. As you can see, I have rewarded you with the last death because you showed the courage to attack first," he said evenly, pausing before continuing. "Now, it's your turn . . . unless, of course, you kill me," Thestos finished in a half laugh.

The man was visibly trembling now, and sweat poured down his face because he knew he was about to die. Eyeing the blade nearest him, he ran toward it and quickly picked it up off the ground. Then he turned and rushed Thestos. Again, Thestos waited for the last possible moment. Then the man made a thrusting motion toward Thestos's abdomen, but Thestos moved with lightning speed, avoiding the blow while at the same time disarming the man of the blade. Then, swiftly moving behind him, he grabbed the man's head and twisted sharply, nearly twisting his head in a 180-degree angle to his body. One loud cracking noise, and the man's limp body fell to the floor in a heap.

Sighing in displeasure and irritation, Thestos exited the room and began preparing his thoughts for what he knew would be an unpleasant meeting with his master.

The two men sat nervously across desk from their leader. Thestos and Detective Deturo had failed to eliminate Mason and were now facing Lord Amahte's disappointment.

"Your incompetence has surprised even me! How could you let Krane get away from you again?" Amahte said angrily as he paced in front of his desk.

"It's strange, but it seems he was protected somehow, my lord," Thestos replied while at the same time lowering his gaze in shame.

"Yes, yes, you told me before what happened, and I still find it difficult to believe your men acted with such stupidity." Amahte sighed deeply before continuing. "Now we must deal with this situation here, which is something I wanted to avoid," he said, flashing an angry glance at both men.

"Excuse me, my lord, but that might not be necessary," Paul said.

"And why is that, Detective Deturo?" Amahte asked with sarcasm heavy in his voice.

"I believe Krane has ended his pursuit for answers due to the attempt on his life. He trusts me, yet since his return, I have heard nothing from him. If he was still on this crusade of his, I believe he would have come to me seeking assistance. Also, he has probably told his family about the attempt on his life, and fearing retribution, he probably hopes to keep them out of danger by not pursuing the matter any further," Paul finished, swallowing hard in fear of his long-winded explanation.

"Lord, I agree with Paul on this. Krane, after all, did find the one responsible for his parents' death, and we are too close to distribution to risk possible exposure of our plans. Krane has no evidence, nor any idea of our plans," Thestos finished.

"Very well, but if he should come to you, Detective, with anything more, I want him and his wife eliminated immediately. You both know what is at stake here, and if we must risk exposure to eliminate a possible threat, then that's exactly what we will do." Changing the subject, Amahte continued, "Thestos, fill me on our progress to date and if we are still on schedule for deployment . . ."

CHAPTER *12*

It had been a few days since Mason had returned home, and both he and Tyler had been to see Jordan many times. Mason spent most of the time just listening to the young man during their visits. Jordan was glad to see him the day he first visited, and they spent most of the time playing board games and just talking. Jordan had been actively asking questions about God and what Mason's spiritual beliefs were. Mason was eager to answer all he could and prayed that God would work in the young man's heart. He could tell that Tyler had shared Scripture with him, and that, combined with his most recent experience, was making Jordan question everything in his life. His life had been full of betrayal, sadness, guilt, and a total absence of love. But in Christ, Mason hoped Jordan would find the trust, relationship, and love that every human being longs for. Mason knew this was Jordan's best chance for a new life.

It was midmorning when Mason sat down to read the morning paper and eat breakfast. Tyler had long since left for work, and Mason decided to spend most of the day with Jordan, since this was going to be his last day at the rehab center. After skimming through the paper, he nearly choked on his coffee when he came to one of the articles. It was actually a follow-up article to something that must have happened while he was gone. Two teenage boys had been reported missing in the area, and the last time they were seen was on their way to school. The police believed that this was a kidnapping because one of the boys' backpacks was found lying on the sidewalk, as if dropped in a hurry. They were asking anyone who had any information on the whereabouts of the two youths to call the local police immediately.

Mason thought he might have his uncle check into this one and then thought better of it. Even if his uncle were to do some poking around, it might tip off those onto him that he was still snooping. He wanted to keep them in the dark and thought it best to just remember the details of this specific incident in line for the next investigative opportunity he may have. Another article caught Mason's attention as well. it turned out that the city had hit an all-time record for pet adoptions, especially cats. Not necessarily newsworthy, but Mason concluded they need to print something positive to contradict all the junk that was happening in the world. He snickered at the odd article, finished up the rest of his breakfast, and headed out the door. He was anxious to see Jordan and couldn't wait till tomorrow when he could bring him home and hopefully help him start a new life. Mason had already spoken with Social Services, and for the time being, he and Tyler would be considered Jordan's foster parents. There were no objections from the state, and Mason and Tyler were hopeful that someday down the road they could adopt Jordan. However, not wanting to rush into anything, they decided the "one day at a time" approach was best.

Grabbing his coat from his office he paused a moment before reaching into his desk drawer and pulling out his father's Bible. He hadn't brought it with him before, but something told him not to leave home without it today. After grabbing the book, he left to spend the day with Jordan at the rehab center.

It was a relatively short drive, and he arrived at the rehab center inside of fifteen minutes. The nurses at the receptionist's desk had become used to seeing him coming in, and when he came through the main entrance, they signed him in and let him through without any questions.

Mason walked down the hallway and was about to enter Jordan's room when he recognized Jordan's voice coming from down the hall. By the sound of it, he was playing a game, and as he entered the recreation room down the hall, his assumptions were validated. Jordan was playing ping pong with another young gentleman and appeared to be putting up quite the fight. When Jordan looked up and saw Mason watching, he held up his finger while speaking.

"Just a second, Mason, I almost got this guy beat," Jordan said with a sly smile.

The other young man served up the ball, and with one huge swing, Jordan sent the ball screaming back across the table at a speed that made it almost impossible to see, let alone hit. Jordan's opponent made his best effort, but the ball hit the corner and bounced out of his reach.

"Good game, man," Jordan said, slapping hands with the other young man before walking over to where Mason was watching.

"You're pretty good," Mason said, motioning toward the table.

"Lots of practice," Jordan replied. "They always have ping pong at the juvie centers and places like this. Do you want to play a game?" Jordan asked.

"Maybe later, I have a couple questions for you. Can we go back to your room and chat?" Mason asked.

"Sure man, it's almost lunch time anyway," Jordan returned.

Mason and Jordan continued back down the hall to Jordan's room in silence. Mason could see that Jordan occasionally glanced at the Bible he was carrying in interest. He hoped he wasn't pressuring the young man just by having it. When they reached their room, Jordan casually strolled toward the bed in the room and laid down, putting his hands behind his back. Then he reached to his night table and grabbed a book from it, showing it to Mason as he spoke.

"Tyler brought this for me the last time she was here," he said, showing Mason a Bible. "I see you got yours there, and by the looks of it, you're ready for a new one," he said, motioning to the old, weathered book in Mason's hand.

"It was my father's," Mason said. "Have you been reading it at all?"

"A little. The last Bible I read I didn't understand. It was full of 'Thous' and all these other uppity words I didn't get. Tyler said this one was easier to understand, and she was right. I don't see any of that weird jive in this one," Jordan replied.

"Yeah, some of those translations use some language that is difficult to understand. The version she got you looks like what's called the New International Version. My father's Bible is a King James Version; it's the one with all the weird lingo," Mason said, smiling.

"So . . . you said you had some questions for me?" Jordan asked.

"Yeah, how is it going in here for you?" Mason said.

"I've been here before, a couple years back, and it didn't do much for me, but this time it's different. I feel like maybe I can try to do something better with myself than get into trouble. Maybe go back to school or get a job, but then again, who'd hire someone like me?" Jordan asked rhetorically.

"I read some of this," Jordan said, holding up the Bible. "That Jesus dude walked around doing all that good stuff. He never messed up. I've already made a mess of things in my life. That's why they wanted to pin that murder on me. I guess no matter how far you run, you can't escape your past." Jordan paused before continuing. "Tyler was talking to me about asking Jesus into my heart and asking for forgiveness for my sins, but I'm not good enough to be a Christian. You guys do everything right. Why would God want somebody who messes up all the time? That's why I figure there's really nothing left to do, but what I've been doing . . . I don't know why I called you that night," he continued, lowering his head.

"Maybe I thought you could help me, but now I feel like I just interrupted your lives. You and Tyler have been so nice to me, and I really don't deserve that . . . I shouldn't have called. I should have just left you alone," he finished, choking back tears.

Mason got up, walked over to the bed, and put his hand on the young man's shoulder. "Jordan, I hate to break it to you, but I am no better than you are. When I was about your age, my uncle caught me smoking some pot and brought me down to one of these places. I saw all these people going through such pain, both emotionally and physically. It scared me and not because I was afraid of becoming addicted but because I could see that most of these people were dealing with this on their own. They had no one to help them, because most of their friends and family were steeped in the same problems. It made me realize something that I read in God's Word. Here, I'll show it to you." Mason took the young man's Bible and flipped through the pages until he came to the passage he wanted Jordan to read. Handing the Bible back to Jordan, he directed him on which passages to read.

"Read Romans 3:22-23," Mason said.

Jordan took the book back and reviewed the page before starting to read the passages out loud. "This righteousness from God comes through faith in Jesus Christ to all who believe. There is no difference, for all have sinned and fall short of the glory of God," Jordan finished, looking back up to Mason.

"You see, Jordan, it doesn't matter who you are or what you have done or haven't done. We are all in the same boat to God. You and I have fallen short, but because God gave his Son's life for us, we can live." Mason paused before continuing. "You think God's people are perfect; I can tell you about a bunch of them who led horrible lives. There was this one guy named David—he was a great king and faithful servant to God, but one day he saw this woman taking a bath, and he wanted her. So he sent her husband in the field of battle where he knew he would be killed so that he could marry her." He saw Jordan's eyes rise in surprise as he continued.

"There was this other guy named Saul; he actually murdered Christians. He went from town to town arresting them and putting them to death, but God forgave him and he became a great man of God." Mason again took the Bible from Jordan and began flipping the pages before coming to another passage.

"Here, read this one Second Corinthians 12:9," Mason finished, handing the Bible back to the young man to read.

Again Jordan took the book and found the passages he had been shown to read. "But he said to me, 'My grace is sufficient for you, for my power is made perfect in weakness.' Therefore I will boast all the more gladly about my weaknesses, so that Christ's power may rest on me," Jordan finished.

"You see, Jordan, God isn't looking for perfect people; he's looking for people who want to have a relationship with him so that his power can work in their lives, and when you join his family it doesn't mean you stop messing up. It just means you try hard to do the things God wants you to do and to ask for forgiveness when you don't," Mason finished.

"So . . . how do I let God know I want in on this?" Jordan asked with a single tear streaming down the left side of his face.

Once again Mason flipped through the book and handed it back to Jordan to read.

"Read Romans 10:9-10," he said.

"That if you confess with your mouth, 'Jesus is Lord,' and believe in your heart that God raised him from the dead, you will be saved. For it is with your heart that you believe and are justified, and it is with your mouth that you confess and are saved," Jordan finished with tears now rolling down his face.

"All you have to do is ask God to forgive you for your sins, confess that you believe in him and the power of his resurrection, and invite him to be the Lord and savior of your life. Would you like to do that, Jordan?" Mason asked hopefully

"Yes, but how? I have never talked to God before; don't I have to be in a church or something?" Jordan replied back in a half sob.

Mason smiled as he replied back. "God is always listening, whether you're in a church, on the street, or in a rehab center. All you need to do is close your eyes, bow your head, and talk to him," Mason said, now grasping the young man's hand.

Jordan responded by grasping Mason's hand back and bowing his head before praying. "God, I know I have done some bad things, and I want to say that I am sorry for doing them. I would like to be a part of your family and be forgiven for the many things I have done wrong. I want your Son Jesus to come into my heart as the Lord of my life. You sent him to die for me, and I want to live the rest of my life in a better way for you." Shuddering for moment, and nearly sobbing, he finished his prayer. "Thank you, God. I hope I don't disappoint you."

"Amen," Mason said.

"Amen," Jordan repeated.

With that the young man raised up his head and instantly embraced Mason in a deep hug as the tears now flowed out of both of them. Mason silently thanked God for working in this young man's life and knew that whatever Jordan had ahead of him, God would be right by his side. They hugged for a long while before they broke away and Jordan wiped the tears from his eyes, but now he had a grin on him that Mason had never seen before and he knew that a life had been changed.

Mason turned and sat back in his chair before continuing. Sitting down and letting out a long sigh, his eyes glazed over as he began to speak. "God has helped me a lot," he began in somber tones. "You know this case I am working on, the one that you helped me with?" Mason said, glancing at Jordan.

"That case is my life, my purpose . . ." Mason paused before continuing. "My parents were murdered right in front of me when I was five years old. I watched these men come into my house and destroy everything my father had worked hard to build. They even took my older brother, and I sat there outside where they couldn't see and did nothing. I went to live with my uncle after that, but I never forgot about that night, and I have been trying to find out what happened ever since. That's what led me to you in a sense," Mason said with a deep sigh.

"How's that?" Jordan returned.

"Well, I saw that one of the men had the tattoo I showed you on his arm, and up until now no one else had ever seen it. You and a young woman from another case are the only other people who have seen the tattoo," Mason finished.

"Where did she see it?" Jordan asked.

Mason swallowed hard and looked to the floor before meeting Jordan's gaze to answer his question. Then, giving another heavy sigh, he answered Jordan's question.

"She was babysitting, and someone broke in and kidnapped the little boy she was babysitting." Mason went silent for what seemed an eternity, contemplating whether or not to tell Jordan about her death.

"She was found with her throat slit and a note under her hand with a rough sketch of the tattoo," Mason finished somberly.

Jordan's eyes widened, and Mason could tell the question that was coming next.

"If they killed her, will they come after me?" he asked with terror in his voice.

"No. They killed her because she was in the way. A witness to the kidnapping and the man you identified was found a week or so ago dead in his house . . . an apparent suicide." Mason said the last piece with sarcasm.

"Man, this is some trippy stuff. So do you think this guy killed your parents and took your bro?" Jordan asked.

"That happened over twenty-five years ago," Mason said, shaking his head. "This guy would have been too young, plus he wasn't alone. There were three of them in the house that night." Mason paused a moment. "Enough about this for now," Mason said quickly before another question could be asked. "You get your rest, and I will be by tomorrow to take you home. We can talk more about this later."

With that there was an uncomfortable moment between the two of them. Mason wanted so much to embrace the young man who had just come to grips with the new opportunities he had been given by accepting Christ, but he didn't want Jordan to feel uncomfortable. Finally he decided a handshake was the best thing to do, but as he held out his hand, Jordan surprised him by grabbing it and pulling him toward him for a quick hug. As he did so, he spoke in Mason's ear.

"Thanks man . . . for everything. I am really going to try hard this time," he said, releasing Mason from the embrace.

Mason smiled back as he responded to the young man.

"I see strength in you, Jordan, and God has a purpose for you. I will do my best to help you find out what it is, but you have taken a step today that I promise you will never regret. You now have Christ with you, and he will always be there . . . always."

With that, Mason left the young man to rest and walked down the hall feeling better than he had in a long time. He knew now that Jordan's chances of making a real life for himself had just improved a thousand fold, and he praised God silently as he walked out of the establishment, filled with the joy that he knew could only come from God.

CHAPTER *13*

It was just past dusk as Mason walked outside of the rehab center and out to his car. He continued to think about, and take joy in, Jordan's recent conversion. Walking on cloud nine, he failed to notice a figure in the shadows watching his every step. As he got to his car, he had barely begun to place the key in the door when he felt something press against his back.

"Mason Krane?" he heard a voice behind him ask in a Middle Eastern accent.

"Who wants to know?" Mason retorted.

"I am in no mood for cattle play, Mr. Krane," The man said with warning in a deep voice. "If you wish to live, you will do as I say or I will kill you; your choice," the man finished.

Mason didn't really have a choice and was disappointed in his lack of attention to his surroundings. However, he didn't want to egg this guy on. Whoever he was, he wanted something from him; otherwise Mason would already be dead. That being said, Mason spoke more gently this time.

"What would you have of me?" Mason said.

"Unlock the passenger side and don't get in the vehicle until I tell you," the man replied.

Mason thought he might be able to overpower the man in a moment of complacency, but he thought better of it. Seeing the man, he could see that he was indeed of Middle Eastern descent of some kind. He was short, probably about five foot three, and had black hair. He also wore black eyeglasses that covered his almond-shaped eyes. Mason could see that although the man had a gun, he looked terrified, like a wild animal that had been trapped for too long. Even though it was relatively cool outside, the man's head and face were covered in sweat, and his eyes shifted erratically in every direction.

Once in the vehicle, Mason turned to the man to get further instructions.

"Drive," the man said in a flat, even tone.

After starting the car, Mason had no idea where this would lead, but for the moment he decided to play along. The man only spoke to give directions, and soon they were on the outskirts of town. It was dark out now, and there was nothing out this far except a couple of trailer parks and a local fishing lake with some campgrounds. Mason prayed silently that he wasn't about to end up in a shallow grave.

"Turn off here, at the lake," the man barked while at the same time shoving an automatic pistol into Mason's side.

Mason did as he was instructed, but he couldn't help but feel a little nervous.

"Park," the man ordered.

As soon as the car was parked, the man got out of the car and instructed Mason to stay put. The man shut the door and then proceeded to get in the backseat directly behind Mason.

"Keep your hands on the wheel and eyes forward," he shouted while resting the gun point to the back of Mason's head.

"You don't know me, Mr. Krane, but I know you," the man started. "You are the seeker of lost children, right? But you look for more than the children, don't you, Mr. Krane? You are seeking the truth of it all, aren't you? Well it's your lucky day, Mr. Krane. I am going to give you the answers you have been seeking so diligently."

Mason wasn't sure what to say or think. Could this be another trap or an attempt to find out what he knew? He just couldn't be sure of anything at this point.

"I'm not sure—" Mason started but was cut off immediately.

"Silence, Krane," he said, pushing the butt of the gun into the back of Mason's head with force. "I brought you here to listen, not to speak." The man said.

With that Mason swallowed the rest of his sentence and kept his eyes forward. Mason could hear the man take a deep breath and blow it out slowly before continuing.

"My name is Jahid Ramesh, and I am a member of the organization that is responsible for the abduction of the many children you have been looking for."

Mason was stunned. Was this the same cult that had existed long before the birth of Christ and was still around seeking firstborns to sacrifice? He questioned the authenticity of this man, and although it wasn't the most intelligent move, he risked a question.

"I'm not sure I know what you mean," Mason stated hesitantly.

The man snickered in sarcasm, and Mason could hear him moving around.

"Do you recognize this, Mr. Krane?" the man said as he shoved the exposed underside portion of his right wrist within Mason's view.

There in plain sight was the symbol Mason had come to know so well. There were no doubts now; this man was a member of the sons of Apep but obviously had some agenda of his own.

"I assume by your silence you have. Everyone one of us is marked, no exceptions. But you probably already figured that out." The man paused, not really expecting an answer before continuing.

"The Sennew Sas Ne Apep or Second Sons, as you know them, have been kidnapping children for centuries, but never has one child been found, not even the bodies. You know why, Mr. Krane? Because they have been disintegrated," he said with fear shaking his voice.

"We have been using children for centuries for two things. One is to destroy the seed of the Christian infidels. The second is to use those children as test subjects to find the ultimate global plague. The goal is to create a virus so deadly that it will destroy a third of the world's population in less than a year." He paused a moment, wiping sweat away from his saturated brow.

"Quite a task, wouldn't you say, Mr. Krane?" he asked, laughing in a mad state.

Mason, awestruck by this recent revelation, didn't know how to respond. With all the research and investigation he had done, he couldn't have dreamed that a plot so comprehensive could be kept hidden for centuries. Many questions entered his mind, but he thought it best to keep those to a minimum. He didn't want to add stress to an already tense situation. There was a purpose for keeping him alive, and Mason responded carefully so as to not irritate the trigger happy man.

"For what purpose?" Mason responded carefully.

The man was taken aback for a second but responded in turn.

"To eliminate the majority of any resistance for the chaos of Apep and to create a new world in which he and his followers will rule," he responded evenly.

"Why tell me all this? I don't understand what you want from me," Mason replied, halfway irritated.

The man instantly became distraught, and the gun shook in his hand. The question poured salt in an already open wound and obviously triggered deep pain and confusion in this man. Calming himself, the man continued.

"Let me tell you a story, Mr. Krane. Thousands of years ago, a group of Egyptian priests, eager to avenge the sudden and untimely death of their sons, forged a pack with an evil god. This god gave them the tools, desire, and motivation to wreak havoc upon the earth in the form of disease.

"Apep," Mason chimed in.

The man's eyebrows raised in surprise. "Well, I can see that you're not totally ignorant on the subject," he said in sarcastic tones. "The goal of this faction was to create a disease that would render the human race so helpless that a single leader could step forward and rule them." The man paused a moment before continuing.

"A leader chosen by Apep to usher in a new era of civilization with the Egyptian god at its center. Unfortunately, while this group possessed the will to perform the task, the technology simply wasn't available to produce such a deadly weapon of destruction. So the group started small with what they knew and proceeded from there."

"I don't understand, what small steps? Are you saying this group already created some kind of deadly virus and let it loose upon the world?" Mason asked.

The man smiled in return, taking pleasure in Mason's and the world's ignorance on the subject.

"Do you realize, Mr. Krane, that almost every major pandemic in human history was a result of the efforts of the sons? In 430 BC, an unknown agent killed a quarter of the Athenian troops and a quarter of the population over a four-year period. In AD 165-180, a virus similar to smallpox killed a quarter of those infected, up to five million. In AD 541, they released the first string of the Bubonic plague. It started in Egypt, no less, and at its peak, it was killing up to ten thousand people a day with a grand total of almost a quarter of the world's population. In the 1300s, the Black Death, as it was called, was a second version of the bubonic plague. More deadly and potent than the first, it killed nearly twenty million people and destroyed nearly a quarter of the world's population. The Spanish

Flu, Hong Kong Flu, and SARS are all other examples of the groups attempt to create the perfect virus. Over the centuries they have continued to perfect the disease, waiting for the time to release it upon an unsuspecting world." The man's head dropped, and he lowered his voice to little more than whisper.

"All of these pale in comparison to the virus that we have recently created. The virus has been given the name '*Mosi*,' or in English, 'Firstborn,' to represent the death that the tenth plague of Moses brought forth on Pharaoh and his faithful followers. This disease will be the most deadly biological force the world has ever seen. That being said, they decided to name it for the retribution for those deaths that occurred many centuries ago.

"All will die, except for those loyal and faithful to *Apep* and his priests. Lord Amahte, which is to say the incarnation of the god Apep in a man, has ensured that all those faithful to him will be protected." he finished, his eyes now completely coming out of his skull and sunken sockets.

Suddenly Mason realized that there must be a purpose in Jahid telling him all this, but what it was, he didn't know.

"Jahid, why would you be a part of such a sinister plot, and why are you telling me all this now? Why not go to the authorities?" Mason asked.

Jahid only smiled in sarcasm before responding. "They own the authorities. Besides, who would believe me anyway?" he said with a forced smile. "I used to live in Egypt with my wife and daughter. Then on a day, like many others during the Six-Day War in 1967, shells from an Israeli plane bombing the Gaza strip killed my family. In the blink of an eye, my life changed forever. Filled with rage, I searched for an opportunity to avenge my family's untimely death. The radical Islamic factions, though motivated, were not what I was looking for. The goals they had were not enough to quench the blood I demanded for the death of my family. That's when they found me," he said with fear in his eyes.

"The Sons recruited me for my knowledge in biological science, as I was a recent graduate of Boston University. Lord Amahte had me brought before him to ask for my loyalty to the Sons." At this point, Jahid became visibly shaken.

"The man is not human. I have seen him do things that are not of this world. He is truly something greater than a mere man. He has powers beyond explanation and destroys anything and anybody in his way," he finished, his bottom lip quivering in fear.

"Anyway, as I stated, children were kidnapped for me and others to test our newest versions of these biological weapons." He paused as if in a daze before continuing.

"At night, I see their faces and hear their screams of terror. At first I was numb to their pleas because I was bloodthirsty for revenge, but I have come to the point where every child's face I see is that of my own daughter. I can no longer continue to torture these innocent youths and wish this carnage to be brought to an end. This is why I have solicited your help, as it were. I know you have been researching the disappearance of many children in the area. You must do something to save them and soon." Lowering his head, he continued, with tears coming down his face. He then began to cough heavily, so much so that Mason could tell the man was now covering his mouth with something. After Jahid's fit subsided, Mason couldn't help but reach out in concern.

"That sounds pretty bad. We should get you to and emergency room," Mason said.

Jahid let out a slight giggle as he replied

"I have seen many doctors, and an advanced stage of tuberculosis is nothing but a slow death sentence. This is another reason I have devised a plan to destroy the facility and all the inhabitants within it. In two weeks, I will detonate a bomb that will destroy the entire lab facility. The blast will destroy everything, including any traces of the virus. You have till then to figure out a way to get the children out safe. Your chances are slim at best, but since my life will be ended in the process, you are on your own. I would rather die in that explosion then succumb to this incessant disease." He paused a moment, stepping out of the vehicle. Mason did the same and looked at him over the top of the car.

"Meet me here again next Thursday if you plan to do anything. I will go over with you some of the details of the site, how to get in, and other pertinent information." With that, he finished and began walking away but suddenly stopped and turned around.

"And, Krane! Whatever you decide, tell no one. Lord Amahte's eyes and ears are everywhere. He must know nothing, or all will be lost. Be back here next Thursday, late, 11:00 p.m., and make sure you are not followed," he finished and began coughing heavily again as he left.

Still in shock from all that had happened, he nodded back to the man, got back in the car, and started what seemed to be the long drive home. Many things ran through his mind, and he could barely drive with any kind of concentration. His thoughts were so heavily engrained. He had already nearly missed two stop signs completely and was relieved when he finally pulled into his driveway.

The lights were on in the home, and as he suspected, Tyler was eagerly waiting for him when he walked in the door.

"What took you so long? You said you would be home over an hour ago," she said, half in concern and half in anger.

Mason let out a long sigh before replying, mostly because he knew telling her the whole truth would only violate the trust he had been given with the information.

"You have to trust me when I say this, hon, but for now let's just say I had a meeting that could not be avoided," Mason replied.

Tyler looked at him and could see that he was struggling to find words. He had always been a person of integrity, and although she wanted to know more, she knew now was not the time to push. Hoping to ease his tension and help him relax, she smiled and quickly changed the subject.

"How was Jordan?" she inquired earnestly.

In all the evening's excitement, Mason had forgotten all about Jordan's choice to join God's family.

"Great. He gave his life over to God!" he said with renewed vigor in his voice.

"That's great, hon! I knew he would come around. We have been spending a lot of time together, and he has become a trusted and unexpected friend," Tyler returned in a half daze before realizing Mason was staring back at her. "Umm . . . Anyway I'm looking forward to him coming to stay with us. I really think he is going to make a change for the better, Lord willing," she added.

Mason smiled as if forced and nodded in return. Much had happened in the last twenty-four hours, and it was hard to find joy after one sentence and returning to his thoughts of this evening's meeting in the next.

Tyler waited for more but could see that Mason was overcome by his thoughts and turned to leave him to them when he called her back.

"Hon . . . I'm sorry I'm a little off tonight, but there is something I need you to know," he said. "I've never been much of a person for words, but I need you to know that I love you very much and I have stumbled on to something much bigger than I could have ever imagined in my worst nightmares. I am not sure if I am going crazy, but I believe God has placed a very dangerous path before me, and I must follow it." He paused a moment, seeing his wife's reaction of fear and worry spread over her face.

"I want you to pack up what things you can and get yourself and Jordon over to Uncle Joe's by the end of the week. I don't think you will be in any danger, but there are some things going on here that are bigger than the police or any law enforcement agency, and I need to know you're safe." Stopping her before her objections, he continued on.

"You and Jordan will be safer with Uncle Joe, and your safety is mandatory for me to focus on what I have to do. I can't tell you anything else except that I am in dire need of prayer. I will speak to Jordan tomorrow, and we will get you over to Uncle Joe's by the end of the week." He sighed heavily before continuing. "One more thing—if you don't hear from me within a week after going to Uncle Joe's, I want you and all of our family to get out of town as soon as possible and as far away as possible," Mason finished.

Tyler's face had emptied of blood as she stood next to him and she took his hand within hers. "You're scaring me, Mason. If something is going to happen, you need to know something," she said, but looking into his sullen eyes, something told her that her news would only serve to distract him from his purpose, and she faltered.

"I . . . I just want you to know that I love you and I'll always love you," she finished with tears in her eyes.

"I love you too, hon . . ." Mason trailed off and pulled her close as tears rolled down his own face.

Mason was exhausted, but he believed wholeheartedly that sharing the details about tonight's encounter could only serve to put his family in danger. Jahid's plan was crazy, but Mason already knew about the leaks in information when going to Paul, but he would have to contact him sooner or later with this information. And what about Jordan? It wasn't fair to send him off after getting out of rehab, but Mason had loved his new friend and didn't want him involved in the matter either.

Mason lifted himself off the couch with a heavy sigh and headed toward his office. He wanted to continue to do some research on what was going on because he believed there had to be a link between the cases, and if those kids were still alive, they had to be found and rescued from whatever forces were holding them prisoner. He still wasn't sure if he believed Jahid's story, but a lot of it made sense, except one major point he couldn't swallow. How could an Egyptian god come to life and take the form of some Amahte character here on earth? He believed in God and Satan, and if it wasn't God, then it was of Satan. Could Satan have used his influences to fool thousands of generations worth of descendants into believing that he was an Egyptian god come back to life? Again, he didn't know or understand.

Mason sat at his desk with his case files spread out in front of him and scanned over them for hours upon hours, looking for any hint of a clue to confirm or deny Jahid's accusations. Just before calling it a night, or early morning as the case may be, he reached for his father's Bible, which had also been lying among the mess of paperwork on his desk. After flipping through the pages, he came to rest in Revelation and was immediately drawn to passages that his father had underlined: "And the four angels were loosed, which were prepared for an hour, and a day, and a month, and a year, for to slay the third part of men" (Rev. 9:15).

Mason had studied some of this text before and knew that from his studies that the angels being referred to here were in fact angels that were thrown out of heaven with Satan. They were demons, doing the work for the evil one. He thought it was interesting that Jahid had mentioned that the goal of the cult was to kill a third of the earth's population, promising a new world after this was done, ruled by those faithful to Apep. But what if Satan was behind this whole thing and Apep was just a way to deceive these hate-filled cult members? *Could Satan being trying to use this to jump start the apocalypse?* Mason wondered. This would also explain Jahid's fear and explanation that this Lord Amahte was some kind of "incarnation" of the god Apep.

Mason sighed deeply as he sat back in his chair and tipped his head back to stare at the ceiling. He began to think about the possibilities and also wondered how he could possibly battle something so powerful. He was just one man, a seeker of lost children. How did he go from that to battling an army that was possibly governed by Satan and his fellow demons? The thought was overwhelming, and he couldn't help but feel a wave of self-doubt wash over him. Perhaps he could just give the information to Paul, take his family, and run to avoid the possible repercussions if the virus was released? Or he could notify the military, but then again they would probably call him crazy anyway, and he wouldn't be surprised if the cult had influence over them as well.

That was another concern—how high up did this go? Could they have infiltrated the military, local governments, or congress? The thoughts were enough to make Mason's fingers go numb from anxiety. Closing his eyes, he prayed silently to God for confidence, protection, and most of all guidance. When he finished, he realized something that had never changed since the day his parents had been murdered: God had put him on this path. For whatever reason, he was here and he had continued on, even when his own doubts told him to stop, so why would this be any different? Mason believed that God doesn't make mistakes, and regardless of circumstances, he had to continue down the path God laid before him.

Instantly Mason remembered another man who had to battle immense odds and doubted himself. It was the same man that God used to bring about the plagues that eventually led to the creation of this cult. Moses succeeded in doing what God had put before him. He led the Hebrews out of slavery from Egypt, and God never left his side. Mason suddenly felt more relaxed, concluding that God had a pretty good track record for following through with his promises. With this in mind, he headed up stairs and focused on tomorrow's plans. Jordan would be coming home, and Mason wanted to make the most of the time he had with him and Tyler before he sent them to his uncle's.

Hardly sleeping a wink, Mason awoke early and tried his best to focus on what today was about. He tried, but his thoughts about bringing Jordan home constantly took a backseat to the revelation of information he was given by Jahid the night before. It took a constant effort for Mason to keep focused on Jordan and what his needs were going to be. He still believed that Jordan's place was with him, and he wasn't going to let anything get in the way of that—not even a possible apocalyptic event.

After wandering downstairs into his office, Mason sat quietly and opened his father's Bible. Again he began to contemplate what he was up against and prayed for wisdom and guidance on what he should do. He couldn't go to the police. Jahid had told them they owned the police, and from what Mason had seen already, he believed him. Then again, he couldn't take on an entire cult alone, but he also couldn't sit back and do nothing.

As these thoughts continued to run amuck in his mind, he decided to think through this logically. Throughout his life he had seen and heard how mankind had tried to destroy itself. There was always trouble in the Middle East, and the United States and other countries had been through their share of wars and diplomatic disputes. Heck, you could even break it down to what people fought for every day— good health care, for example. People thought they paid too much, and then you have the insurance companies and hospitals holding out there hands as well.

But suddenly it occurred to Mason that the motivation behind these things was never just about killing people. Wars erupted because of disagreements over foreign policy or holocaust situations, some would even speculate over natural resources, and while the Middle East battles had continued for centuries, they had always been about religion for the most part and people giving their lives or taking them in the name of Allah. But this cult, who had been around for centuries, was not interested in money, natural resources, policy, or even religion. Its purpose, according to Jahid, was to kill as many people as possible in the swiftest and most efficient manner, believing that this would make the world weak enough to be ruled by them. Mason knew that, theoretically speaking, a virus could not target a specific race, creed, or color, and it certainly couldn't target individuals belonging to a specific religion. So what was the motivation for the Second Sons efforts? Did they really believe in some ancient Egyptian god? From what Mason had gathered from Jahid, he could tell that they believed it, but in order to be plausible their leader, this Lord Amahte, was either the greatest con-man ever or he possessed some kind of power that really was supernatural.

Mason leaned back in his chair for a moment on that thought, while still holding his father's Bible. Was that really so hard to believe?

Mason had obviously been protected by something that couldn't easily be explained. Those spiders should have killed him, yet he had not one bite. Why couldn't evil exert supernatural powers as well? Remembering studies he had done, there were numerous occasions in the Bible where people had been possessed by demons and practiced some kind of ungodly sorcery. There was only one problem with this theory, Mason thought, and that was in order for this to be true, this guy was drawing his power from an Egyptian god, and Mason couldn't and refused to believe such a god existed. With that thought still hanging, he opened the Bible miscellaneously and suddenly caught a passage his father had not only underlined but highlighted in bright orange, something he had never really seen before. It read, "For we wrestle not against flesh and blood, but against principalities, against powers, against the rulers of the darkness of this world, against spiritual wickedness in high places" (Eph. 6:12).

Mason raised his head and turned his chair, focusing on the wall as he thought. He was concentrating so hard, he didn't even notice that Tyler had entered the room, and when she cleared her throat, he jumped with such force that the Bible tumbled to the floor in a flurry and he almost fell out of his chair.

"Sorry, hon, I didn't mean to startle you," she said.

Mason blew a sigh of relief as he replied.

"It's okay, you just caught me off guard is all," Mason returned with a halfway faked smile.

"I was going to make some breakfast. Would you like something to eat?" Tyler asked.

"Sure, hon, that sounds great. Let me know when it's ready. I have a few more things I want to check out in here," Mason finished.

Tyler nodded her understanding and left the room, giving Mason the privacy she knew that he was asking for without being rude or overbearing.

As Tyler left the room, Mason continued to his chain of thought and found there was little more information gathering he could do at this point, but then he was sure that the name Amahte was Egyptian, and he was curious what it meant. This so-called Lord Amahte's name must have had a purpose, and so it did. After about fifteen minutes on the web, Mason located the information he was looking for. The word Amahte in English meant, "To have power over."

There was no big surprise there, and it became painfully obvious that this wasn't his real name. In fact, Mason spent a considerable amount of time trying to figure out through the web if there was any information on this guy at all, but he found nothing. Again he wasn't surprised, but since he seemed to be wielding power over those committed to the cult, his choice of names was perfect and was probably even chosen as additional means to drive fear into the hearts of those who served him. As for the supernatural, Mason believed there were only two possible explanations for supernatural activity. One explanation was divine intervention from God; the other was demonic intervention from Satan.

Things were becoming clearer to him, but he knew he would learn more from his next meeting with Jahid, next Thursday. This put Mason at ease a bit more. Some how he felt he would learn enough information there to complete a plan based off what Jahid was going to do, the layout of the headquarters, and what the goals would be. Once this was final in his mind, it was much easier for him to let it go for the moment and begin to focus on a more joyful subject: Jordan coming home from the rehab center.

Just then, Tyler hollered that breakfast was ready, and as he sat down to a warm plate of food, he knew he had to give Tyler something to give her peace in her heart as well. As she continued to move back and forth from the kitchen, she set a glass of juice in front of him, and Mason took the opportunity to grab her gently and gestured for her sit down for a second. She sat down across from him silently but with a face that expressed concern and a desire to have many questions answered.

"Ty, I know I was a bit tight-lipped last night, and I'm sorry. I didn't want to scare you, but obviously that wasn't accomplished either. This investigation is taking a very dangerous turn, I have found out. I have a source that has confided that the Second Sons exists here, in our own city, and that they are planning to do some very terrible things. Kidnapping children was just the start, but I need you to know that I am working on this, and I trust God and his guidance. Things are going to be okay, I promise, and while I know I can't give you peace about it, we both need to be strong right now for Jordan." he finished, as if waiting for Tyler to comment.

"You really scared me last night, Mason, but it's clear in my heart that God is working in your life right now and using you actively to further His cause. I fear for your safety, but I take comfort in the knowledge that God is guiding you, and I believe he will keep you safe." She finished with a smile and then turned to continue. "Plus, I've got to get someone around here to kick your butt in ping pong, and I believe Jordan is just the one to put you in your place," she said with a chuckle.

With that, the subject didn't come up again, and they continued to make plans for the day's primary activity which was to go pick up Jordan from the rehab center and get him well established in his new home.

CHAPTER 14

It was almost midday by the time Mason made it to the rehab center. Tyler had to work, but she promised to be home as early as possible to welcome Jordan back.

It was amazing to Mason how things had worked themselves out. His thoughts had completely flipped the moment he pulled into the parking lot. He no longer concerned himself with the near-impossible task he knew was coming. He was now solely focused on the well-being and care of Jordan. It was clear to him that God needed Jordan for some purpose, if nothing more to be a part of the body of Christ, and Mason was going to do everything he could to ensure the young man's safety, regardless of the circumstances.

As Mason entered the facility, Jordan was already ready and waiting in the lobby. He looked so much different, Mason thought to himself. It was definitely Jordan, but there was a light behind his eyes, something that wasn't there before. You could tell that this young man had been to hell and back. He was thin, and his eyes were still a bit sunken, but there was a new strength about him, something beyond physical that was very apparent.

Jordan greeted him with a wide-brimmed smile, which he returned as they embraced lightly.

"Ready to go?" Mason asked.

"Yeah, I'm good," Jordan returned as he nodded at the lady seated at the reception desk.

They didn't speak a whole lot on the trip home as Jordan's attention was constantly gripped by the places they drove by. Jordan reminded Mason of a young child experiencing a train ride for the first time, taking in scenery that he had never seen before. As they pulled into the driveway, Mason realized he was going to have to break the news to Jordan sooner rather than later about sending him and Tyler to his uncle's place. He had pushed it off as long as he could, and he dreaded having to bring this up. Jordan had been abandoned so many times. Mason didn't want him to think he was doing it to him again, but before he could speak, Jordan spoke out loud as soon as the car was shut off.

"I had a dream about you last night . . ." Jordan hesitated a moment.

Mason was caught off guard by the rather odd topic but figured indulging Jordan's current train of thought would be a good segue to break the news to him. "Did I win the lottery?" Mason prodded with a playful snicker.

Jordan smiled briefly, and then his smile faded as he stared straight ahead, obviously trying to recount the images accurately.

"No. It was bunch of images scattered—you know how dreams are—but one thing I saw clearly was you getting beat down bad by some guy. And there was this other dude in there, just watching and laughing. That's all I can remember, but it seemed so real. I don't know; guess it's still some of that junk lingering in my body or somethin'," Jordan finished.

Mason knew the power of dreams all too well. They had haunted him his whole life, but in this case, he had to agree. Who knows what lingering thoughts get thrown together for no reason at all, but for his sake, he hoped that a dream was all it was and decided to treat it as such.

"Yeah, I've had some pretty crazy dreams too, but sometimes I think our brains just get full of leftovers—you know, like the scraps on your dinner plate you never finish. We scrape them off into the trash, and they get thrown away. I think that's the way dreams work sometimes. It's just a bunch of lingering thoughts, sights, and sounds that all get thrown together," Mason finished.

"Yeah, I suppose you're right," Jordan stated in agreement as he went to open the car door.

"Jordan?" Mason started.

"Yeah," Jordan replied, halting midstream from exiting the vehicle.

"In a week or so I have to take care of something, and I need you to do me a big favor."

"Sure, anything, man, just name it," Jordan replied with curiosity.

"I'm sending Tyler to go stay at my uncle's, just for a little while, and I want you to go with her. I know it seems like things are just settling down, but something urgent has come my way, and I need to know that you and her are safe. I can't say anything right now and I know that's tough, but I need you to trust me on this—plus you would be doing me a big favor by looking after her," Mason finished with a forced grin on his face.

Jordan let out a deep sigh and then looked Mason in the eye as he responded. "When?"

"In a week or so," Mason said stated flatly.

"That's cool, man. Me and Ty . . . we tight, but I hope you're not going to look for trouble without your best tag team partner," he said with a smile.

"Not if I can help it," Mason responded warmly, and with that they got out of the car and headed inside. Once inside, Jordan rushed in and gave Tyler a large embrace, who had managed to get off early and beat them home. They locked eyes for a moment as if to speak a secret language—not as lovers do but as the closest of friends. Mason didn't understand how close the two had become until that moment, and his heart rejoiced because of it. For the rest of the night, Mason forgot about his impending meeting, and the night was filled with laughter and peace as Tyler and Mason each took turns telling funny stories from their youth. It was a sight and sound that warmed the heart, but elsewhere evil stirred and those who served it prepared for a great awakening that would shatter the very existence of peace.

Thestos continued down the dark corridor he knew all too well. He was eager to share the good news with his master. As a matter of fact, it was the only time anyone would be eager to share news with Lord Amahte. As he approached the large double doors, a heavy sound signaled the doors automatically opening. Thestos entered the room and got on one knee, in front of the desk, bowing his head in submission as he spoke.

"I have the latest update, my lord," he stated flatly.

A figure stood on the other side of the desk, his back to Thestos, but when he spoke, it was as if his voice came from all directions.

"Rise and report," Lord Amahte said as he turned to face his faithful servant.

Thestos arose just as his master turned to face him. The only light in the room came from a fireplace on his left side, and from this angle,

Thestos swore his master's face contorted into different shapes in time with the flickering of the flames.

"The final tests have been completed, and the virus is ready for distribution, ahead of schedule." He was testing the waters with that last bit but couldn't resist.

"You have done well, Thestos, and you shall be rewarded for your continued faithfulness." He paused for a moment before continuing and turned his back toward his audience. "And what news of Krane?" He said the name with heavy disdain.

"No news, my lord. It appears that the attempt on his life was enough to frighten him into seclusion."

Lord Amahte turned rapidly, and with eyes red with anger, his voice seemed to shake the very foundation of the building.

"Appears! Appears! I am not interested in appearances. I want facts! I have known many men like Krane over the centuries, and there is one thing I am sure of. It's not fear that keeps them from action; it's the type of fear." Anger withdrew from the sound of his voice as he spoke that last sentence. Turning to face Thestos once again before speaking, he also brought his hands together, rapping his fingertips against each other.

"We have come too far to become careless. I want to ensure that Krane is out of the picture. Before we send out the Kamenwati, I have a special job for you and Detective Deturo," he said with an evil grin as his eyes once again flashed blood red.

Mason had never been a patient man, and in all his years, he had never wanted a week to go by more slowly but have it pass so quickly. Tomorrow night he would meet Jahid again to learn about the details of the compound. He was anxious, to say the least, and he couldn't let go of thought that he might never see Tyler, Jordan, and Uncle Joe again. Tyler and Jordan would be leaving for Uncle Joe's, and Mason had given strict orders for them not to try to contact him at the house or any other way. Getting Uncle Joe to agree to this would be near impossible, so Mason took the tactic of not informing him of anything. Tyler would explain everything when she arrived. Uncle Joe would have to accept that any attempts to contact Mason at the house or any other way could place him and the rest of the family in great danger. He didn't like it, but he couldn't think of any other way to accomplish keeping his family safe without betraying the man who had raised him since his parents' death.

As he rolled his head sideways on the pillow, Mason silently watched Tyler sleep. She had never looked as beautiful to him as she did now. He watched the covers rise and fall in a deep, rhythmic pattern as she slept soundly, and it became almost hypnotic. He had to catch himself from breaking into tears as he was afraid this would wake her, and he wanted to cherish this moment for as long as possible. He memorized the contours of her face and the way a few strands of her strawberry-blonde hair draped over her forehead. He analyzed ever bump, every eyebrow, and every dimple and then silently thanked God for placing her in his life. Suddenly her eyelids flickered open, and she smiled at him as his eyes could no longer hold the tears that had gathered, and like a small, flowing creek, they slid down this face. Maintaining her smile, she reached up gently and wiped the way the tears with her thumb as one of her hands cupped his face, and then she drew close and kissed him. No words needed to be shared; it would have been a waste of time. They spent the next moments enjoying each other as God intended.

Half an hour later, Mason came downstairs to find that Jordan was already awake. He was at the kitchen table eating a bowl of cereal. It had only been a week, but it was truly great having Jordan there. Even though Mason had worked his whole life to find children, he and Tyler had yet to have one of their own. Even so, he felt he would at least have some clue as to how to guide and support Jordan, but early on he found there were a great many things he took for granted. He smirked as one of them came to mind—that he had no idea teenagers could eat so much food. As Jordan continued to lift spoonfuls of cereal to his mouth, Mason would bet money it wasn't his first bowl. As he thought for a moment, he realized he didn't have the slightest clue what it felt like to be a father, but he assumed that the pride he felt in Jordan's accomplishments was something close to it.

Suddenly, Jordan looked up from his bowl, milk still staining his smiling lips.

"Did you save any for me?" asked Mason teasingly.

Jordan sported a huge grin as he nodded toward the top of the refrigerator where the cereal was kept. Mason got his own bowl, and the two sat silently sharing a cornflake moment together.

The rest of the day was spent packing and spending time together. Mason and Jordan even went downstairs and worked out for a couple of hours. Mason was amazed at how quickly and easily Jordan was able to improve his technique. He was clearly ten times the student Mason had been. Jordan was even able to do the gun removal drill a few times without getting hit by the pellets. As Mason recalled, it had taken him a year to do that without getting nailed. Before they all knew it, though, the time had come for Jordan and Tyler to leave, and saying good-bye was hard on all of them.

Even Jordan, who had learned the hard way to keep his emotions hidden, could not stifle the tears. He had tried on many occasions to get Mason to tell him more about what was going on, but true to his nature, Mason never faltered and only thanked him for his interest and concern. They all prayed together, holding one another and asking God for protection and guidance before loading up the car with their belongings and starting up the vehicle. Watching them pull out of the driveway was one of the hardest things Mason had to do, and as soon as they were out of sight, he broke down completely and wept uncontrollably. He knew he might never see them again, but regardless of the outcome, he knew he had a chance, albeit slim, to save their lives and others by giving his own. He realized at that moment that it was far easier to throw yourself in front of a car to save a life than having a week to dwell on sacrificing yourself. He was afraid, but nonetheless he was determined to see this through.

After taking a deep breath, he felt a little better and peered down at his watch. It was just after 9:00 p.m., and he needed to make sure he was at the lake to meet Jahid by 11:00. He had plenty of time, but Mason wanted to ensure he didn't forget anything he might need. He thought about bringing his recorder but thought better of it. Based on how nervous Jahid had been on their last visit, Mason didn't think he would be receptive to the prospect of being recorded. A good old-fashioned pen and notepad would have to do. Gathering up his thoughts and his things, he readied himself for his appointment.

As he headed indoors and distracted by his thoughts, Mason failed to notice a black sedan follow after Tyler and Jordan as they disappeared around the corner.

CHAPTER 15

The drive to the lake took half the time Mason thought it would, but he had no intention of being the slightest bit late. He had taken a side track to the airport and even went through the parking garage purposefully to shake anyone he thought might be following him. Since it was a weekday, there was no one here; in fact, Mason saw no other vehicles parked where he and Jahid had met last week. This didn't worry Mason because Jahid had stalked off in another direction last time. He had probably parked his vehicle on the other side of the lake or hidden somewhere close.

As Mason exited his car, he realized how quiet it was. All he could hear was crickets and the occasional bullfrog. When he got out of his car and walked to the rear of the vehicle to wait, he felt as if his footsteps were sonic booms. As he rested on the car's back bumper, he glanced at his watch. He was a good twenty minutes early. Mason detested waiting, and he let out a large sigh, which amplified his impatience. As he looked up at the stars and the half moon showing, he felt a sense of peace. Up there, there wasn't any chaos or death; just the light show of an immense galaxy God had created. Mason forgot how much he loved looking up at the night sky; it's why he loved camping so much when he was a kid. Whenever he felt angry or frustrated, he could look up at the stars and see no wrong in them. They were just simply there, so far away that they couldn't be harmed by man's need to exploit every possible resource for whatever motive suited them. There were no hurt feelings, raised voices, wars, or even disgruntled looks from an angry driver; just God and his saints.

"It's curious, don't you think, how easily we forget how beautiful they are?" a voice said, nearly giving Mason a heart attack. As he turned, Mason saw Jahid walking toward him, once again coughing a bit and holding a handkerchief to his mouth as he did. Jahid must have read his face based on his next comment.

"I've been here for over an hour, Mr. Krane." He waved Mason's expression off. "I wanted to ensure you weren't followed," he finished with a grin and then exploded into a coughing fit, which produced blood on the hanky he had been using. Mason must have looked concerned, because again Jahid waved him off as if to still his actions. "I'm fine," he said after taking several deep breaths without a problem.

"My plans have changed a bit, Mr. Krane, but I think what I have in mind should be in your favor, as I see you're interested in saving those children."

"I am," Mason replied.

"Well then, let's get down to business, shall we?"

Over the next hour and a half, Jahid went into complete detail of what was happening and showed Mason some actual maps he had drawn of the facility. The amount of information was staggering. Apparently the date that the Sons had chosen to execute their plan had been moved up and with an increased measure of security. This meant Jahid would have to set off some smaller explosions first as a distraction so that the larger bomb could be detonated in a secure area that would completely annihilate the virus. This would actually benefit Mason because it would give security personnel on site something to occupy their time and give him more time to get the children out of the facility safely.

"How do they plan to distribute the virus?" Mason asked.

Jahid gave a smirk and stifled a cough before answering.

"Lord Amahte has selected, out of many volunteers, twenty of his most faithful servants. They are called the Kamenwati or 'Dark Rebels.' Since the virus has to incubate in the host for five to seven days, if they are injected with it, they will not become contagious for at least a week. By then, each of them will have traveled to major transportation hubs all over the world, most of them airports. There they will they stay, moving, coughing, and spreading the virus with each wipe of the nose or exhale of a breath. They will refuse medical treatment and continue to travel all over the world until they are no longer able to breathe. By then it will be too late to put into place any effective quarantine, let alone for doctors to even identify what they are dealing with." He paused a moment, looking down.

"We estimate that within a month, at least one billion will be dead or dying."

Mason, so shocked by the scope of this planned atrocity had to remind himself to breathe. "How will they die?"

"It will start out like a cold and then spread quickly to the lungs, where it will cause pneumonia-like symptoms, high fever, and cold sweats. The victims will slowly deteriorate into a state of shock, in which the central nervous system will be attacked, causing severe breathing issues, loss of control of the bowels, and even loss of the ability to walk. Soon after that, the body will shut down due to lack of oxygen," Jahid finished in robot like fashion. One could tell as he rattled off the symptoms that emotion and the pure horror of what had been created was not a factor.

"Shut down! You make it sound as if these innocent people are machines. These are lives we are talking about!" Mason finished in ire.

As he stared off at the lake, Jahid responded with a sort of peace that was almost creepy but very sincere. "You forget, Krane; I wasn't recruited to kill people. I was recruited to kick start an apocalypse. Morality never factored into it; it would have been a hindrance to any value I could provide. I was full of rage and had no concern for the consequences of my actions. That's why they chose me. That's why I was perfect," Jahid finished with a deep sigh, followed by another relentless coughing fit.

Mason, fighting the urge to lash out again, focused on the issue at hand. It would do little good to debate morality or goals at this point in time. He had the opportunity to help save lives, billions if successful, and he needed to be perfectly focused to do so. Forcing himself to concentrate, he looked again at the map Jahid had drawn up and pointed to the main chamber where the remainder of the children were being kept and suddenly realized another problem that made the blood drain from his face in fear.

"This place here," he said pointing at a specific place on the map, "this is where the children are being kept, but have any of them been infected with the virus?" he asked, praying the answer to the question was no.

"Mason, you're going to see some things you don't like in there, no doubt about it. However, those not dead in their cells have yet to be infected, meaning they are free from the virus and have been spared, probably due to the fact that the virus was ready ahead of schedule. As far as what they have planned for them, I don't know, but if they're alive when you get there, you can assume they're safe," he finished with a light smile.

They continued to go over the map of the facility, and Jahid's plan really wasn't that complicated. Jahid had managed to gain an extra active security card with an active code so Mason could gain entry into one of two entrances into the facility. To Mason's surprise, the library would be the safest place to enter. The whole facility had been built underground, but there was a second entrance to the facility a mile away in the warehouse district. This would be the best way to get the children out of the facility because it had less security and would look less suspicious. Plus, by the time he had the kids, he would need to exit quickly, and the alternate entrance had vehicles he could easily use to load up the kids and hopefully escape. It was at this point that Mason learned of a shocking compromise he would have to make.

"Krane . . . there is one thing that you must do to enter into the facility without any suspicion," Jahid said, rolling up his right sleeve and showing the symbol once again.

Mason started to shake his head.

"It can't be a fake, and it must have this chemical added to the ink, but just around the outline. When you enter the facility, there is a checkpoint, at which time they will shine a light on it. If the chemicals are not there or are distorted, you will be discovered and probably killed on site," Jahid said while handing Mason a small vial of clear liquid.

This was becoming harder and harder to take. Not only would he be expected to save the lives of all these children, but he would also have to fully assume the identity of the very organization that had hunted the children he had tried so hard to save—the very organization that had murdered his whole family. He thought back to the tattoo shop he had visited just before he had met Jordan. He remembered the man inside said he could duplicate the tat, and Mason believed this was a person who was used to keeping secrets.

"Given the timing and the time needed to heal, I suggest that you get this done immediately. Ours were always done internally, so you have to find someone who will do this good, accurately, and quickly with no questions. If it looks as if it were just done, it could pose a real problem, but as far as I know, there is no size limit. Mine took less than two hours to do, but I'm sure yours, depending on the location, could be done a bit smaller. Mine took about a week to heal, which is about what you'll have, as they plan to send the Kamenwati out next Thursday at midnight. The blast must kill them all, including all the plans and data repositories, so that the data cannot be sent to another installation."

"Another installation? You mean there are others? How many? Where?" Mason asked frantically.

"Lord Amahte is the only one with that information, but fortunately we are the only ones with the responsibility of the virus. The others have been given other focused goals, to which only he has the details."

"This is getting better by the minute," Mason said.

Mason paused for a moment; he had no more questions and felt he had a good grasp on the plan. It was a long shot at best, but he felt he could execute what had been outlined to the best of his ability. His feelings now turned to Jahid. It was obvious with all his planning that he thought he would be either discovered or killed by one of the explosives he planned on planting, and no matter how much he tried, Mason couldn't get comfortable with this man's outlook. Even if his health condition was irreversible, this kind of death didn't seem right. As Mason turned to Jahid with concern, he could already see that Jahid was reading his body language, and his body tensed as if about to defend himself.

"Jahid—"

"Save your breath, Mr. Krane. I am not interested in your sentiments, conscience, or any other thoughts you have on my safety. I made my peace with this decision long before I came to you. Be thankful I chose to include you on it for the children's sake," he finished coldly.

"Very well," Mason said, reluctantly stifling his objections. "But the fact you felt a need to save these kids tells me that there is something in your heart worth redeeming, and I will pray for you whether you like or not," he finished with a smile.

"As you wish." Jahid shrugged and began to pack up the maps and other materials. He made a point to test Mason over and over during the time they spent because he thought it was too dangerous to leave him with the actual maps. If someone were to find them, it could thwart the whole plan, and that was something Jahid was not willing to risk.

As he finished gathering his items, Jahid turned to Mason with an open hand. "Good luck, Mr. Krane. We will have no further contact either way."

"And good luck to you, Jahid. May God be with you," Mason said.

With a sarcastic grin, Jahid finished his firm handshake and disappeared down the embankment, leaving Mason alone with his thoughts.

Mason wasted no time in his next steps. On the way back from the lake, he decided to stop at the tattoo parlor he had dropped in at on that fateful day he had first met Jordan. He wasn't sure it would be open this late, but he decided that this would be the best and least suspicious time to have the tattoo done. After pulling up to the curb, he leaned forward to view the familiar sign reading "Dragon Tattoo," only now it was all lit up with neon lights. As he walked into the empty establishment, he saw the same character he had run into the last time he was there.

"Perfect," Mason said with satisfaction. The last thing he wanted was an audience to what he was about to do.

The man noticed him walk in and looked at him cockeyed as he approached. The man looked almost identical as he had last time. He was short and stocky, with the same goatee and white tank top he had worn before, presumably to show off his own many tattoos. The only difference, Mason noticed, was this time the man was not wearing any sunglasses, and one of his eyelids drooped as if he had sustained a lasting injury.

"Do I know you?" the man said with a Mexican accent.

"Let's just say we've seen each other before," Mason said, laying the paper on the counter that showed the design of the tattoo. The man's expression turned to recognition as he looked back up at Mason.

"Ahh yeah. I remember this one . . . but I told you, homes, I never did this," the man responded.

"No, but you did offer to duplicate it," Mason countered squarely.

The man reviewed the design again carefully and then returned Mason's glance.

"Sure, I can do this. Where do you want it?" the man asked.

Mason had to be careful about this part and he decided the best way to ensure secrecy with this individual was money. That's why he had made a stop off at an ATM before coming here.

"I want it here," Mason stated, pointing to the top of his left wrist. The man nodded and gestured for Mason to have a seat.

"A couple more things . . ." Mason started. "I want it small enough that it can be covered by a large watch, and I need you to add this chemical to the outline of the design. This part needs to be absolutely perfect, and I also want this kept between us with no questions." With that Mason placed a large wad of cash on the table along with the vial of liquid Jahid had given him.

The man glanced back at Mason in surprise and then glanced down at the large amount of cash along with the vial before speaking.

"No problem, I can do that. I will mix this in with the outline color, and it will come in without any blemishes. Have a seat." The man gestured again to the chair.

The next hour and half was silent except for the buzzing sound of the needle that pined away at Mason's skin, slowly turning into the symbol he had come to know so well. Mason had to admit that there was a lot more to this than he thought. It took an extreme amount of concentration and focus, and many times he could see the same level of attention on the man's face as he imagined a surgeon would have performing open heart surgery. It didn't hurt that much, though there were a couple times when Mason grinded his teeth when a nerve was hit. The needle felt much like having sunburn and then having someone with sharp fingernails scratch it. When he was finished, the man delicately bandaged up the wrist and explained to Mason what he had to do to ensure that it would not get infected or scab up incorrectly, ensuring it would heal quickly and with complete accuracy.

As he reached the door to leave, Mason turned and eyed the man carefully one more time.

"Remember, I was never here," Mason stated.

"I've never seen you before, man," the man said with a wide smile, holding up the wad of cash he had just earned.

Stopping by the drugstore on the way home, Mason picked up some of the healing moisturizing lotion that the tattoo artist said would need to be applied twice a day to keep it from scabbing up incorrectly. He also said not to scratch it once it started to itch. When

Mason inquired why, the man explain that if you pulled off the scab or any of the skin that had not fully healed, you could accidently pull parts of the skin that had been inked, thereby distorting the image of the tattoo. He even went as far as to show Mason an example of one of his tattoos he hadn't had the time to touch up where this had happened, and this was a defect that Mason definitely wanted to avoid. He had a week to get this thing looking as good as possible, and he was going to follow every piece of advice, to the letter, on top of praying to ensure it looked perfect for the day it would be needed.

CHAPTER *16*

The time had finally come, and Mason was making last-minute preparations for a near-impossible task. Mason had spent the whole week training, praying, nursing his tattoo, and memorizing the plan over and over in his head. He desperately had wanted to talk to Tyler and Jordan, but he knew any such attempt to contact them would put them in serious danger. Since they had done as they were told and hadn't contacted him, he assumed that they were safe from any plot aimed at thwarting the plan to bring down the Sons.

Mason went downstairs to retrieve a weapon to bring with him for protection. He dressed in all-black jeans with a nice button-up black shirt with no tie. He wanted to be stealthy but not look like an assassin. As he opened his weapons cabinet downstairs, he decided to slide a small knife into his boot and a small 9mm pistol that he kept in a hidden holster on his right ankle. With this he raised his wrist and looked at the time on his new watch, one bought specifically to cover his new tattoo. As he lifted up the watch, he saw that the tattoo had healed very nicely and showed no signs of infection or inflammation. He replaced the watch and glanced at the time once again. It was 4:30 p.m. and time for him to be on his way. Dropping to his knees, Mason opened his father's Bible to a verse that had kept repeating itself in his head all week: "Let those who love the Lord, hate evil, for He guards the lives of His faithful ones and delivers them from the hand of the wicked" (Ps. 97:10).

Then Mason prayed. "Dear Lord, you know what evil lurks in this world better than me. I have neither the power nor the wisdom to do this alone, and I beg for your divine intervention. I feel like a reed being bent backward, almost uprooted, by a powerful storm that blows with unbelievable power and strength. I pray that you would guard me as I go into battle and provide protection to the billions of lives that are at stake. I am scared, Lord, but I know that you are with me, and I pray that you would use me as a tool to deliver those who are innocent from the hands of the wicked. Whatever may happen, Lord, please know that I trust in you, and I pray you would help me to be the evidence of what your grace can do. In the name of your Son, Jesus, I ask it. Amen."

After rising to his feet, Mason went through the plan one last time in his mind as he packed up and left the house to the library. The plan was relatively simple. He would enter the library just prior to 5:00 p.m. Being as inconspicuous as possible, he would make his way to the secret entrance, which was located in the bathroom at the library. After they verified that he was legit, they would let him in and he would travel down the pathway to the elevator.

Once there, he would travel to the lowest level of the temple and wait in a hallway closet until the first of four explosions occurred. These explosions would theoretically draw security away and allow him a much better chance of getting to the children who were in the observatory portion of the floor. He expected to encounter a few guards and would do his best to avoid them, but he had decided already that if deadly force was necessary to get past them, he would use it. Once the fourth explosion went off, he would have approximately twenty minutes before the real bomb would go off, which would destroy the entire facility.

Jahid had purposely made it a point not to tell him where the bombs were located because Jahid didn't trust Mason to try to disarm them for more time. He only said they would be well hidden and could not be found without specific directions. The cells the children were held in were air sealed and had oxygen and other items pumped directly into them, obviously to protect those on the outside from the dangerous virus that could be released. Jahid had explained to Mason in detail how to open the cells. Once he had the kids, they would have to make their way through a ventilation shaft from the observatory to another set of elevators on the other side of the floor that would exit to the other entrance to the temple. This access point was a warehouse, and Jahid explained there would be a van with the keys in it to get them out of there as soon as possible.

Though it seemed simple enough, Mason understood that there were several major points where the slightest error could cause the plan to fail. For one, Mason brought up that he had been to the library on multiple occasions and would almost certainly be recognized by the receptionist there. He now understood her odd behavior on the day he was researching information on Egyptian history. Mason had an idea of how to get around this, but if it faltered, he knew he would be in trouble. He also had to get past security. This would be a test of his composure as well as his newfound tattoo artist's abilities.

The final and most deadly challenge would be leaving the facility with the children. The last security checkpoint to get out would almost certainly know that something was up at this point, and Jahid could not provide any ideas on how to get past them. He said there would be at least five armed guards, and once they saw him coming down the corridor with all those children, the jig would be up. Mason ran through a couple of scenarios in his mind but settled on two things. First, he would hit them swiftly before they could react to the confusion of the scene, and second, he would need God's help. There was also a massive amount of "what ifs?" What if Jahid changed his mind? What if the bombs didn't detonate? What if this was all one big setup? He contemplated all of these all week but still came to the same conclusion. He couldn't risk the loss of life that would most certainly occur should he do nothing. He had considered contacting Paul, but he knew the police had a leak somewhere, and there was too much red tape anyway to get anything done immediately.

Arriving at the library shortly before 5:00 p.m., Mason took a deep breath as he prepared to enter the building. After meeting with Jahid a week before, Mason knew the receptionist at the library was basically the first line of security for the temple. She kept an eye on who came in and who left and would alert security if something seemed suspicious. Mason also knew she would recognize him on sight and that would be the end of it. He had to get past her as if he were a normal library patron. To do anything else would jeopardize his cover and could blow the whole plan. That being said, Mason decided to go with a disguise and timed his entry so that he was walking in with some others who were entering the facility. In preparation for this, he had grown out his facial hair, put on dark sunglasses, and wore a nice fedora-type hat. He prayed that this combined with walking in with some other people would be enough to get him past the desk undetected.

As he put on his disguise, he waited for an opportunity to enter the building, and he didn't have to wait long. Just as he finished, a lady pulled into the parking lot with three children who appeared to range in ages from eight to sixteen. Seeing his opportunity, Mason exited his vehicle and slowly approached the building but paced himself evenly so he was just slightly ahead of the family of four. As he reached the door, he opened it and held it open for the woman and her children. She thanked him as she and her children passed, and better yet, they headed directly for the reception desk. Mason followed behind them and as nonchalantly as possible turned the corner and walked down the first path that took him deeper into the library. He couldn't have even been in the receptionist's line of sight for more than a second, and better yet, she was immediately preoccupied by assisting the family that had come in.

It could not have worked more perfectly, and Mason let out a deep sigh as he took off his sunglasses and headed for the men's room. He felt confident his ruse had worked, but only time would tell. The next part would truly test his composure, and he said a quick prayer as he opened up the bathroom door. Recalling the details Jahid provided, Mason entered the last stall, which was larger than the others and marked with the handicap signal on the front. Closing the door, he faced the blank, solid wall to the left of the door. Next, Mason removed his watch and held up his wrist, which sported the new tattoo, in front of the wall, while at the same time trying to calm his heart, which was beating a mile a minute and sounded like thunder.

Suddenly a light shone out from the wall, illuminating the tattoo. Then it shut off. For a moment, Mason thought he had done something wrong because there was nothing but dead silence, but then a piece of wall pushed back and slid open, revealing a secret passage, exactly as Jahid had described. As soon as he made his way through the entrance, he could hear the wall being pushed back into place behind him. As he traveled down the torch-lighted path, he finally came to a junction where he could see actual people and armed soldiers. Mason felt beads of sweat forming on his forehead and began to wish he had worn a short-sleeved shirt. One of the soldiers approached Mason casually and gave a motion as if he wished to frisk him. Again Mason was alarmed because he was packing a 9mm pistol as well as a knife in his boot, but he tried his best to act as nonchalantly as possible. The guard wasn't very thorough; however, he did catch Mason's ankle holster but simply pulled it off, slipped it inside on a shelf, and said he could pick it up on his way out. Mason nodded as if he was used to this, though inside he was ready to burst. The guard looked him over once more and then waved for him to continue.

Well, no gun, but I've got the knife, Mason thought to himself.

Mason passed the security door and continued down a narrow pathway. The walking path was paved; the walls and ceiling were dirt with a wooden support every few feet, just like a mine shaft. Torches lit the way, and Mason couldn't help but wonder if the rest of the place was like this how the Sons could possibly have the facilities necessary to accomplish such an elaborate scheme. But the assumptions were laid to rest when he saw the path end at an elevator door. There was only one button, and it pointed down. Mason turned to make sure he wasn't being followed, but he did see a camera watching the elevator door and calmly pushed the button and waited.

He didn't have to wait long; he could hear the elevator moving up swiftly and eventually announcing its stop with a prominent ringing sound. When the door opened, he was met with a few surprises, the least of which was a group of people staring back at him blankly. Then finally one man in a white lab coat gave Mason a look as if he was waiting for him to do the something, and then he spoke in a not-so-polite tone.

"If you don't mind moving," the man said, gesturing that he wished to pass.

Mason felt like an idiot. They just wished to get off, and Mason, apologizing while he did it, quickly moved to the side to let everyone off. He noticed that most of them were dressed as the man in front was, in white lab coats. However, toward the rear of the pack were a couple of men dressed like the guards at the desk. Thinking everyone had exited the elevator, Mason took his first step inside and came face to face with Paul. He was about to open his mouth in shock, but he saw Paul shake his head quickly and motion with his eyes to the upper rear corner of the elevator. There was another camera there, and Mason got the cue. He regained his composure, quickly turned his back to the camera, and was about to select a floor according to his plan, but Paul pushed one first and whispered in his ear.

"Go with me on this," he said softly, leaning in to hit the button. Then he settled back into position slightly behind Mason and continued quietly, "There's no microphone. As long as we keep our backs to the camera, they can't hear us."

Mason tried desperately to keep his composure but honestly didn't know what to think.

"What the hell are you doing here?" he asked Paul quietly but with vigor.

"I got a tip and followed it up. There's something bad going on here. I wanted to let you in on it, but there wasn't time," Paul returned.

"How did you get in here?" Mason queried.

"The same way you did. I was about to leave and get some backup down here, but when I saw you, I knew I couldn't just walk past you. It could have blown our covers, and we would both be dead."

There were only a couple floors left before they would reach what looked like the lowest level.

"Look, we don't have much time; we need to get some kids being held hostage here and get out." Mason stated the last with extreme urgency.

"Sounds good. How much time before the bomb goes off?"

The elevator was now slowing to a stop and was just about to ding when Mason realized he had never said anything about a bomb to Paul and there was no way Jahid would have said anything to the police or anyone else, for that matter. Then he heard Paul let out a deep sigh as the elevator rang and the doors began to open.

"Guess I put my foot in my mouth on that one, eh?" Paul said, now shoving a pistol into the back of Mason's head. "Don't even think about moving or you'll be the next slab of meat on the coroner's table," Paul stated with a cold tone Mason had never heard from him before.

"You know, I thought I had you figured for sure. All that back and forth and you searching me in the locker room—which was very clever, by the way—but you still couldn't nail it down." Paul paused a moment before continuing. "Turn around and I'll show you how this one got past you."

Mason turned slowly. He was anxious to figure out how Paul could be working for the Sons and how he could have missed the tattoo. When Mason turned fully around, Paul gave him another order.

"Put your hands on the back of your head," Paul stated and Mason cautiously did as he was told.

Paul backed up a few paces and then used both of his hands to peel back the inside of his bottom lip. Clear as day, tattooed on the inside of his lip was the symbol Mason had come to know so well. Mason was furious. He couldn't believe he could have missed such a detail, and his blood began to boil.

"Turn back around and put your hands down!" Paul ordered. When Mason finished, Paul continued, "You could have lived the hero, Krane. Now you're going to make your wife a widow instead, but not till you have a little chat with Lord Amahte first." With that Paul struck Mason in the back of the head with the butt of the gun, and Mason's world went black.

CHAPTER 17

Mason fought the urge to stay down as his head began to pound with pain from the blow he had taken earlier. He slowly began to open his eyes, and at first he thought he still might be out because everything was very dark and very blurry. He was lying on the floor, and he tried to reach back to rub the spot where he had been struck, only to find that he had been shackled, each arm to the floor. As his vision cleared, he found himself in totally unfamiliar surroundings. He was in a long, rectangular room, which he appeared to be just inside the entryway of, as there was a set of large, black double doors behind him and a desk at the far end in front of him. All the walls were black, and what light there was came from small lights shining from the floor and a fireplace. The ceilings were high, but it got so dark when you looked up that it was as if it turned into the night sky.

Gathering himself to his knees, he realized his shirt had been taken and he was shivering despite a fire crackling in the large fireplace on one side of the room. As he looked himself over, he realized blood was dripping from the shackles on his wrists; however, there was no pain or even any bruises yet. Since the blood was not Mason's, he concluded there had recently been someone else in these shackles, and he must have put up quite a fight. As he tested the steel shackles' length, he deduced that not only was he not going to be able to break free, but the length at which they were bolted to the floor would not give him enough room to stand. He did manage to rub the spot on the back of his head by placing his head practically face first on the floor. As he rubbed it for a moment, he could feel a nice lump coming in, but when he brought his hand into view, he saw no blood.

"I'm sorry we didn't have time to clean those before bringing you here, Mr. Krane," a voice boomed and seemed to be coming from every direction. Mason looked around but saw no one.

Suddenly the double doors behind him made a loud click that echoed through the room. Mason turned to watch because it sounded as if the doors were being unlocked. When the doors didn't move, he returned his gaze forward, and now there was a figure standing before him. He was short and had on a black cloak with red trimming on the edges. The hood was up, so Mason could not see any facial features except for part of the man's beard, which was sticking out a bit. He had a cane in his right hand and slowly walked toward Mason. As he got closer, Mason could distinguish more and more of his features. He had dark, sunken eyes and a brown, narrow face with many wrinkles and a couple liver spots, giving the impression this man was at least sixty-five, if not older. Mason thought he looked Middle Eastern as well, which matched the accent of the voice he heard speak just a moment ago.

"You must be Lord Amahte, I'm gathering?" Mason queried.

The figured continued to move forward, but he seemed to glide as he walked. Even with the cane, his movements were smooth, quiet, and deliberate. He continued forward until he was a few feet away from Mason and then turned to face the fireplace. This gave Mason his best view yet of the man's face. It was amazing, Mason thought, this little figure of a man, yet his face and those eyes held immense power, prowess, and seemingly incalculable intelligence.

"So what else did our little lab rat tell you?" Amahte slyly countered.

Mason thought carefully. He was sure he would be dead by now if not for the fact that they needed something from him. He didn't want to reveal anything that he thought might assist them in any way. That being said, Mason decided his strategy would be to reveal what he knew Amahte already had knowledge of. Amahte might slip and provide some useful information Mason was unaware of.

"Enough. He told me you are planning on killing a third of the world's population by using human guinea pigs to carry your virus all over the world. You must have some hold over these blind followers," Mason finished smugly, trying to goad the figure into anger, but in return all he got was laughter—deep, evil laughter—and it continued as Amahte turned to face him.

"Blind? Blind you say? Is it not your religion, Mr. Krane, that says by faith, not by sight? You have been blind your whole life." He paused a bit before continuing. "Your parents were murdered, your brother kidnapped, and you have faith. You run around the city for years trying to find answers to questions you've had your whole life, without success, and still you have faith. Even now as you consider never seeing your wife again, you have faith. Your kind has always been the blind ones. That is why we must do something to wake you up from your delusions of grandeur!" he yelled this last point and brought his face directly in line with Mason's as his eyes glowed a deep red, so much so that no pupil or any other part of it could be seen. His sockets seemed to be bulbs of fire.

Mason was in complete shock and awe. His bones began to feel a chill, as if they were being frozen from the inside out, and he couldn't ignore the presence of pure evil in this room. It was then that Mason suddenly put everything together and realized who it was he was really dealing with. It took all the courage he had, but he looked into those eyes and began a little laughter of his own, mostly forced but also a little mad. As his laughter tapered off, Lord Amahte's eyes returned to normal before Mason spoke.

"It must disgust you to put on such a façade, pretending to be the human incarnation of some old Egyptian god so that you can fool those around you into submission through fear and awe. Evil wears many faces and uses many tactics, but it all comes back to one owner, one entity that is responsible for every evil thing in this world, and you're either him or one of his brothers." Mason got more confident as he spoke, and he could tell by the look on the man's face that he was hitting a nerve.

"I mean, let's face it, human possession is so . . . Old Testament. Why would you want to go into a human body when you can just manifest yourself into something you think will be convincing enough? The real question is, are you Lucifer himself or one of the pathetic creatures that followed him out of heaven?" With that the room burst into a bright light, and Mason shut his eyes tight. It felt as if a bomb had detonated right in front of him. The burst threw him backward. He landed on his back and stretched the shackles' full length. Then in an instant it was over.

Mason was holding his arms over his face and slowly lowered them so he could peek through his squinting eyelids. For what seemed an eternity, all he could see was a bright spot, but eventually that faded and the darkness of the room returned, only to hold a new sight. Standing before him now was a human-like figure over six and half feet tall with a huge set of almost-black wings on his back. His musculature was perfect, and with his eerie gray skin color, he looked as if he were chiseled out of solid stone. His face was that of someone in their mid-twenties, with a wide brow, square jaw, and black hair. His eyes, the most astonishing feature besides the wings, seem to glow white, except for the black pupils in the middle, which were little more than specks.

Mason also noticed a large scar on the left side of his face, which started at the forehead above the left eye and slid down to the middle of his left cheek. It appeared that when the wound was inflicted, it damaged the left eye as well, as it seemed slightly off color and was sagging. He wasn't wearing any clothes except for some red cloth wrapped around his waist that started below the bellybutton and dropped down to mid thigh with a black belt holding it on. Before he spoke, he took a few steps, and then the wings on his back seemed to slightly extend and then snap back into a tucked position, which shot out a quick breeze that blew the hair back on Mason's head.

"Very impressive, Mr. Krane," he said with young, booming voice. It was very different than the accent-riddled speech of the figure Amahte was assuming. "You're right, this feels much more comfortable," he stated with a sneer.

Mason was shocked. Even though logically he figured this was a fallen angel, he never suspected that a demon would reveal its true form to him. Seeing that Mason wasn't about to speak anytime soon, the creature continued.

"Since I've dropped the charade, I'm going to ask that you do the same and just tell me what your disease-ridden partner could not," he said

"I don't understand. What did you do to Jahid?" Mason asked.

"Not much. He couldn't take much pain, and his life ended before I was able to have any real fun." With that he jumped back behind the desk with amazing speed and strength, picked up a body lying on the floor where it could not be seen, and hurled it toward Mason. The dead body slammed into the floor with a heavy thud as it came to rest just in front of Mason. It was Jahid, and from the looks of it, a combination of blunt force and his tuberculosis killed him. Blood was still draining out of his mouth, but his eyes, ears, and nose were bleeding as well. Oddly, though, Jahid seemed to have died with a slight grin on his face.

"But look at you!" the creature said as he stared at Mason like a lion stares at its prey. "You're young, healthy, and in good shape. I wonder how much pain you can take before you tell me what I want to know." He finished the last with his teeth grinding. "I'm only going to ask once, and don't lie or I'll know it." It paused before continuing. "Where are the explosives hidden?"

Mason now understood how Jahid could have died with a smile on his face. No matter what happened to Jahid or Mason, the explosives were going to bring this place down. Jahid purposefully didn't tell Mason where they were hidden, and now it seemed Jahid's plan was going to be executed perfectly.

"If you know the truth when I speak it, then you'll know I'm not lying when I tell you I don't have a clue," Mason countered.

The demon flapped his wings in irritation as he stared at Mason.

"I will tell you this, though. I am a servant of Christ, and as his disciple, he will not allow me to be harmed by you," Mason said with confidence, noticing the creature wince at the name. Then its face changed to a hopeless look, and he let out a deep sigh before he replied.

"You're right, Krane. I guess I can't make you talk. But I can offer you an exchange . . ." It paused a moment before continuing. "Since the beginning, you've been looking for something you lost. No. Wait, I take that back, you've been looking for something that was taken," it finished with a fiendish grin on its face.

Mason's face turned as white as a ghost as he thought of his brother. Eyeing Mason, the demon could see a nerve had been touched. He began to tap his long, talon like finger to his lips as if thinking hard as he spoke.

"Let's see . . . his name was . . . Jason, was it not?" It didn't wait for a response before continuing. "What if I offered to give him back to you and you can tell me where the explosives are at?" the demon queried.

Mason didn't know how to respond. He had searched his whole life and had never once found anything resembling a clue that his brother was on this continent, let alone still alive. Still, Mason didn't have the answer, and even if he did, he would not sacrifice a host of lives for his brother. It would destroy him, but in the end, his faith to see this through and to follow God's path was his mission.

"Even if I knew, I wouldn't tell you, and if Jason were alive, he would understand that," Mason said the last as he eyed the demon with disdain.

The demon watched Mason carefully and then moved to face the fireplace while sighing deeply.

"Perhaps you're right, Mr. Krane. As I recall, I drank your brother's blood during a very moving ceremony," the demon said, smiling as Mason's whole body tensed with anger. "Purely ridiculous to us who are aware of the truth, but to those souls who need something to follow, it spoke volumes. Those days have passed, but we still needed the children, and they served both as motivation for our many members and as subjects for our—how should I put it?—gift to the world," the demon said with an evil smirk.

"But I digress. None of this is relevant except for the part about loss. You see, Mr. Krane, I think you've forgotten exactly what it means to lose something precious, and since I hold something precious of yours, perhaps you will reconsider how my questions are answered," he finished, turning to the door, and within the blink of an eye, the old figure with the cane stood before him again.

"Enter, Detective," Amahte shouted with the voice and accent true to form.

Mason heard the doors unlock and begin to open, and as he turned to see who was entering, he noticed a ring of keys hanging from the wall, probably the ones that unlocked the shackles he was in. Continuing to turn and face the doors behind him, the wind was nearly knocked out of him by what he saw. First he saw a middle-aged, dark-skinned man enter without a shirt. He was carrying a small knife and appeared to have blood all over him. Mason assumed this was the one who had tried to make Jahid talk. Next he expected to see Paul come walking through the doors, but instead he saw Tyler and Jordan being hustled into the room. Paul was behind them, shoving them forward while holding a gun on them at the same time.

Gesturing toward the first individual who entered the room, Amahte began introductions.

"This is Thestos, my second in command, and I can think of no one on this earth who enjoys inflicting pain more than him."

Mason glanced at the man, and a cold hard stare and slight nod was what he got in return as the man approached. Suddenly, without warning and with incalculable speed, the man punched Mason square in the face. Even though he was already on his knees, Mason sprawled to the floor, and blood began to pour out of his mouth as he heard Amahte speaking in the background.

"Now, now, Thestos, we will get into more intimate engagements shortly," Amahte said mockingly as he continued to introduce the others in the room.

"Let us continue. I believe you know Detective Deturo, who has done us the extreme pleasure of bringing your wife and your young friend."

For the first time Mason truly gazed upon Tyler and Jordan. Tyler's face was streaming with tears, and her eyes were puffy, as if all she had done for the last few hours was weep. Mason shifted his gaze to Jordan, who he could tell was scared, but at the same time he remained very calm, as if studying the situation. Turning back to Amahte, Mason pleaded for their release.

"Please, they have nothing to do with this. I'll do whatever you want. Just let them go."

Amahte paced back and forth a few times before answering Mason's plea. "I've got a better idea. I'm going to let Thestos beat you to within an inch of your life while they watch and then . . ." He paused a moment, allowing an evil grin to cover his face. "I'm going to let you watch as I let Thestos slowly and painfully kill your knew friend, your wife, and your unborn child."

Shock filled Mason's face as he looked at Tyler for confirmation. While her lips quivered, she mouthed the words, "I'm sorry," as tears continued to stream down her face. Amahte studied Mason's reaction and the nonverbal exchange. Realizing Mason had no knowledge of his wife's pregnancy, he began a deep, throbbing laugh that filled the room as if it were coming from all sides. Still smiling widely, Amahte continued in half laughter.

"You didn't know . . . well, this should be very interesting indeed. My patience is at an end, Krane, so I'm going to make this very simple. I think you know the truth when you hear it, so I won't bother trying to tempt you by saying you can save them, but I promise you all a quick, painless death if you tell me what I want to know," Amahte finished, now standing directly in front of Mason.

Confusion, anguish, and terror filled Mason's thoughts. When he had decided to move forward with this, the one thing he wanted to make sure of and take peace in was the fact that whatever happened, Tyler and Jordan would be safe. He was further torn by the fact that he had just learned that his wife was pregnant, which brought on a whole load of emotions. He was oddly joyful, but the joy took a backseat to the sorrow and fear he had for the impending situation. For the first time in his life, Mason felt like giving up. There was literally nothing he could do to make this anything but a lose-lose situation. With his thoughts and emotions overwhelming him, he hung his head in his still-shackled hands and began to sob uncontrollably while internally he prayed. After a few moments, he raised his head up and gathered himself before replying to this offer.

"I told you before, I don't know where the bombs are, and as for the rest, I leave it in God's hands," Mason finished.

Amahte stared at Mason for a few moments in obvious frustration before turning to Thestos.

"Well, it looks like Mr. Krane has chosen the way of pain," Amahte said, gesturing for Thestos to do his worst.

While Mason was still on his knees, Thestos walked over and kicked him square in the ribs. The blow nearly lifted Mason off the ground, and then he fell flat as he recoiled from the kick.

"Leave him alone!" Tyler screamed as Amahte laughed in the background.

Thestos walked over to the wall and pulled the keys down from the place Mason had seen earlier.

"We are going to need some more room to do this properly," Thestos finished with ice in his voice.

After grabbing the keys, Thestos walked over to where Mason lay flat on the floor and rolled him over with his foot. With Mason now flat on his back, Thestos placed his right foot on Mason's chest and pulled the middle link of the shackles between Mason's hands. This had a stretching effect, and Thestos pulled upward so hard that Mason screamed in pain because it felt as if his arms were going to pop out of their sockets. Thestos was clearly enjoying this; he would pause for a moment and then start all over again. Finally, after about the fifth time, Thestos held the pressure steady while using his other hand to unlock the shackles. As soon as they came loose, Mason slumped back to the floor like a rag doll. He glanced at his wrists and recognized the bloody marks on his own wrists as they mimicked those on Jahid's body. He found it difficult to breathe and was totally conflicted on what he should do. Any attempt to fight back would be met with Paul pulling the trigger on Tyler and Jordan. For the moment, he concluded he had no choice but to try to survive and pray that God would intervene.

"Please, you're killing him!" Tyler screamed again as Paul held the gun steady on her.

"Yeah, man, he would kick your butt if you would let him fight back," Jordan added.

Thestos walked over to Mason and pulled him up by his hair as he spoke.

"Is that so . . . I love a good fight, but unfortunately, he's in no condition to fight back," Thestos finished the last, directing his response at Jordan.

Still holding onto Mason's hair, Thestos punched him repeatedly in the face and then let Mason fall to the floor, his face a bloody pulp.

"Time for step two, eh, Mr. Krane?" Thestos stated while pulling out the knife Mason had seen him enter with earlier.

As Mason watched him through swollen eyes, he suddenly remembered that he had a knife. When he was searched upon entering, they hadn't found the knife he had hidden in his right boot. Could it still be there? He didn't want to give it away, but there was still the fact that Tyler and Jordan would be in danger should he counter in any way. He looked back at Tyler and Jordan, and suddenly everything seemed to go in slow motion. His gaze focused in on Jordan, how he was standing, and the way he positioned his body. Jordan was preparing to try to remove the gun from Paul's hand, but the problem was that the gun was pointed at Tyler, not Jordan. The move Mason had taught him called for the gun to be pointed directly at him, and before Mason could get the word out, Jordan struck.

"Noooooooo . . ." Mason screamed, but it was too late.

Jordan moved with light speed as he reached for the gun and began to spin it, as he had practiced with Mason a hundred times. It all happened so quickly. Mason was in front of Paul and Jordan and couldn't see what exactly happened except he heard two gunshots, one right after the other. Everything was silent for a moment, and then Paul fell to the floor in a heap. As he fell, Mason could see Jordan and Tyler still standing and felt hope that they survived the incident unscathed.

But then Mason saw Jordan look down, and examine himself. His green shirt began to grow darker in the area of his abdomen. Jordan looked up at Mason in surprise and slowly started to wobble, and Tyler guided him to a sitting position. Mason was about to rush to Jordan's side when it seemed a thunderclap went off somewhere nearby, making the whole room shake to the point where dust from the ceiling fell. Mason concluded the first bomb had gone off, which signified the countdown had begun. Mason turned to Thestos and Amahte to see what they intended to do next. Amahte's lip curled in rage, and he suddenly exploded in anger as he spoke.

"Kill them! Kill them all!" Amahte screamed, and then, like a flash of lightning, he was gone.

Thestos, wasting no time, approached Mason with knife in hand. Seeing him approaching, Mason carefully planned his movements. He knew in his current state he would be unable to mount a capable defense, and he suddenly remembered one of his favorite Scriptures: "My grace is sufficient for thee: for my strength is made perfect in weakness" (2 Cor. 12:9).

What Mason was about to do would take amazing timing, tolerance, and speed, but most of all, God's intervention. As Thestos raised the knife above his head, his pace quickened. In response, Mason rose to his left knee, sliding his right hand to his right ankle. Mason raised his left arm over his face with the perceived vain effort to block the incoming stab. When Thestos reached Mason, he came down hard with the knife in his right hand. Mason hoped this was the attack that would be coming, and he grinded his teeth and bore down for the excruciating pain that would be coming. As Mason turned his forearm flat, the blade buried itself into Mason's arm all the way to the hilt, missing the bones. The tip came out the other side, only inches from Mason's face.

Mason screamed in pain as he used the adrenaline pumping in his body to catch his opponent off guard. As Thestos tried to remove the knife for a second blow, Mason, in one swift motion, stood up, pulling the knife from his boot with his right hand and shoved the blade threw the bottom of Thestos's chin till it could go no further. Thestos immediately let go of the blade in shock and stumbled backward, clasping the hilt of the blade that was lodged through the bottom half of his skull. Mason, now fully erect, walked slowly up to his adversary. Then, spinning clockwise, he landed a kick to Thestos's chest, sending him flying backward into the fireplace, where he was instantly engulfed in flame. With the exception of the sudden roar of flame, there was no sound and no movement.

Mason stared into the flames a moment longer and then turned and made his way to where Tyler was sitting against a wall with Jordan. Just then a second explosion could be heard going off, closer this time, and again the structure shook. Mason looked up for a second then made his way over to Tyler with a little more hustle this time. When he reached Tyler and Jordan, he knelt down in front of Jordan to take a look. Jordan had a small but steady stream of blood coming down the side of his mouth. Tyler had gotten up and was walking around to check Mason's arm, which still held the blade.

"We are going to have to get this out now," Tyler stated evenly while at the same time tearing a piece of fabric from her dress.

"Put your arm here and try your best to pull the blade straight out." She gestured to her knees. Mason placed his arm across her knees with the knife in the middle and then he grabbed the hilt of the knife while looking Tyler square in the eyes. With teeth grinding and a loud growl, Mason pulled the knife free. As soon as he got it free, Tyler instantly began to tend the wound. She was bandaging the entry would tightly and also making a tight tourniquet a little higher up his arm. She hoped this would slow the blood flow from his wound until they could get out of here. Mason looked over at Jordan as he was being tended to. Jordan returned his look with a long smile before he spoke in a half whisper.

"Pretty neat, man . . . I've never seen anything like that. You'll need to teach me that one," he said, still smiling, but he seemed to be in a haze, as if he were drunk but not. Mason instantly forgot about his own injuries. His only concern now was Jordan.

"Is he going to be all right?" he whispered to Tyler. Tyler met his gaze with an unconfident look.

"He's lost a lot of blood, and he can't be moved," she finished, turning her head to shed a quick tear.

"Hey, you two . . . you don't got to worry about me. I shot for the gold. You may think I never got a chance to read the Bible you gave me, but I did, and I remembered one passage just before I tried to take that gun. It went something like there is no greater love than the man who lays down his life for his friends . . . so I figure God's going to take care of me," Jordan finished.

"That's right, Jordan, that's from the book of John, and if it hadn't been for you, we would be dead. Try not to talk. Just rest a moment," he said as Tyler could hold back the tears no longer.

Jordan held out his hands one to each of them. Mason and Tyler quickly went to each side of him to hold his hands and be with him.

"You two love each other, you hear . . ." They both nodded as he continued. "Teach your child what you taught me . . . that there is hope in this world. Sometimes you just have to look real hard, but it's there . . ." Jordan's breathing began to slow drastically. "For the first time in my life I'm not afraid, even now, I feel . . . God . . . is . . . with . . . meeee."

And with that, Jordan was gone. Tyler broke down sobbing as Mason shut Jordan's eyes and kissed him ever so gently on the forehead. Again, another explosion rocked the building, and Mason could now here people screaming and yelling instructions just outside the door. There was still time to save the children, but they had to hurry. Grabbing Tyler by the shoulders, he stood her up but winced feeling the pain from the knife wound for the first time.

"Ty, we have to hurry. There are kids in here being held hostage. We have to get them and get out of here before this whole place comes down," Mason said, shaking Tyler slightly to get her to snap out of her grief-stricken state. She finally nodded and grabbed his hand as he led the way.

Somehow Mason remembered every detail of the structure from the maps Jahid had provided. Mason and Tyler weaved in and out of office rooms and staircases. Even among the chaos, Mason was eyed warily, but when he thought he was being eyed a little too closely, he simply flashed the tattoo on his wrist and was waved aside.

Finally, they approached a lab door that would only open by a code key. Mason pulled the code key from his boot where he had hid it and quickly slid it through the reader. With that the door slid open, allowing Mason and Tyler to enter. Mason was slightly prepared for what he saw, but he was somewhat taken a back when he saw children trapped in clear cells lined on each wall staring back at him through tear-streaked faces. Except for the children, the room appeared to be empty. Mason wasted no time and ran to one side to pull off two lab coats from a rack.

"Put this on," he instructed as he tossed her one of the lab coats. Tyler did as she was instructed.

Mason buttoned his up because he wasn't wearing a shirt and wanted to look as least suspicious as possible. Suddenly another explosion rocked the structure, and the power went out. Emergency lights soon came on, but Mason knew that if he didn't get these kids out of here now, none of them would survive.

"Tyler, I am going to let them out and send them to you. I want you to keep them quiet until I can release all of them. Tell them we are here to get them out safely." Tyler nodded in confirmation.

Mason went from cell to cell, releasing every child who was alive. As they came out, he told each of them to keep quiet and to go see the lady that was waiting for them. He also noticed that a few of them seemed to be missing their index fingers. Then he came upon a face he recognized, David Grafton. Quickly Mason slid the code key and the door to David's cell opened. David was hesitant to move and seemed traumatized, like a wild animal.

"David, it's okay. You're going to be safe now," Mason said calmly.

"How do you know my name?" the boy replied.

"Your parents sent me to find you, along with these other kids. I need your help to keep the other children calm and quiet. That's my wife, Tyler. She is here to help you as well," Mason finished, reaching out his hand. The boy grabbed Mason's hand and quickly moved to where the other children were gathered with Tyler.

Mason continued down the cells, letting out all the children he could. He reached the final cell and was about to open the door when he noticed that the child in this cell, a little girl, was lying face down on the floor, possibly sleeping. Mason banged on the cell wall, trying to get any reaction or to wake the child up, but there was no response. Mason turned to the children as he spoke.

"Do any of you know how long she's been like this?" Mason asked hopefully.

David stepped forward. "The last time they brought her food was a couple days ago. She was very sick."

Mason's heart sank. This one could not be saved, and opening the cell would mean a death sentence for them all. He turned and surveyed the situation. It appeared they had around fifteen children, roughly what he had planned for, but he had no real clue on how he was going to get them out of here. There wasn't enough time to use the air duct as originally planned. He could only pray an idea would come to him, as Mason believed they weren't just going to let him walk right out. Mason walked back to where Tyler had gathered up the children, some of them in shock. Others were frightened and crying.

"Okay, we have very little time, so I need you all to listen to me very carefully," Mason began to instruct. "I want you to form a single-file line forming behind me and follow me wherever I go. You need to move as quickly and quietly as possible. Tyler, I want you to bring up the rear. Don't stop for anything or anybody. Does everybody understand?" Mason queried. The children all nodded in confirmation. Tyler did as well.

Mason knew the exit wasn't far, but he also didn't know what stood in their way. No one alive knew about the final bomb that would destroy this whole facility, so perhaps the distractions and the lab coats would be enough for them to concoct a story to get past a guard station he knew would be waiting for them. As he slid the code key once again to exit the lab room, he came face to face with two individuals, both in lab coats, who obviously were concerned about what they saw.

"What are you doing? Where are you taking these subjects?" one of the men asked.

Mason thought quickly and came up with the only answer he could, hoping it would work. "Lord Amahte asked me personally to escort these subjects to an alternate location, since there may be some kind of sabotage at work here."

"I received no such orders, and I've never seen you here before," the man stated with suspicion.

"I'm from another facility, and these subjects have to be moved immediately in case they are still needed to finish testing," Mason finished the last by holding up his wrist, showing the symbol tattooed on his wrist.

"Very well, get them out of here," the man ordered.

Mason was amazed the ruse had worked but didn't waste any time congratulating himself. Moving swiftly through the corridors and hallways, Mason, the children, and Tyler made their way to the last guard checkpoint before the exit. As he approached the last guard station, he noticed two guards. One of them who saw them approaching placed himself in the way and held up his hand.

"I'm sorry, Doctor, but the temple is on lockdown until we can find the source of the explosions and contain the situation," the guard said with conviction.

"You don't understand—I am on director orders from Lord Amahte himself to evacuate these test subjects to a safer facility until this blows over. You have to let us pass," Mason pleaded.

"I'm sorry, but I will have to confirm your authorization. It's protocol," the guard stated.

Mason glanced back at Tyler, who was giving him an impatient look. She knew as well as Mason that this place could go up any minute. Mason, left with no choice, had to act. As the guard shifted his attention to his partner, Mason grabbed him from behind in a headlock, slowly choking the oxygen from his brain. If he could make the guard go unconscious, it would give him all the time he needed. However, the other guard, seeing what was happening, pulled a gun and was about to fire on him. Mason turned quickly, using the guard he was holding as a shield. The other guard shot twice, striking his partner both times in the chest. Mason took advantage of the other guard's shock at having just shot his partner and pushed the body of the guard he was holding into the other. Then, swiftly moving toward the guard, who had now been knocked to the floor, Mason kicked the gun from his hand and landed several punches to face, knocking the man unconscious.

Mason glanced back at his followers and quickly waved for them to follow. They entered a large lift, and as soon as everyone was in, Mason hit the button to take them to the surface. According to Jahid, this would take them to the other entry/exit to the facility, where a vehicle could be commandeered for their escape. Mason entertained the notion that they might make it until, with a floor left to go, the lift stopped, probably due to the power outage. He looked frantically for an alternative and saw a ladder leading up.

"Let's go, everyone up the ladder, quickly now!" Mason ordered.

The arm Mason had sustained an injury to was now next to useless. He could see blood soaking through the lab coat he was wearing and had to use his right arm only to climb. It took a good five minutes of climbing before Mason pushed open a latch above him and crawled out into what appeared to be a typical warehouse. As he stood at the top, he quickly helped each of the children and his wife out of the shaft. There, as Jahid had described, were a few vans that were used to transport supplies and the kidnapped children. Mason found one with the keys in the ignition and quickly loaded all the children and his wife into the vehicle.

Suddenly the ground rumbled, but it was different this time; it felt as if the floor was going to fall out directly beneath them. Mason concluded that the large bomb had been detonated and they had only seconds before it would reach the top floors.

"Hang on!" Mason screamed as he started the van and floored it toward the closed garage door.

The van raced with incredible speed toward the door, which Mason prayed would give way to the fast-moving vehicle. Just as the van reached the door, a large ball of fire launched the van with even more force like a cannon through the aluminum garage door and sent the van hurtling through the air at least a couple hundred feet from the building. The children screamed in terror as the vehicle landed on its side and slid across the street, sending sparks flying as metal on asphalt created a light show before the vehicle came to a complete stop another hundred yards away from where the explosion had occurred. All the screams and cries came to an end as the van came to a halt. Now, with exception of the occasional whimper and moan, there was complete silence.

EPILOGUE

Mason stood looking out the window of the hospital room, waiting for the nurses to bring the newcomer to their family. Tyler was resting silently in the nearby hospital bed as Mason continued to collect his thoughts.

Eight months had passed since the night the Sons' temple had been destroyed, and Mason was still reeling from the plethora of emotions that culminated in such a short period of time. With the exception of a view scrapes and bruises, everyone in the van had escaped that night unharmed. Mason underwent extensive surgery on his arm, and although he had lost feeling in a few of his fingers because of nerve damage, he still had the full use of his left hand.

When the authorities arrived, along with every other emergency vehicle imaginable, Mason filled them in on every piece of information he had, with the exception of seeing a demon. He felt that piece of information would only serve to confuse people, especially since the FBI was now involved. The facility, as Jahid had planned, was completely destroyed, along with any trace of the virus and anyone inside. The only person detained in connection with the cult who was not inside the building when it was destroyed was the librarian. As it turned out, she was the one who had abducted the child from Mason's church. Thankfully he was among the survivors Mason rescued in the van. In the end, the FBI listed the Second Sons as a new terrorist threat, which Mason was thankful for. With the resources the feds had, they would be able to track any leads much better than any local authorities could, plus they could look at things from a global perspective.

As for Jordan, Mason and Tyler grieved many months for him. Mason was upset about Jordan's death. It was not because of where he ended up, because Mason knew in his heart Jordan was with God.

It was because Jordan had not really had a chance to experience life. They set up a headstone at the cemetery next to Mason's brother, Jason, for Jordan. Mason visited it at least once a week; he missed Jordan so much and was so grateful that God had given him the opportunity to have a relationship with such a great individual. Jordan had taught Mason more about himself than anyone he had ever known, and not having him around was going to be difficult, to say the least. Tyler was upset too, but once she began to show signs of her pregnancy, her focus quickly changed to nesting routines.

As the time passed, Mason and Tyler focused more and more on their expected family member. When the day finally came, Mason was so excited, he could hardly sit still. The birth went smoothly, and it had been a good twelve hours since Tyler had given birth to a beautiful baby boy.

Tyler began to stir in her bed, and her eyes opened to see Mason still staring out the window.

"What do you see?" Tyler asked in a sleepy voice.

Mason snapped out of his daze and looked back at her with a large smile.

"Nothing, just blue sky and your beautiful face," he said as he approached the bed. He sat next to the bed and held her hand.

Just then, the nurse wheeled in their son in one of those little baskets, and behind the nurse was Uncle Joe. He came in with a bright smile as the nurse handed the baby to Tyler.

"So did you all come up with a name yet?" Uncle Joe asked excitedly.

Mason and Tyler looked at each other before Tyler looked back to answer.

"His name is J. J. Krane." Seeing the confusion on Uncle Joe's face, she continued, "It's short for Jordan Joseph."

Uncle Joe smiled brightly as he reached out to hold the baby.

"May I?" he asked. Tyler nodded, and Mason's uncle reached down and picked up the baby.

"Looks like you're a godfather again," Mason said jokingly.

"I would be honored," he returned, and with that Mason grabbed a camera off the end table to grab a photo of his son with his uncle.

"We need to make this official. Smile," Mason instructed as he took several snapshots of his uncle holding the baby. When Mason finished, his uncle approached with the baby.

"Your turn," Mason's uncle said, handing the baby to Mason as he grabbed the camera.

Mason's uncle snapped a few photos and then went to speak with Tyler.

Mason wandered back to the window and began to think about what waited out there. He had seen the true evils of this world, and now he had to raise his son to live in a world filled with them. As he looked down at his son, his eyes drifted to the tattoo, which he hadn't had time yet to get removed, or perhaps there was a part of him that wanted to keep it. Jahid had spoken of other installations across the world that had "different goals." What could they be, and what horrors awaited the world if they weren't stopped? Again he looked down at his son and then back out the window. Mason sighed deeply and then looked up to God with his heart and said a prayer that whatever evil lurked in the world, mankind, including himself, would find the faith, grace, and love to overcome it.

CPSIA information can be obtained
at www.ICGtesting.com
Printed in the USA
BVHW031054100519
547857BV00012B/4/P